The Hunt for Sonya Dufrette

THE HUNT FOR SONYA DUFRETTE

R. T. Raichev

CARROLL & GRAF PUBLISHERS
New York

Carroll & Graf Publishers
An imprint of Avalon Publishing Group, Inc.
245 W. 17th Street
11th Floor
New York, NY 10011-5300
www.carrollandgraf.com

First published in the UK by Constable,
an imprint of Constable & Robinson Ltd 2006

First Carroll & Graf edition 2006

ISBN-13: 978-0-78671-734-7
ISBN-10: 0-7867-1734-3

Printed and bound in the EU

For Emma Tennant

Author's Note

This is a work of fiction. All the characters are imaginary and bear no relation to any living person. I am indebted to N. H. for a particularly inventive though rather awful joke.

R. T. R.

Contents

1

By the Pricking of My Thumbs

A death that is yet to take place but is believed to have happened some twenty years earlier? Antonia was to think afterwards that it was the kind of ingenious idea crime writers played around with in their idle hours, while luxuriating in a hot bath, or scanning the *Times* obituaries, beguiled by the seeming impossibility of it, but later discarded as too fanciful, not really worth working through and weaving a whole novel around.

It was 28th July. In the evening, her first back in London since she had returned from her walking tour in Germany's Black Forest, her son and daughter-in-law paid her a visit, bringing with them her beloved granddaughter Emma. Antonia was delighted to see them. She was also glad of the diversion. Something had been troubling her the whole day – she had felt inexplicable twinges of anxiety, the odd sensation of standing under a dark cloud. Once or twice she had even felt like crying.

Emma seemed to have grown bigger in her absence, as bright and happy a child as could be, looking enchanting in her black shirt and baggy blue trousers, her golden curls peeping from under a black beret.

'Look at her. She's destined for the catwalk,' David said.

'No way,' Bethany, her daughter-in-law, said. 'She'll be a

writer, like Granny.' Bethany was a former model and strikingly beautiful. David had met her four years before, in Cannes, where he had been sent by *Tatler* on a photographic assignment. Bethany was disillusioned with the whole *prêt-à-porter* business and regarded the two years she had devoted to it as wasted.

'One book does not a writer make,' said Antonia with a smile. 'Still, sweet of you to say so.'

'Why-tah!' Emma cried and banged her fists on the table. *'Why-tah!'* She banged them again.

'Yes. A writer, like Granny. Don't do that, sweetheart . . . How is the new book going?'

'Very slowly. Not well. Don't ask.' Antonia poured out tea and distributed pieces of Bakewell tart. She hadn't been able to write a single word the whole day.

'Gwanna!' Emma cried. Antonia hugged her.

'Aren't detective stories –' Bethany broke off.

Antonia looked at her. 'Easier to write? Because they are easier to read? Well, they aren't.'

'Actually they are extremely hard to do,' David said. 'The kind my mother writes. Mystifying and enlightening at the same time. Having to play fair. Trying to be original. That's probably the hardest – given that every trick has been done.' He turned towards his mother. 'That's correct, isn't it?'

'Pretty much. At any rate no one thinks in terms of tricks any more. At least no one admits to it.'

'You do want to get out of the library, don't you?' Bethany said. She put Bakewell tart in Emma's mouth.

'Well, I love the library dearly, but, yes, I would very much prefer to be able to write full-time.'

Antonia had for several years been librarian at the Military Club in St James's. David went on, 'As libraries go, that is the place to be – a highly desirable address within striking distance of Clarence House. Watering hole to the Great and the Good.'

'And the not so good,' Antonia said.

David gasped in mock horror. 'You don't mean there are old boys who *misbehave*?'

'Well, somebody was found entertaining a young friend in his room – it turned out they had met only an hour earlier in Piccadilly.'

'Ah, those military types – notoriously starved of affection. The Queen Mum used to visit some of her old chums there, didn't she, while she could still get about with a stick? Wasn't it suggested that she had a beau at the club, some not-so-moth-eaten commodore?'

'Can't say. Before my time.'

David had visited his mother at the club and loved every minute of it. He described it as an edifice designed exclusively for manly, or rather, gentlemanly habitation in the Edwardian manner. One walked into a haze of costly cigar smoke – the 'heathen's frankincense'. (He claimed he had actually heard one of the club members call it that.) The polished parquet floors were the colour of best-quality *halvah* and they had been covered with Persian rugs in soft greys, greens and muted yellows – slightly murky London shades. Oak-panelled walls. Winged armchairs. Revolving bookcases. *Spittoons* – had Beth ever seen a spittoon? (She hadn't.) The coffee had been excellent – real Turkish coffee – so had the chocolate éclairs.

'Nobody spits,' Antonia pointed out. 'They use them as ashtrays.'

'The walls are covered with Spy cartoons and ancient royal photographs. Lord and Lady Mountbatten in the most incredible Ruritanian-looking robes. You know the one? Edwina looks pencil-thin, freakishly thin, almost anorexic –'

'Was she a model?' Bethany asked.

'No, my sweet. She was a vicereine. She had affairs with Nehru and people. They also have the Goddesses cycle. Where did they get them? I mean Madame Yevonde's thirties society ladies dressed up as goddesses. Lady Rattendone as Euterpe, Lady Diana Cooper as Aurora, Mrs

Syrie Maugham as Artemis – it is the most *un*selfconscious high camp I've ever seen!'

'Colonel Haslett bought them at an auction at Christie's. Colonel Haslett is my boss,' Antonia explained with a smile. 'He's at least eighty-five.'

'I'd love to come again and take photos at the club. *A la recherche du temps perdu* kind of cycle. The old boys look like extras in a Merchant–Ivory film. Hairy tweeds and regimental ties. Some of them creaked alarmingly as they moved. Too good to be true. Must do it before they start kicking their respective buckets. You've noticed of course how they read *The Times*?'

'They go to the obituaries first. Well, after a certain age one does, I suppose.'

'Have you had any deaths recently?' David suddenly asked. 'I mean among resident members?'

Antonia frowned. 'Several, yes.'

'Your friend, the intellectual Major, no doubt suspects foul play? What was his name? My mother has an admirer,' he told Bethany.

'I have nothing of the sort.' Antonia felt herself reddening.

'Yes, you have. What was his name?'

'I don't know who you mean.'

'Come *on*. I was there. I saw him making sheep's eyes at you. He was chatting you up. All that rigmarole about murder mysteries resembling baroque opera was only a pretext to get your attention. He *must* know you've written a murder mystery.'

There was a pause. 'He was right, actually,' Antonia said. 'Sex and power, jealousy and rage, despair, menace, violent death – you find them in baroque opera and in most murder mysteries. Especially violent death. That was clever of him.'

'Death,' Emma said. Amazingly she pronounced that one word perfectly.

'What was his name? No, don't tell me. Penderby. Major Horace Penderby.'

'Don't be silly. It's Payne. Hugh Payne.' Antonia found herself looking at Emma. For some reason her heart had started beating fast.

'Major Payne. Oh yes. You fancy him too, don't you? Well, he was a presentable sort of chap. Better-looking than Dad. Not as ancient as the others. Can't be more than fifty-three or four. They say that fifty is the new forty.'

'If fifty is the new forty, then forty's the new thirty – which means twenty is the new ten, right?' Bethany said. 'Which means that I am fourteen. You are married to a girl of fourteen and have fathered a daughter by her. You've broken the law.'

'No, no, it doesn't work that way at all . . . What is Major Payne? Divorced? Bachelor?'

'Widower. His wife died last year.'

'There you are.'

'What do you mean – there you are?'

'Has he got any children?'

'A son. In the Guards.'

'Forgot to tell you. I saw Dad the other day. He didn't seem at all well.'

'Oh? What's the matter? Did he tell you?'

'I was on the top of a bus in Oxford Street.'

'Was Sally –' Antonia bit her lip. It still hurt, each time she recalled that her husband had left her for a young woman of Bethany's age. What was it now? Nearly two years ago.

'No, she wasn't with him. He was walking by himself. He looked pale and haggard – older. I tried to phone later but no one answered.'

'I wonder if –' Antonia began. If Sally's left him, she was going to say but didn't. Well, she'd always maintained that this kind of thing wouldn't last. Richard, after all, was old enough to be Sally's father. She felt a thrill at the thought that she'd been proved right, and she didn't like it. She told herself it wouldn't do to gloat – that giving way to *schadenfreude* was beneath her.

'Do they allow women in the club?' Bethany asked.

'They didn't use to, but now they do. Wives and sisters and, I suspect, mistresses. One can't always tell which is which.'

'Don't mistresses have a certain . . . air?' David said.

'I don't know. I may be entirely wrong, but I think they tend to *laugh* a lot. Exhilaration, exultation – or nerves. I don't know. There are widows of club members too. One of them, Mrs Vollard, relic of Admiral Vollard RN, was rumoured to have started a secret brothel on the premises. It's an apocryphal story. Part of the club mythology.'

'Hookers or rent boys?' Bethany said.

They all laughed.

Afterwards Antonia was to remember what a happy occasion it had been up till that moment. Emma had stomped around the place, keeping up her prattle of separate words, kissing her grandmother with exaggerated affection and allowing, nay demanding, to be kissed in return, being charming to Antonia's two cats and generally lovable. Then, suddenly, and without the slightest provocation, it turned to tempestuous tears, shrieks, ugly anger and violence. Reaching out, she swept two teacups off the table, causing them to smash. She then kicked the pieces.

Emma's face had become dark and suffused, the usually friendly eyes flashed alien and hostile. In the stunned silence that followed she picked up a slice of Bakewell tart from the cake stand and flung it at her grandmother. It hit Antonia on the chest and disintegrated on her lap. Never having seen this side of her granddaughter before, Antonia was appalled and distressed.

'She's just tired, it's nothing,' Bethany said in a matter-of-fact voice, picking Emma up, only to have her face hammered at by two vicious little fists. David intervened at once, taking Emma away and slapping her bottom lightly. The child screeched and jabbered and tried to claw at his face, writhing like a snake the while. Then she started sobbing uncontrollably. Despite their reassuring smiles, Antonia could see that David and Bethany were discomposed and puzzled. Soon after, they left. She felt shaken up by Emma's outburst, more than she thought possible. She had imagined an accusatory glint in Emma's eyes. For a moment Emma had reminded her of somebody . . .

Antonia's mind became clouded by a certain unidentifiable sense of dread that wouldn't go away. She had the very palpable feeling of – well, the only way to describe it was, of something having been *unleashed*.

She knew it was absurd of her to feel like that and sought a rational explanation. No doubt the tantrum had been the sort that three-year-olds experience every day. She was overreacting – she was being neurotic, getting things out of all proportion. She was still smarting from her divorce. Her confidence had been dealt a blow. She hadn't recovered yet. The trip abroad hadn't really done the trick. She was in a fragile state. She was still feeling tired after her long plane journey. (There had been a four-hour delay and they had arrived at Heathrow at three in the morning.) She had also drunk champagne on the plane, which she shouldn't have done. She was a poor drinker. She should have resisted the Roscoes' well-meant attempts to cheer her up. And why had she needed cheering up? Well, she had been depressed. She had burst into tears. *That* hadn't had anything to do with her marriage. She had convinced herself that she could never possibly put pen to paper again.

'Unleashed,' she said aloud. 'Nonsense.'

But the dark cloud wouldn't go away. Tired. That was it. Terribly tired. That was the reason. When she was tired she became subject to odd fancies, like a pregnant woman – a proclivity she did not always succeed in keeping well under control. It had all happened before. The fact that she was going back to work tomorrow morning and had to write a report for the club committee by the end of the week didn't help either.

Antonia sat down and listened to a Haydn sonata. She managed to persuade herself that that was the salve she had needed. (Haydn's common sense had 'penetrated', was how she thought of it.) She then glanced at the twenty pages of the novel she had started writing and thought the whole thing implausible in the extreme – rather silly, actually. She had got the premise of self-imposed amnesia – of repressed memory that turns out to be false memory – from an article she had read in *The Times*, but she didn't seem to have been able to do much with it. Did people behave like that? Did people *think* like that? Did that sort of thing *happen* to people? Why had she chosen a subject she knew nothing about?

Exasperated, she opened the bottom drawer of her desk and pushed the pages in. The bottom drawer was the one she opened only when she wanted to get rid – no, to *half* get rid of something. It contained various discarded papers. She was waiting for it to get full before she made a bonfire in the back yard and burnt its contents. (Not an entirely rational thing to do, but then she had to admit she wasn't an entirely rational person.)

The drawer wouldn't shut. There was something at the back that had got jammed. After two attempts, she gave up, leaving the drawer gaping. She refused to take that as a sign, though she did imagine it might be a sign. She vaguely wondered what it was that had caused the jamming but felt reluctant to investigate.

'Hate writing but love having written. Dorothy Parker said that. Well, not true – I hate *both*,' Antonia told her cats as she fed them a little while later. 'I am afraid this is a writer's block from which I may never recover. My first novel will also be my last. I may be going mad too.'

The cats looked back at her with indifference and licked their whiskers.

She had a cup of hot milk, took two sleeping pills, turned off all the lights and went to bed.

Antonia hadn't expected to sleep well and she didn't.

She woke up in the middle of the night, feeling hot,

drowsy and confused, her heart thumping in her chest. She turned on the bedside lamp and reached out for her glass of water. Once more she had a sense of foreboding. She also felt consumed by guilt. And this wasn't the familiar dread of facing a lonely future, nor the guilty feeling she had had over her failed marriage. She was conscious of having done something appalling. Something that had resulted in disaster – no, not the disaster of losing a husband to a younger woman, something worse. Much worse.

Falling back on her pillow and shutting her eyes, Antonia found herself remembering, of all things, a production of Eliot's *The Family Reunion* which she had seen a couple of years back. In it the Eumenides had been presented as children, which she had thought an extremely spooky and effective decision on the part of the director. One didn't expect children to look and sound menacing, accusatory, slyly knowing . . .

Violence and children . . . one particular child . . . something unresolved . . . a death that could have been prevented . . . something she had allowed to happen . . . a little girl . . . no, *not* Emma . . .

As she drifted into an uneasy sleep, she heard a man's voice hum, *'When I am King, Dilly, Dilly, You shall be Queen . . .'*

She saw a doll floating on a river . . . blood coming out of a hollow in the middle of an ancient tree . . . a Mary Poppins-like figure disappearing into the sky . . .

2

The Day the Earth Stood Still

It was the following morning as she took the Tube to work that she knew what it was her subconscious had been trying to tell her. Somebody standing beside her on the platform was reading the *Metro* and she saw the date.

29th July. My God, she thought, it's twenty years. To the day. Did she hear a woman's voice behind her say that it was the anniversary of the royal wedding, or did she only imagine it? Well, for some people the day of the royal wedding still meant only one thing: Charles and Diana walking up the aisle. Wild cheering crowds. Flags and flowers and fireworks. A fairy-tale come true. The wedding of the century. A hopeful nation. A hopeful world. If statistics were to be believed, 730 million viewers worldwide had watched it on television.

That was when it had happened. If they hadn't been sitting glued to the TV, Sonya would have been alive now. Alive and, very possibly, given the progress medicine had made over the past twenty years, well too. Yes, why not? Sonya might have been completely cured of whatever she had had wrong with her, leading a normal life, a happy, healthy life with a husband and children. Instead of which . . .

Once more the smell of the river came to her nostrils and she heard Lena's accusatory voice: 'It was all your fault. It was you who showed her the way – she'd never have gone there if you hadn't shown her the way.'

No, she didn't want to dwell on it. She mustn't think about it. She had managed not to so far. There would be no point. She would only get upset and that would never do – not on her first day back at work, not after the bad night she had had. There was nothing to be gained by getting upset over a twenty-year-old event – was there? Well, she could have prevented the tragedy. If only she had been less selfish – if only she had taken David with her! Lady Mortlock had said she could. David would never have allowed Sonya to go to the river by herself. Antonia had wanted a holiday – a *proper* holiday. She had been selfish and because of her selfishness a child had died –

Stop it, she told herself. Don't be melodramatic.

She edged her way into the carriage and eventually found a suitable place where she could stand and read her book. She had deliberately picked up a book on library lore before she had left the house. She had meant to take Daphne du Maurier's *Don't Look Now*, but had decided against it. The library lore book was as dry and unappetizing as sawdust. The discarded Daphne du Maurier, on the other hand, was one of her old favourites. Not all the stories were as good as the title one. The title story of course was the best of du Maurier's short fiction – her most effective excursion into the macabre, her most atmospheric. Venice in the twilight – running steps alongside the narrow canal – cellar entrances looking like coffins – a lonely church – a little hooded figure skipping from boat to boat.

Was there any particular reason why she had decided against it? Could it be because it too dealt with the drowning of a young girl? (A psychiatrist would have a field day, should she ever decide to consult one!)

Twenty years. Sonya would have been twenty-seven. Just a bit older than David. What a lovely summer's day it had been. The house party at Twiston. The scent of roses and freshly mown grass wafting in through the open windows, mingling with the smell of beeswax. Bowls of flowers everywhere. Lilies festooning a portrait of the Queen in the hall. Sheikh Umair heaving a sigh: 'Now I *know* what old England is like.' The servants in their Union Jack hats. Balloons and party poppers. (The excitement at one point reaching fever pitch as discussion turned to the footman and the maid who had chosen the day to get married themselves at the local church.) The giant TV set, specially hired for the occasion. Lawrence Dufrette shaking his forefinger: 'There she comes, the silly young goose, in her doomed glory!' Sir Michael clearing his throat: 'It's a bit too early for a drink, but do help yourselves, if you feel like having one. After all, it's a special occasion.' Bill Kavanagh pointing out the Countess Spencer. 'I used to know Raine jolly well before she married Johnny. Remarkable woman. What a shame the Spencer children never got to appreciate her properly.' Lena screaming at her: 'You showed her the way to the river! You as good as killed her! It was all your fault.'

No, no – that had come *later*. Antonia opened her eyes.

The train was crowded – well, it always was. Even late in the morning it was the same, though they said the Piccadilly line wasn't as bad as some of the others. There were no more poems on the walls, sadly. What vacant expressions people had on their faces. Those who were not gazing into space were drinking Coke out of cans or biting at sandwiches and buns. As it happened, they were all young people, of David and Bethany's age. They should have had a proper breakfast before they left home, or failing that, they could have stopped at a café. Besides, it was bad manners, eating on a crowded train, didn't they know that? Some of them looked hung-over, or tired from partying till late, or more likely sitting in front of their computers, e-mailing, surfing the net, or joining chat rooms. Major Payne had made the suggestion that she consider the sinister potential of chat rooms for a possible novel. A chameleon-like figure – a man assuming multiple identities – changing his age and gender depending on whom he was chatting to – targeting the vulnerable and the lonely – winkling secrets.

Major Payne was always giving her ideas. Well, he *had* ideas, unlike her former husband. He actually read books – had insatiable curiosity about things.

None of the young people, she noticed, was reading. They hadn't the energy, she supposed. It didn't look as though they were curious about anything. Such pasty faces – and *must* they pierce their noses?

Antonia smiled. That was Miss Pettigrew speaking and Miss Pettigrew always made her smile. Miss Pettigrew invariably put in an appearance at times of emotional upheaval, she had noticed. Miss Pettigrew seemed able to provide her with a safety valve of sorts. Antonia had been toying with the idea of having Miss Pettigrew playing the amateur sleuth in a series of novels she might write one day, though Major Payne hadn't cared much about it. Heaven knew there were enough musty elderly spinster detectives already. He wanted her to use a sleuthing couple – now why didn't she do that? A husband and wife team. They would be endowed with equal deductive powers *and* they could take it in turns to play the detective and the Watson.

Miss Pettigrew had arrived fully evolved at the time Antonia started work at the Military Club library. She was a much older woman than Antonia and, apart from the fact that both worked in a library, her complete antithesis. (Major Payne had warned Antonia against turning into a Miss Pettigrew – that was when she had told him off for spilling pipe tobacco over a biography of Younghusband, the improbably named Victorian explorer.) Well, Miss Pettigrew wasn't a particularly likeable character. The librarian spinster par excellence, genteel, even lady-like, frustrated, chronically disapproving, rigidly adhering to archaic codes of behaviour, an anachronistic throwback to a previous age. Her favourite authors were Trollope and Barbara Pym, and, when not reading those, she perused books on library lore of the kind Antonia held in her hand at that very moment.

Miss Pettigrew crusaded through her little world, making sure people were provided with suitable reading matter; she had the energy both to read herself, even in the most adverse conditions, as when finding herself in the middle of a crowd, and to encourage others to do so. The trouble was that she was so volubly and forcefully full of suggestions that patrons tended to drift away after a while. Miss Pettigrew also tried to give her ideas for novels, which Antonia invariably dismissed as too far-fetched.

On the positive side – well, yes, there *was* a positive side – Miss Pettigrew was a forthright, practical, no-nonsense type, who had little patience with displays of irrational emotionalism. She was good at times of crisis. Hers – frequently, though not always – was the voice of reason.

It's ludicrous that you should be blaming yourself, dear. You are too sensitive for your own good. (Antonia improvised.) *What happened twenty years ago had nothing to do with you. It wasn't your fault – in the same way that your failed marriage is not your fault, but we won't go into that one. That poor girl, Sonya, needed lots of care – proper care, round-the-clock care – if she was autistic. Well, her parents were there, but they neglected her badly – that's the upper classes for you. Her nanny shouldn't have left in the first place. You did your very best. You had a child of the same age, that's what made it so difficult for you. I fully understand, but, really, you couldn't have kept a watch over her. What she was doing in the garden while everybody else was inside is what I would like to know. Criminal negligence. I blame the parents – entirely! I know it's dreadful – the death of any child is a dreadful thing – but it had nothing to do with you. Nothing at all.*

The crowd was thinning. At the next stop Antonia, feeling much calmer, sidled up the carriage to one of the vacated seats. The train rumbled on. Ten more minutes and they were at Green Park station. Stowing away her book, she made for the opening doors.

* * *

It was a pleasant sunny morning, much warmer than the day before. Walking through St James's, London's clubland, was always a delight. Every time it felt like entering a different world. A group of Japanese tourists were standing at the corner, snapping away with their cameras. There was Lock, the legendary hatter, now more than three hundred years old. She looked through the window – still no signs of modernity. If they used computers, they concealed them carefully. All she could see was handwritten ledgers, sinister-looking wooden moulds and shop assistants wearing morning coats and winged collars. Major Payne had bought a polo cap from them, also a fez. Putting on the fez, he had recited verses from Kipling. Antonia smiled at the memory. On the other side of the street was John Lobb – quality handmade shoes and boots. She looked up. That was where Lord Byron had once held a bachelor establishment –

Suddenly she came to a halt. She thought she had seen a familiar figure go up the steps at White's. Tall, distinguished-looking in a dark pinstriped suit and an old-fashioned Homburg, grey gloves, a rolled-up umbrella.

Her heart was beating fast. Lawrence Dufrette? Surely not? Before she could take a closer look, the man had disappeared inside the club. He had always hated London, he had told her so himself. Well, that was twenty years ago. She hadn't seen him since the fatal day. She hadn't seen Lena either . . . Lena had been hysterical, deranged with grief, which was odd, to say the least, given that, prior to the tragedy, she had paid her daughter only scant attention. 'Run along, darling, Mamma's terribly busy.' (Busy leafing through the Harrods catalogue – busy drinking a spritzer – busy eating a chocolate gateau as high as Mont Blanc – busy painting her fingernails scarlet – busy watching television.)

Where did the Dufrettes live? St John's Wood, someone had said. Or had they separated? She seemed to remember a rumour to that effect. Would Lawrence Dufrette be in central London on this day of all days, this tragic anniversary, twenty years since his daughter's death?

Could Lawrence Dufrette be looking for her, Antonia? Was there going to be a commemorative service perhaps? Or was it possible that there had been . . . developments? She couldn't say what developments exactly she had in mind, but if that had been the case, surely it would have been the police looking for her, not Lawrence Dufrette? Though why should the police want *her*?

I am being reclaimed by my past, Antonia thought. She knew this was nonsense. She was becoming paranoid. Perhaps she should seek medical help?

She entered the Military Club.

3

Taste of Fears

She could still feel a little surge of excitement when she arrived at the club library. She relished the 'unknown factor', the uncertainty as to what might turn up, the possibility that it might be something really exciting. It was the detective story writer and mystery enthusiast in her as much as the librarian. One never knew. The library users sometimes had very interesting enquiries, out of which there emerged the most fascinating stories.

There had been the old boy who had known T.E. Lawrence in the short while before that fatal motorbike accident, which of course, he claimed, hadn't been an accident at all; the chap whose aunt had been a nanny to the children of King Zog of Albania; the retired MI6 officer who told Antonia in great detail how he had foiled a plot to kill the Dalai Lama. The books themselves – Antonia tended to think of the books almost as people – often yielded surprises too, especially those that were brought in as donations. Old volumes of memoirs, frequently privately published, of the two world wars, of travels in the East when it had really been the 'mysterious Orient', and in Africa. Then there were the old personal archives, which she got to investigate from time to time.

'Ah, Miss Darcy. You are back.'

'Good morning, Mr Lodge,' responded Antonia. She had been about to close the library door behind her. Mr Lodge was the club secretary: a small man in his late forties, rubicund and dapper, invariably sporting a bow tie, a polka-dotted one this time.

'You look as though you've had an excellent holiday, if you don't mind my saying so. You look tanned and fitter than before you left.'

'Thank you. I had a very good time.'

'I am glad to hear it. You did seem in need of a holiday. We've had upheavals here while you've been away.'

'Really?'

He glanced over his shoulder. 'New management on the way. It looks like war,' he whispered. In his normal voice he said, 'I have some more books for you. More donations.'

'Oh, *good*. Thank you, Mr Lodge.' They had known each other for three years, but somehow there was no question of first name terms ever being established between them.

He was holding a cardboard box containing a number of books. 'Brigadier Shipton left them for you, in case they were of interest. It's a mixed bunch. There is a rather unusual recipe book . . . Not for the squeamish!' Antonia at once thought of cannibals but it turned out to be for dishes favoured by the ancient Mongols.

Now inside her inner sanctum, she stood beside her desk and looked at the pile of letters that had accumulated in her absence. The one at the top was addressed to *Mrs Antonia Rushton, c/o the Military Club, St James's, W1.*

Antonia stared. Rushton? She had reverted to her maiden name, Darcy, after her divorce, and she had been using it for the past six months. The handwriting seemed familiar, though it might be her imagination. Could it be something to do with Sonya? It didn't look like an official envelope, so it couldn't be the police. It *was* somebody from the past – Lena? – who had written to her. Somebody who didn't know about her change of circumstances.

Now this won't do at all. There's no one out there who wants to get you. Pull yourself together, girl. Snap out of it.

Mr Lodge appeared at the door once more. 'I am sorry,

Miss Darcy. I keep bothering you. I have received the new *Who's Who*. Would you like last year's edition?'

'Thank you. It would be very useful.'

'Here you are . . . So heavy, aren't they? Someone's cranium could easily be smashed with this. The perfect murder weapon, eh?' He gave her a knowing look and left. Major Payne had told her that it was common knowledge now that she had penned a mystery yarn. On an impulse she opened *Who's Who* and went to D.

Dufrette, Lawrence – well, last year, at least, he had been alive. He would be seventy-one in September. He lived in South Kensington and listed as his interests 'the Babylonian brotherhood and walking'.

Hearing the sound of running steps, she looked up. It was Martin, the porter. 'Oh, ma'am, look what I've got!' He was carrying three large hardbacks. 'These came back for you, at last! I thought we'd never see them again.'

Grinning with genuine pleasure, he showed her the books. Of course. She'd completely forgotten about them. The memoirs of various cricketers, which Martin, a keen amateur sportsman, had been borrowing and slowly but delightedly reading, regaling everybody who would listen with anecdotes. Their absence from the library shelves had hit him and his fund of stories hard. 'They were left on the table in the hall, Miss Darcy. Can you imagine?'

Antonia tut-tutted and shook her head. (What *was* the Babylonian brotherhood?)

'They should have brought them here, shouldn't they? What can they be thinking of?' The porter tapped his forehead significantly. 'Some of these old codgers . . .'

'Don't talk like that, Martin,' she reprimanded him.

On the floor beside her desk there were more books in cardboard boxes, some of them sticking out of the heap at crazy angles. More donations, left for her by various well-meaning club members while she had been away. Buchan's *Greenmantle*. *They Die With Their Boots Clean* by Gerald Kersh. MacDonald Fraser's *Flashman*. Anthony Powell's *The Military Philosophers*. So far so predictable. Her brows went up. *Lesbia's Little Blunder* by Frederick Warne. She picked it up. The blurb promised 'two ripping school yarns'. The book had been published in 1934 – the picture on the cover showed two smiling girls, bursting with rude health and holding hockey sticks. She leafed through it. No, it wasn't a spoof – it wasn't what the title suggested either. All perfectly innocent, actually.

Pushing the boxes out of the way, she sat down in her swivel chair. She found she was still holding the letter from the top of the pile, but postponed opening it. All around her apparent chaos ruled. In the days leading up to her holiday she had felt too unwell to do anything about it. The wooden table topped with red tooled leather on her right was covered with uncatalogued books and sprinkled with notes on little bits of paper, pens, pencils and equipment for labelling books. Another, smaller, table was stacked high with yellowing papers, most of which bore copperplate writing, apparently from another age. The shelves above contained filing boxes, heaps of typewritten paper and variegated volumes.

Her 'office' was situated underneath a staircase and so the ceiling tapered down to the floor at the back. The space in which no one could stand up straight was occupied by piles of enormous ledgers, bound in red or black leather, some of them with brass corners, some ancient and mouldering, some in uniform sequences, some not. The organizing of all this material was part of her work.

She looked down at the letter. Coming to a sudden decision, she picked up the paperknife, slit open the envelope and extracted the folded sheet.

Antonia gave a sigh of relief, seeing it was only an invitation for a class reunion. It was thirty-five years since she had left the Sempersand School for Girls. The letter was short. It had been written by Isabel Bradley, one of her former classmates, whom Antonia did not remember. I won't go, she thought, crumpling up the letter and dropping it into her waste paper basket. She had been to her twentieth anniversary and had hated every moment of it.

This one would be worse. Women did not improve with age. A gaggle of middle-aged matrons, prying into each other's business, complaining about indifferent, critical or wayward husbands, hinting at affairs on either side, some of them getting embarrassingly drunk and, as likely as not, making desperate passes at the waiters.

Twenty minutes later she was sipping a cup of coffee and examining some notes she had made a fortnight before. One of the notes bore the words: *A Rec. Fest. Vol.15/2.* She took down from the shelves on the wall a large reference book and started flicking through the pages until she found the phone number of a nearby specialist library. Balancing the book on her lap and holding the note with her left hand, she reached for the telephone. Just as she was about to lift the receiver, it rang.

It was a colleague from a parallel institution. He wanted to know how she was getting on with the map.

Antonia knew at once what map he meant. (What a sad life hers was!) 'Ah. Very well indeed,' she said. 'I've shown it to one or two of our members and they were extremely interested. I think I have made some progress in identifying a few of the buildings. Two people separately identified the same one, so that's fairly promising, isn't it?'

'Marvellous!' What her fellow librarian then suggested was a meeting in the near future when they could actually look at the map properly, to which Antonia agreed with great alacrity.

A couple of minutes later she finished with the reference book on her lap and replaced it on the shelf.

'Excuse me, are you the librarian?'

An elderly gentleman of imposing height stood before her. He had a mane of silver-white hair, carefully brushed back. He was dressed in a dark pinstriped suit. He had taken off his black Homburg. In his other hand he held a shabby Gladstone bag and a rolled-up umbrella.

Lawrence Dufrette? No, it couldn't be . . .

As she continued staring at him, he said impatiently, 'Are you the librarian or an owl?' He didn't seem to be in a very good mood. He had a Duke of Wellington nose, a mean choleric mouth and a ruddy complexion. He rapped his knuckles against the desk.

'Sorry. I am the librarian, yes. What can I do for you?'

'Have you got any books on the Himalayas?'

'We do have a section on Geography and Travel, not a very large one, I am afraid. It contains memoirs of mountaineers and explorers.' Her voice sounded odd, Antonia knew. 'Amongst the regimental histories you will find quite a few about the Ghurkas, which describe their background in Nepal. There are also atlases. Let me show you.'

She led the way to the appropriate section, telling herself that this wasn't Lawrence Dufrette. Of course it wasn't him, though it did look like him. How could she be certain either way though, after twenty years? Was her mind playing her tricks? That was what happened, they said, when you had somebody on your mind – you kept seeing them. Was the old boy the same one she had observed entering White's earlier that morning? One could never tell with a certain type of Englishman – they looked so similar.

From the corner of her eye she watched him as he lingered beside her desk, muttering to himself, shaking his head, poking among the books inside one of the boxes, opening and closing his bag. He wasn't stealing her books, was he? When he joined her, she managed to ask whether his interest was theoretical or practical.

He said, 'My nephew's going trekking in the Himalayas next month. The book's for him. My trekking days are over. Thank you very much indeed. I'll take a look.' He turned his back on her.

He *did* sound like Lawrence Dufrette . . . Was the alpinist nephew an invention? She remembered Lady Mortlock telling her that Lawrence Dufrette had quarrelled with all his relatives. That was twenty years ago. He hadn't shown a flicker of recognition, but he might be pretending. She didn't think she had changed so much . . . Perhaps it wasn't Lawrence Dufrette after all.

Suddenly she stood very still. She had actually written a detailed account of the tragedy, she remembered. She had done it first by hand, then she had typed it up. She had covered a great number of pages, which she had put inside a folder. Every year at the end of July she started looking for the folder, but never managed to find it, after which she forgot about it. (Was that deliberate? Talking about self-imposed amnesia!) It was somewhere at home, she knew, in some drawer. She determined to do her very best this time, dig up her account without fail and read it. She felt she had to. She knew she would have another bad night if she didn't.

Twenty years. She owed it to Sonya.

An hour later she heard a familiar booming voice outside the library door. 'Scrambled duck egg with smoked eel – not bad at all. Bloody good in fact. You must try it, Wakefield. Be adventurous, that's my motto. What? Splendid idea, yes. Haven't told her yet. I'll tell her now. No better time than the present.' The door opened. 'Miss Darcy! Miss Darcy! Are you in there?'

Antonia rose. 'Good morning, Colonel Haslett,' she greeted her boss brightly. Despite his advanced years Colonel Haslett OBE, DSO dealt with every matter at top speed before passing on to the next item on his always-extensive list. In his wake he left ripples, which tended to develop later into a large backwash of things to do.

'Ah, Miss D., you are back. Good, excellent. How have you been getting on with the Gresham papers?' Colonel Haslett was leaning heavily on his silver-topped cane and craning his head forward, half-moon glasses at the tip of his nose, his hand cupping his right ear. At his neck he had a starched damask napkin; it was clear he had had a late breakfast in the club's dining room. He frequently forgot to remove his napkin. It was Colonel Haslett's record with the Number One Commandos on the French coast early in the war and in North Africa and Burma that had won him a reputation for outstanding leadership. He had been nicknamed 'Junior' because another Haslett, a first cousin of his, had been a commanding officer.

'Well, Colonel Haslett, the Gresham papers are proving a bit –'

'The reason I ask is that we may have a contact at the Historical Manuscripts Commission. A friend of m'wife's, actually. A Miss . . . um . . . Can't remember her name, but she is the right person for this kind of job. She's been highly recommended. On the highest authority. She could help us with them, you know. I mean, take the Gresham papers off your hands, Miss D. Good idea, what? I can see you have lots to do, lots to do.' He was peering round her office, at the heaps of unprocessed books and mounds of paper. 'Not to worry.'

'Well, I suppose it would make sense to –'

'Good, excellent. She'll be round quite soon, tomorrow as likely as not. She's that sort of woman. Damned efficient. Puts us all to shame, what? Cathcart, that's it. Her name's Cathcart. Miss – or Mrs Cathcart. Don't know which. Actually she comes round our place occasionally and we play bridge together. You know her?'

'I'm afraid not –'

'You haven't got very far with the Gresham papers, have you? Been an arduous task, I imagine.'

'Well, actually –'

'Never mind, never mind. I can see how much there is to do here. You'd better get on with it. Get cracking.'

He patted her arm bracingly and, despite his stick and gammy leg, marched swiftly out of the room with amazing agility.

I was quite enjoying the job, Antonia finished the sentence to herself. Looking down at the box filled with books that stood beside her desk, she noticed that the one at the top bore the title, *The Greatest Secret*. It had been placed on top of *Greenmantle*. Had it been there earlier on? She had the feeling that it hadn't. Underneath the main title was written, *No one who reads this book will ever be the same again*.

4

Six Characters in Search of an Author

There are some events, Antonia reflected, of which each circumstance and surrounding detail seem to stay with us for the rest of our lives, even though we may have convinced ourselves we have forgotten all about them – and so it was with the drowning of little Sonya Dufrette. As she started leafing through her twenty-year-old account that evening, everything came back to her with stark clarity, in vivid Technicolor, as though it had all happened only yesterday. (She had found the folder containing it at the back of the bottom drawer as she had known she would. It was something else, some other papers, that had caused the jamming – not that that changed anything.)

What she had written was more than a mere account. Some of it read like a diary, some like a story. She leafed through the pages. She had actually *researched* the main protagonists' backgrounds, she saw with surprise. Twiston, she had made clear, had once belonged to the Jourdains, who were Lady Mortlock's ancestors, not Sir Michael's. She had recorded her thoughts and feelings on various subjects. She had described the river, the oak tree, the hideous hollow and the outfits worn by Lena and Veronica. She had mentioned the fact that Major Nagle smoked Egyptian cigarettes out of a monogrammed Asprey's slide-action silver case. She had told how Sonya loved 'Lavender's Blue' to be sung to her. She had even quoted Tennyson. It was curious how many details had managed to impress themselves on her mind, but then, she supposed, she must already have decided that she wanted to be a writer.

It had been the month and the year of the royal wedding. July 1981. Antonia had been married for eight years – happily, or so she had believed. Her son David had been six and a half and she had intended to take him with her to Twiston, Sir Michael and Lady Mortlock's country house outside Richmond-on-Thames. Lady Mortlock had assured her it would be perfectly all right as there was going to be another child there. A little girl who was the same age as David. However, at the eleventh hour she had decided to leave David with her mother in Hatfield. She had persuaded herself that she needed a proper break.

Things might have been different if David had been able to go with her. David had been extremely mature for his age. He would never have allowed Sonya to walk down to the river by herself – never. He'd have been aware that there was something wrong with Sonya, that she was not like other children. He would have been very protective of her, Antonia felt sure. Richard too had been invited and Antonia had dearly wanted him to be there, but he had had to go to France on a business trip. (It was only later, much later, that she learnt the truth, namely that he had been at a hotel in Reading with his mistress of the moment.)

She had been included in the weekend party at Twiston as a matter of course. She had already been spending time there helping write Lady Mortlock's family history. She saw she had described Twiston as *the best sort of doll's house come to life – a masterpiece of Jacobean exuberance, all mellow red brickwork, elaborate chimneys, extravagant gables, fantastical griffins and gargoyles.*

She had become very fond of both the house and its owners, Sir Michael and Lady Mortlock, then in their late sixties. Tall, imperious, austere, Lady Mortlock looked like the headmistress of a girls' public school and indeed had been one until some six years earlier. She was always impeccably turned out – she had worn a very desirable silk dress on the day of the royal wedding – and was noted for her acerbic wit. Her father, Frederick Jourdain, had been a famous if controversial consultant who specialized in rare blood diseases. In the 1930s he had become a dedicated believer in the 'German miracle' and he had managed to infuse (some said 'infect') his daughter with some of his pet theories. It wasn't a subject Lady Mortlock was ever willing to discuss, though Antonia had seen books on eugenics and euthanasia on her study bookshelves, even one favourable account of the Final Solution. Lady Mortlock had also been extremely interested in the welfare of the several girls who came to clean the house and had tried to help them in various ways, but had not met with any great success. Antonia had observed the girls put their heads together, whisper and giggle. Not a very happy woman, Antonia had decided.

Sir Michael had retired from his top MI5 job only the year before, but was already showing signs of mental and physical decline; the once keen intelligence was no longer in evidence and he had turned into an amiable old buffer who pottered about his house and garden dressed in shabby country tweeds, cigar in hand, and liked nothing better than to sit reading P.G. Wodehouse or simply dozing in the sun, like an ancient lizard.

It was Sir Michael who had invited the Dufrettes, a decison which had angered Lady Mortlock so much that, in a rare outburst, she had referred to it as 'extremely ill-judged, bordering on the feeble-minded'. Lawrence Dufrette had been working in MI5, in what, prior to his retirement, had been Sir Michael's department.

Antonia had never met the Dufrettes before, but they already held a fascination for her. (The allure of the freak show?) Lady Mortlock had warned her to expect the worst. Lawrence she had described as 'cranky and cantankerous' while she had been positively horrified at the prospect of having Lena stay at Twiston. A previous visit had been termed a 'disaster'. Apparently Lena had smoked between courses and had nearly started a fire by dropping her cigarette amongst the sofa cushions and leaving it there. She was fat and slovenly, far from bright, indiscreet. The derogatory epithets had rolled off Lady Mortlock's tongue. Lena and Lawrence had little regard for anyone and invariably conducted their rows in the most public manner imaginable. The LL double act, somebody had called it.

Lawrence Dufrette had already carved a reputation for himself as a maverick and something of a loose cannon – by all accounts a picaresque and eccentric figure on the fringes of the Old Establishment. From Burke's Landed Gentry Antonia had discovered that Dufrette was born in 1930, the elder son of Jasper Dufrette, a landowner and high court judge in Malaya, and Millicent Herbert. He had been educated at Harrow and Trinity College, Cambridge, where he read history. He served as a lieutenant in the Intelligence Corps in 1951 and was stationed for a while in post-war Berlin. His extensive knowledge of heraldry had led to his appointment as Bluemantle Pursuivant of Arms and, consequently, he played an important role in many great state occasions. At the Coronation in 1953 he had been standing near the Throne – 'closer than all but the great officers of state', as Harold Nicolson had put it in his diary.

Another diarist, society photographer Cecil Beaton, had described young Lawrence Dufrette's appearance in some detail. 'With his light blue eyes, sand-coloured hair, quartered tunic of scarlet, blue and gold and sombre stockings, holding the two Sceptres in his pale ivory hands, he was the perfect work of art. He has a long, pale, lovelorn face. He seems to be burnt with some romantic passion.' Dufrette had been the Earl Marshal's press secretary throughout Coronation year.

He had been given a job at the College of Arms and might even have become Chester Herald, but, in Lady

Mortlock's words, 'Lawrence's absurdly haughty and cavalier attitude to his colleagues and irresponsibility over money led to his enforced resignation. He thought he was better than all of them put together. *Primus inter pares*. That kind of rot . . . He hasn't improved with age. You should hear how he talks about his colleagues in MI5. Men of straw, operating in a blizzard of displacement activity! I don't see how Michael puts up with it.' At the start of his career in the Intelligence Service, he had been considered brilliant but eventually caused consternation with his erratic and unpredictable behaviour. He also developed an obsessive interest in conspiracy theories.

The Babylonian brotherhood, Antonia suddenly remembered. What *was* the Babylonian brotherhood?

Sheikh Umair had described Dufrette as 'a clever but extremely dangerous man. Talks about flogging and hanging and bloody foreigners and niggers – equally to shock and to get a reaction, I think. He has a strong exhibitionist streak. He carries a gun. He said he needed to protect himself against his enemies. He pointed the gun at my head and made a popping sound. It is exceedingly difficult to know when he jokes and when he is serious, but then that is a very *English* kind of thing, isn't it?'

Enemies . . . Antonia looked up with a frown. One enemy at least . . . The incident at breakfast. (She had given an account of it somewhere later on.) Dufrette quarrelled with one of the other guests. Some military type. Stocky and pouchy-eyed, small trimmed moustache, great heavy hands, amazingly well-tended fingernails the colour of oysters . . . Dufrette had said something that had infuriated him . . . Major Nagle? Yes. 'Tommy' Nagle. Major Nagle had made a lot of fuss over a signet ring he had lost. He had been in a real state about it, she remembered.

In 1954 Dufrette had married the Hon. Pamela Wigham, the 'deb of the season'. (Antonia had since seen pictures of the two newly-weds, looking solemnly distinguished, almost regal, in an old number of *Country Life*.) However, the marriage had been dissolved only two years later.

There had been no children. Then in 1960 Dufrette married for the second time, an exiled Russian countess, or, as Lady Mortlock had put it, 'a woman who *claimed* to be one'. The new bride's name was Lena Sugarev-Drushinski. Antonia's subsequent research had proved that Lena's title was genuine, albeit acquired as a result of a four-month marriage to a certain Count Poliakoff. As a matter of fact Lena had the dubious distinction of being descended from the mad Yusupovs on her mother's side. Prince Yusupov had been heir to one of the most fabulous fortunes in pre-revolutionary Russia and, of course, he had cut out his niche in history as the man who shot Rasputin an inordinate number of times in the winter of 1916.

As a young woman, Lena (born in 1938) had been a voluptuous blonde, vivacious and fun-loving – as the pictures Antonia had seen in *Tatler* testified – and, though greatly impoverished at the time of her marriage, she had managed to make Dufrette very happy for a couple of years. However, by 1981 the marriage gave every impression of bursting at the seams. The Dufrettes detested one another and never bothered to conceal the fact.

When Antonia finally met her, Lena was forty-three, but she looked older, the years of excess having taken their toll. She was plump, puffy-eyed and over-painted. She clearly strove to be uncompromisingly exotic. Her eyebrows had been plucked in the style of the 1930s – thin arches high above the natural line of the brow. The effect should have been one of perpetual comic surprise but Lena's kohl-ringed blue eyes gave her a slightly sinister appearance. She was dressed in a kaftan, sported a cornucopia of costume jewellery and had an emerald-green scarf tied round her henna-dyed hair. She was smoking through an ivory cigarette holder and drinking vermouth.

When a grim-faced and rather pale Lady Mortlock had completed the introductions, Lena stood peering at Antonia. She said, 'It is *my* life you should be writing up. I am unlike anyone you have ever met. You wouldn't believe some of the things that have happened to me. My first marriage was a disaster. A German aunt of mine predicted this with chilling accuracy, though I never listened to her. I've been told that I have God in one eye and the Devil in the other.' Cigarette smoke curled from her nostrils. Although educated at an English school, she spoke with a pronounced Russian accent. 'There was a sign when I was born. (I was born on Bastille Day at the Paris Ritz.) That night a fiery meteor burst across the sky –'

'How could they tell which was which?' Dufrette had interrupted in his mocking voice. 'The sky must have been ablaze with fireworks.'

'Lawrence always tries to undermine me,' Lena told Antonia. 'It happens every time. He wants to make me look a fool in front of people.'

Antonia continued smiling politely. She had the awkward feeling that she was not behaving quite as she should, but then how *did* one respond to the embarrassing confessions of strangers?

'Not a bit of it, my precious one,' Dufrette had said. '*Le bon Dieu* has already taken care of that.'

'If Lawrence only knew how much I despised him, he would want to go and hang himself. He would want to cut his throat from ear to ear.' Lena had accompanied her words with an eloquent gesture.

'Not before I had cut yours, ducky!' Dufrette had raised his neck as if his collar was too tight and twisted his head slightly to the left – it was a tic he had. It made him feel authoritative, Antonia imagined.

Part Strindberg, part Punch-and-Judy show – that was how Lady Mortlock had described the Dufrette marriage. Even mild-mannered Sir Michael had conceded in private that things weren't working terribly well, and that 'Lawrence would have been better off if he'd stuck with the Wigham girl.' Sir Michael had been unflaggingly nice to both Dufrette and Lena. He had actually taken the trouble to talk to Lena and given every indication of enjoying the experience – something few others had done.

There had been much unkind speculation as to what the offspring of such a 'gruesome twosome', as someone called it, would turn out to be – if they had any, that was.

It was not until 1974, when he was forty-four and Lena thirty-six, that the Dufrettes produced a child, a daughter, whom they named Sonya. Reading what she had written about Sonya Dufrette, Antonia felt her eyes filling with tears.

5

Baby Doll

A tiny, frail child, like a live doll. She is seven but looks about five, if not younger. Flaxen-haired, light brown eyes, ethereal, gentle-tempered and trusting. She has the sweetest smile. She had picked some flowers in the garden, a straggly bunch, which she held out to me as soon as she saw me. Her eyes are slightly unfocused. Her nanny – a Miss Haywood – was with her, holding her by the hand. A youngish woman with a hooked nose, sallow-faced, not particularly prepossessing. She had dyed her hair blonde and, like many other young girls, had had it cut and styled like our future Princess of Wales. Miss Haywood struck me as extremely tense and preoccupied-looking. Lady Mortlock later told me that her mother was gravely ill, in hospital. Lady Mortlock said she had great admiration for the poor girl, whom she described as 'having the patience of a saint – wonderfully suited to the care of a backward child'.

Sonya made me feel extremely protective towards her. I had to resist the urge to pick her up and hold her tight. She had such a 'lost' look about her! She couldn't speak, just the odd word, baby talk, really. It was also the way she walked. She didn't seem to have much awareness of the world around her. Compared to David, who at six and a half is so articulate and so competent. It then dawned on me that there was something seriously wrong with the girl. Well, Miss Haywood referred to Sonya vaguely as 'young for her age', which is an understatement. It is clear Sonya suffers from some kind of arrested development.

After lunch on the 28th I was taking a stroll in the garden, which is not only beautiful but remarkable in that it is full of surprises. One is constantly led from one scene to another, into long vistas and little enclosures, which seem infinite. This is odd since the garden doesn't cover many acres. It abounds in flowers and plants that have been brought from the most outlandish places in Asia and Africa.

I was walking towards the ancient oak tree when I ran into Lena.

She was wearing a pink dress with lots of frills and bows, ankle-length lace socks and gold sandals of an elaborate design. Around her neck she had a gold crucifix. She had just finished painting her nails (an uncompromising scarlet) and was flapping her hands in the air. She said, 'I saw the way you were looking at my kotik. *You have such kind eyes. You are a simpatico sort of person. I don't often meet simpatico people. I am always misunderstood and frequently reviled. I haven't had fifty-two days' happiness in my life. Sometimes I wonder I am still alive. My first husband was a foot fetishist. He loved me with a truly terrifying passion.'*

She leant towards me. 'Now I am going to say something that is bound to shock you. My daughter is subnormal. That is God's truth. Sounds awful, I know, but that is God's truth.'

I smelled brandy on her breath. 'It must be difficult for you,' I felt compelled to say.

Difficult? She shook her head slowly from side to side and sighed deeply. It was clear I had disappointed her. So even a simpatico person like me didn't understand! Well, no one understood. It had been hell. She hadn't had a moment of peace. (She spoke unemphatically, in lugubrious tones.) Children like her poor Sonya were an open wound, a millstone around the neck, an albatross, a trial, a torture and a punishment. It was terrible when they grew up for – didn't I see? – they never grew up.

'Can't doctors help?'

Lena waved a dismissive hand. 'Doctors. Don't talk to me about doctors. We've seen everybody. The cream of Harley Street. The best of the very best. We've paid a fortune in consulting fees, money that could have been spent on better things, only to be told that Sonya will remain as she is. She may even take a turn for the worse. It is her poor little head. It is a delicate piece of machinery. If only the tiniest screw were to become loose . . .' Lena paused significantly. 'I am punished for the sins of the Yusupovs. I never doubted it would be so. Prince Felix used to wear drag, did you know? I too have this terrible duality in my nature. That is why I am punished. I have been bad, oh so bad, you can't imagine how bad. Ask Hermione Mortlock. She knows me well – better than anybody. She will tell you. She has no illusions about me.'

It was a hot day and we were standing in the shade of the oak. Lena said, 'I don't like this tree. It has the face of a very old, very evil man who gapes and grins. You don't see it, do you?' She seemed irritated that I had failed to see. 'I hate that hollow! It wants to swallow me up, I am sure of it.' She touched her crucifix as though for protection. 'I always see things like that – terrible, vile things. I never see anything beautiful. I am not meant to be happy.' She then turned round and started walking in the direction of the house.

'Some women must never be allowed to become mothers.' It was another of my fellow guests who had addressed me thus: a Mrs Vorodin. Veronica Vorodin. 'You too think it, don't you?' I nodded. She took off her dark glasses and looked at me out of lavender eyes. 'Lena used to amuse me, but now she only fills me with horror. She'd do anything for money. Cranked up, did you realize?'

'Was she? I thought she was merely drunk.'

'That too . . . They used to call her LSD, you know.'

'Lena Sugarev-Drushinski? Oh, you mean – Really?'

'Yes. She had quite an addiction.'

As it happens, Veronica and Lena are distant cousins, but the contrast couldn't have been greater. Veronica was wearing an ice-blue dress, which simply shrieked designer. All her clothes are made by Oscar de la Renta, couturier to Nancy Reagan and Princess Grace of Monaco, among others, Mrs Falconer had informed me. Both Veronica and her husband Anatole (also of Russian extraction) spend most of their time commuting between Florida, London, Rome and the South of France, in each of which they have houses. Fabulously rich, Lady Mortlock had said. They have their own jet, apparently, also a yacht.

(Vorodin – corruption of 'Borodin'?)

Well, the Vorodins are the epitome of cosmopolitan sophistication – slim, suave, accentless, with those glowing perma-tans. Though I understood them to be thirty-nine and thirty-eight respectively, they look barely out of their teens. They give the impression of being typical jet-setting wastrels and professional bon vivants. The kind of people who have drawing rooms that take half an hour to cross, Monets and Picassos hanging in the lavatory, truffles and Beluga caviar for dinner, which they eat with a spoon. However, looks can be very deceptive. Lady Mortlock told me that they were generous to a fault, philanthropists with a number of charities named after them. Most of the charities are for children.

As Sonya and Miss Haywood passed by, Veronica said, 'She looks like an angel, doesn't she? Such a sweet little girl. Helplessness personified.'

'I always thought angels looked confident and a bit smug – if Christmas cards are anything to go by. What is wrong with her exactly, do you know?'

'She is said to be autistic. I wish Lawrence and Lena would do something about it. They haven't really seen "everybody". It doesn't all start and end with Harley Street. There are good specialists abroad . . . If I had a child like that, I'd love her more than I would a normal one!' Veronica spoke vehemently, with genuine passion. 'A mentally handicapped child is a very special child – a gift from God. A child like that would help me preserve my humanity – would prevent me from getting spoilt, keep me to the ground.'

How odd it is that one woman should consider a gift what another describes as punishment.

'I love children, so does Anatole,' Veronica went on. She had been a beauty queen and an actress, but she spoke simply and naturally, without the slightest trace of affectation. I found myself warming to her. 'We don't have any children, sadly. Do you?'

I told her I had a boy of Sonya's age. Her face lit up. 'A little boy! How wonderful for you. And he is – fine? He is in good health? I am so glad! You must be very happy. I'd love to meet him. What's his name?'

'David. I nearly brought him here with me.'

'Oh, why didn't you? I must send him something – some little present. How about a pair of platinum cuff links with the initial D?'

'Oh, that's very kind of you but I couldn't possibly –'

'Of course you can. It's nothing. He can use them when he grows up. I have them in my room. We always carry two boxes full of cuff links that have all the letters of the alphabet on them. I carry the ones with A to K, Anatole has the rest. We present them to deserving little boys. I hope you won't think us too peculiar!' She laughed. 'We have things for girls too.' A shadow passed over her face. 'We'd give anything to have a child. If you only knew what it means to us –' She broke off, then changed the subject. 'Twiston is a lovely house, isn't it? One thing we haven't got is an English country house. Sorry, this sounds terribly spoilt of me!'

'It is the kind of place exiles think of when they dream of home,' I said.

'Beautifully put . . . Perhaps one day I will buy this house and live in it.'

Lawrence Dufrette had strolled along and he was joined by Miss Haywood and Sonya. We watched him pick up Sonya and swing her round by her hands, making her scream with laughter. He then put her on his shoulder and unexpectedly broke into song.

> *'Some to make hay, Dilly, Dilly,*
> *Some to cut corn,*
> *While you and I, Dilly, Dilly,*
> *Keep ourselves warm.'*

Sonya clapped her hands. She looked delighted.

Lawrence Dufrette was wearing a white shantung suit and a Panama hat, which he allowed Sonya to take off his head and throw down to the ground. This was repeated several times. She laughed. Her brown eyes were bright. He laughed too. I was amazed since I hadn't thought Lawrence Dufrette capable of laughing like that. His whole face changed. He looked happy and relaxed. More importantly, it was clear to me at that moment that he loved his daughter. I said as much.

'Oh yes, he loves her all right,' Veronica said in a toneless voice. 'Lawrence is nothing like Lena in that respect.'

Three men wearing overalls were walking towards the ancient oak tree. Veronica asked what they were doing, did I know? I did – Sir Michael had told me. 'The tree is something of a historical monument. It was planted by James I. They are going to provide it with a cement base in an effort to preserve it. It is entirely hollow inside. It's starting to disintegrate.'

'It looks horrid. If it were up to me, I'd have it removed. Wasn't there a poem about a hollow? Do you know the one? It always gives me the creeps when I remember it.'

'Would that be Tennyson's Maud*?'*

She looked blank. '"I hate the dreadful hollow behind the little wood . . ." How did it go on?'

I completed it for her:

'Its lips in the field above are dabbled with blood and heath,
The red ribb'd ledges drip with a silent horror of blood
And Echo there, whatever is ask'd her, answers "Death".'

6

The Royal Wedding

The cuff links had been left on her dressing table, in a charming presentation box with an onyx lid. She had found them later that day. She gave them to David on his twenty-first birthday, though she hadn't seen him wear them very often . . .

How many people had there been altogether? Antonia was standing in her kitchen now, heating some excellent Marks and Spencer's asparagus soup in a pan. Ten? Twelve? Excluding Sir Michael and Lady Mortlock, that was. She counted on her fingers. The Dufrettes, the Vorodins, Major Nagle, somebody called Bill Kavanagh, whose bald head and thick black-rimmed glasses brought to mind a bank manager, um, Sheikh Umair, several FO types and their wives. A couple called Falconer and another called Lynch-Marquis. She remembered Mrs L-M. as a large woman with a Roedean voice, wearing a long white silk robe with black stripes from the shoulders down both sides of the skirt.

The argument. For some reason she kept thinking about the argument. It had taken place at breakfast on the morning of the 29th. Lawrence Dufrette and Major Nagle had been no strangers to one another. For a while they had worked together in the same department. Neither man could stand the other, it had soon become apparent to everyone. (Sir Michael should never have asked the two of them together. What could he have been thinking of?) The reason for the animosity? 'Some sort of rivalry, the usual office in-fighting,' Lady Mortlock had said dismissively. 'That, and Lawrence's tendency to poke his nose into other people's affairs.'

Nagle, it transpired, had asked to be transferred to another department because of Dufrette. It had been as bad as that. The argument had started as a result of Dufrette making some disparaging remark about the royal family and Nagle countering it. Dufrette didn't like to be contradicted and he had said something very personal and extremely inflammatory – something about Nagle's wife?

After finishing her soup and feeding the cats, Antonia went back to the sitting room. Should she spend some time on her novel? Standing beside her desk, she looked down at the bottom drawer, which was now closed. She hadn't made *any* progress with her novel. She did need to work out the details of the rather complicated plot; it was at a stage when everything appeared hopelessly absurd . . . No, the drowning of Sonya Dufrette first.

She resumed reading.

It had been a most unsettled morning – the morning of the royal wedding. It had started promisingly enough. At eight o'clock Antonia had been woken up by birdsong and had drawn her curtains made of rich, pea-green moiré silk, fringed with appliqué galloon three inches broad, upheld by stout clasps of gold foliage and draped and tasselled festoons, to see the sun shining from a cloudless blue sky. From her window she could see the river. The sun's slanting rays had turned it into a stream of shimmering molten gold. A light rain had fallen during the night and the air was brighter and fresher than the day before, with the sweet scent of roses and honeysuckle wafting in from the garden. Somewhere a sprinkler hissed. She felt happy and at peace, but also exhilarated. She reflected sentimentally on the sweet young girl who would one day be Queen and remembered the eve of her own wedding. She thought wistfully of Richard, wishing more than ever that he was with her at that moment . . .

Things started to go wrong when Miss Haywood left Twiston with the speed of lightning, in a cab. Antonia heard the story when the maid who had received the phone call, a kindly-looking middle-aged woman, brought her tea. 'Poor girl. Her mother was rushed to hospital an hour ago. Suspected kidney failure. They phoned her from the hospital. At half-past seven! Came as a shock to the poor girl. Apparently her mother was fit as a fiddle the last time she saw her. Today of all days. Terrible.'

Miss Haywood wasn't the only one who left. So did the Vorodins, in their car. At least their departure was pre-planned; they were flying to the USA later in the day.

The row between Major Nagle and Lawrence Dufrette occurred at quarter to nine and resulted in Major Nagle declaring that he wasn't staying under the same roof as Dufrette a moment longer. Nagle rushed out of the dining room and reappeared several minutes later, his face the colour of beetroot, a suitcase in one hand, his car keys in the other. It took Sir Michael all his diplomatic skills to persuade him to stay. Nagle did stay, though he spent the whole morning in his room, 'covered in shame', as an unrepentant Dufrette gloatingly told Antonia, who had only just sat down at the breakfast table.

'You missed my coup. I managed to reduce old Nagle to a quivering jelly by making public a jolly murky episode from his very private life. He didn't like it – what with Michael and Bill Kavanagh and the Falconers *and* Sheikh Umair listening. Bill's the greatest gossip the FO has ever known!'

Dufrette gave a delighted croak. 'I thought Nagle was about to explode. If looks could kill! Well, I do tend to acquire interesting information about people. In this particular instance, I ran into someone at my club, a chap whose late stepsister turned out to have been the first Mrs Nagle. He was of the opinion that Nagle was a monster.

I said, what a coincidence, I was of that opinion too. That broke the ice. It turned out that the day before her death his stepsister had confided in him – told him what treatment she had been receiving at Nagle's hands. Well, after a couple of scotches he spilled the beans. Nagle had been having an affair and he'd been flaunting it in front of his wife. Twice he made sure she found him and his mistress in bed together. Mrs Nagle then committed suicide. Hurled herself under a train. She'd had a history of mental illness of one kind or another, but there is no doubt that it was Nagle who drove her to it. He as good as killed her. Something of a sadist, old Nagle. He's married his mistress since but it seems things are far from blissful. Nagle enjoys treating his women roughly, especially at bedtime, if you know what I mean – but that's another story.'

It was at that point that a ghostly tinkling sound had been heard and Sonya walked into the dining room in her somnambulist manner, carrying a doll that was almost as big as her. Both girl and doll wore similar dresses: white and gold, with tiny bells at the waist – one of Lena's dafter ideas, Antonia imagined. Sonya reached out and took Antonia's hand. She started pulling her towards the open french windows that led into the garden. Antonia looked at Dufrette and received an approving nod. 'It's a lovely day, Mrs Rushton. Go and pick some flowers, why don't you? She likes that.'

They walked out into the garden and Antonia made a daisy chain, which she placed on Sonya's golden head. She pointed things out to her: a comic magpie, a busy squirrel, a strutting wood pigeon, but Sonya paid little attention – she was cooing to her doll. Happening to glance up at the house, Antonia saw Major Nagle standing stock-still at his open window, smoking. It was one of the south windows from which the garden layout of symmetrical beds, stone gate plinths and ironwork could be seen at its best, but she didn't think Nagle was admiring the view. His eyes seemed fixed on them. Feeling somewhat disturbed, Antonia had steered the way briskly down a path leading to the river bank. Sonya had prattled the while, incomprehensible baby talk, directed exclusively at her doll. Beside the river it had felt pleasantly cool.

Antonia raised her brow again. *Could* Major Nagle –? No, no guesses – too early.

They had spent no more than a minute on the river bank, watching the dragonflies circle and the skitterbugs skate across the smoothish green surface of the river, before making their way back to the garden. There they stopped for another minute and Sonya picked some more flowers while Antonia watched the men in blue overalls pour cement into the hollow of the ancient oak. They were talking about Sir Michael's weakness for 'large ladies'. They had seen the Rubens in his study, apparently, and were making ribald jokes about it.

'Will a cement base prevent the tree from decaying?' she asked. The men shrugged and one of them said that the boss – he meant Sir Michael – certainly seemed to think that was the right thing to do. The man was clearly amused by Sir Michael calling the tree a 'historical monument' for he chuckled each time he uttered the phrase. Antonia and Sonya had then returned to the house.

And then?

She had let go of Sonya's hand only when they reached the hall. That was the last time Antonia had seen Sonya. She had heard Lena say, 'Run along, darling, Mamma's terribly busy at the moment.' She had not turned round to see where Sonya had gone but had walked into the sitting room in search of orange juice – she had been extremely thirsty.

Had Sonya, left unattended, wandered out of the front door and back into the garden? The door had certainly been open. Later Lena told the police that she had no recollection, that she hadn't seen where Sonya had gone, but she was pretty sure it hadn't been up the great staircase.

(*Criminal negligence*, Miss Pettigrew had called it.)

In the wake of the Nagle–Dufrette contretemps, the house party had been subdued. Sir Michael tried cheering them up by playing numbers from Fred Astaire's film *Royal Wedding*, with a reminder that the broadcast was about to begin in a quarter of an hour. Would they care to take their seats? Everybody – with the exception of Major Nagle – was there and they complied.

The sitting room was the size of a barn, filled with comfortable chairs and sofas, with ancestral portraits hanging from claret-coloured ropes with tassels against beige neutral silk walls. There was a giant TV set, as well as strategically positioned small tables with plates of sandwiches, bowls of smoked almonds and peanuts and stands containing canapés of various kinds. There were bottles of gin, whisky and brandy on two side tables, old-fashioned siphons, also two coffee percolators and a tea urn. Through the window Antonia had observed the men in blue overalls walking briskly in the direction of the servants' hall, where, she knew, there was another TV set. Sir Michael was as considerate an employer as he was gracious a host. She remembered the whirring of an ancient electric fan in one corner of the room.

'One of your wives is at St Paul's, isn't that so, old boy?' Bill Kavanagh had addressed Sheikh Umair.

'Indeed she is. It was Her Majesty the Queen Mother who provided the pass. The Queen Mother is a very old and valued friend. We both have a passion for horses. My wife is exceedingly fond of weddings. I am not, I must confess. You will probably argue that it has something to do with the fact that I have already attended several of my very own.'

'A certain sense of ennui sets in after a while, eh?'

Lynch-Marquis said with a sigh he knew the feeling well – though he had been married only once.

Dufrette perched on the arm of a chair close to the television set and shook his forefinger at the festive crowds filling Ludgate Hill. 'Look at them – just look at them! The singing, chattering fools in their ridiculous Union Jack hats! What they really should be doing on a day like this is storming the palace, like the Russkies did in 1917.'

And he hadn't stopped there. It soon became apparent that Lawrence Dufrette had taken it upon himself to provide his hosts and fellow guests with a running commentary on the event. Everything he said was noted for its anti-monarchist bias. How he had transmogrified from an ardent royalist to a rabid enemy of the Crown was a mystery, though Lady Mortlock hinted that it had something to do with a snub he had received from the Duke of Kent, that mildest of royals, during a shooting party in 1969. Dufrette, it appeared, did not forgive easily.

'I am no great admirer of my wife's fellow Russkies as a rule, but I take my hat off to them for shooting the Tsar and the Tsarina *and* their brood like a bunch of dogs.'

'Why do you always say such awful things?' Lena had been sipping a Bloody Mary, but she put down her glass and crossed herself. 'That was the greatest calamity to befall Russia. There is a church there now, on the very spot the Romanovs' blood was spilled. Do you know what it is called?' She paused significantly and looked round. 'It is called the Church of the Spilt Blood.'

'Oh, how remarkably original!'

'Pilgrims trekked hundreds of miles on foot to Yekaterinburg for the consecration. They carried crosses and icons. They burnt so much incense that day, the sun disappeared in the fumes. They saw that as an omen.'

'It's been said that if people treat their royalty badly, a kind of curse is visited on them,' Mrs Falconer – a tall woman in a tomato-coloured dress with high winged shoulders – said. 'D'you think that's true?'

'True enough about the Russians.' Lynch-Marquis nodded. 'The French too. They guillotined the King and Queen and tortured the Dauphin, and look at them – not a single decent government since!'

'Serves them jolly well right,' Bill Kavanagh said. 'Let's drink to it.'

Mrs Lynch-Marquis said tentatively, 'We killed our King too . . .'

'Ah, Charles the Cavalier, with his zeal for his creed, his

expensive demands and silk underwear!' Dufrette croaked. 'Cromwell did a damned good job.'

'*Have* we got a decent government?' Mrs Falconer asked.

The night before, Antonia had heard Dufrette refer to the '*Gräfin* of Grantham', or it might have been the 'Griffon of Grantham', or even the 'Gryphon of Grantham', so she expected another disparaging comment, but what this perverse person said now was, 'Of course we have. Ma Thatcher is a goddess and I will personally shoot anyone who dares suggest otherwise.'

Lena pointed to the TV screen. 'Is the glass coach bulletproof? Is it made of fortified glass? What if somebody decides to shoot at dear sweet Diana? There might be a sniper hiding somewhere! The IRA –'

'*That* would be the day!'

'So young, so fresh, so beautiful.' Lena dabbed at her eyes with her handkerchief. 'So innocent-looking. Do you know who Diana reminds me of? She reminds me of *me*.'

Dufrette said with a smile that she must be thinking of somebody else. She had never been innocent. Young and beautiful yes, about two hundred and fifty-five years ago. Innocent – *never*. 'Shall I remind you what one of your party tricks used to be? Better not – we are after all in polite society.'

'Do you know what I want to do, Lawrence? I want to throw my glass at you and smash your face,' Lena slurred.

'You are most likely to miss, my sweet, but do you know what will happen if you do a crazy thing like that? I will strangle you with the curtain cord.'

Sheikh Umair had been looking immensely bored, but at this last lively exchange he perked up. Antonia saw his hooded eyes fix speculatively on the window curtains. The rest of them, being terribly English and well bred, pretended nothing untoward had happened.

'Drink, anyone?' Sir Michael called out. Antonia saw his

faded brown eyes fix anxiously on Lena. He seemed to be the only one who took her seriously.

'When you die, Lawrence, I shall dance on your grave,' Lena declared. 'Then I shall dig you up and feed you to the dogs.'

Antonia remembered thinking that it all put *Who's Afraid of Virginia Woolf?* in the shade.

'Poor Johnny looks dreadful,' Sir Michael had said as a beaming, if painfully slow Earl Spencer led his daughter up the steps of St Paul's and along the aisle.

'Go back, you slippered pantaloon! Shoo! Shoo! Go back before it is too late! You don't know what you are letting your daughter in for! Go back, I say!' Dufrette flapped his hands. He could be very funny, Antonia had to admit, though his particular brand of humour wasn't to everybody's taste – if Lady Mortlock's face was anything to go by.

'That silly goose. Just look at her. Observe how she simpers in her doomed glory. She has no idea. The Windsors will eat her alive. Shoo! Back! Back, I say!'

'Why don't you have a drink, Dufrette?' Sir Michael suggested in a mild attempt at deflection.

'Ivory silk . . . That's so beautiful.' Lena brushed away a tear.

Bill Kavanagh said, 'I used to know Raine Spencer very well at one time – before she married Johnny. When she was married to Dartmouth. Remarkable woman. Shame the Spencer children never got to appreciate her properly.'

'Just imagine . . .' Lawrence Dufrette raised his voice. 'Just imagine that instead of landing two earls, Raine had married and divorced the following: Lord Rayne, Prince Georg of Saxe-Gotha, the King of Spain, Baron Kommer, Dr Johnny Gaynor, Tommy Nutter and Sir Robin Day, she'd have been called – now you need to pay *very* close attention – *Raine Rayne Gotha Spain Kommer Gaynor Nutter Day . . .*'

That was met with some appreciative laughter. Only

Lady Mortlock's expression remained morose while Sheikh Umair merely looked puzzled.

How long had it taken him to work that one out? Antonia wondered. It wasn't exactly spur-of-the-moment wit. He must have prepared it well in advance.

'What a drip Charlie boy looks.' Dufrette had spoken again. 'And there's Mrs P-B. How she must be wishing it was her walking up the aisle!'

'That was never terribly likely, was it?' Mrs Lynch-Marquis said.

'Not terribly likely, no,' Mrs Falconer agreed.

'If he had lived in my country,' Sheikh Umair pointed out, 'the Prince of Wales would have been able to marry them *both*. There would have been no problem at all.'

'I always understood Camilla was a cracking bird,' Mr Lynch-Marquis said. 'Parker-Bowles is a lucky fellow.'

'The question is, does she curtsey before she jumps into bed? Does she call him "sir"? It's a well-documented fact that her great-grandmama did.' Dufrette gave a histrionic little cough. 'Of course, as the redoubtable Mrs Keppel herself put it, things were done so much better in her day.'

7

Death by Drowning

It was about an hour and a half later, when the broadcast was over, that they had become aware of Sonya's absence. As it happened, it was Antonia who raised the question and subsequently the alarm. 'Oh, she loves to hide, the naughty *kotik*,' Lena said dismissively, at first quite unperturbed. She continued sipping from her glass. 'She's got herself into a cupboard somewhere, or under a bed, or behind a curtain. It is an annoying habit she has.'

So they looked inside all the cupboards and under all the beds and behind all the curtains, then everywhere else around the house. They checked all the rooms. Everybody – hosts, guests, servants, workmen – took part in the search, the only exception being Major Nagle.

Major Nagle remained in his room. He hadn't left it for a moment, or so he said. When they knocked on his door, he was looking for his signet ring. His face was very red. He seemed more concerned about the loss of his ring than about the little girl who had vanished. Then they searched the garden. They walked around, calling out Sonya's name . . .

Antonia looked up. She was remembering the sick feeling at the pit of her stomach, the convulsive pounding of her heart against her ribs, the ringing sound in her ears, the dizziness, the sudden dryness in her throat, the nausea . . .

Sonya's bracelet was discovered on the path leading down to the river, her daisy chain on a bush. It had come to Antonia as something of a shock to see the river. Only two hours earlier it had been smooth and calm and golden – now it was darker, olive-green and turbulent. The banks leading down to the water were rather steep, she had noticed for the first time, and they were overhung by trees, silver birches, a box elder, a copper beech. She looked across at the armies of reeds and rushes, sword-shaped and yellow-green in colour. She felt the cool rising off the water – also a 'green' smell, like moss. She shuddered.

'*Kotik! Kotik!* Where are you? Mamma loves you so much. Mamma can't live without her *kotik*!' Lena lurched about on her high heels, wailing piteously. 'Where are you? Come out – speak to Mamma!' The next instant she screamed and pointed.

The small body was floating on the river surface, face up. It had got entangled in some tree roots that crept into the river across the bank. Lena, her red hair wild in the wind, the mascara running down her cheeks, collapsed in a heap on the ground. She beat her fists against the river bank, rattling her bracelets. She shook her head and rocked her body forward and backward, wailing, '*Kotik, kotik!*' Then, casting her face heavenwards, she threw up her arms and cried, 'Why, oh God? Why? *Why?* Why deprive me of the one thing I loved best in this world?'

Antonia had seen the Falconers exchange cynical looks. Dufrette stood some distance away, very still, and stared at the body in the river, his face deadly pale.

It was Antonia who said, 'That's not Sonya. It's her doll. It's only her doll.'

Lena raised her head. 'But she couldn't be parted from her doll! Don't you see what happened? They both fell into the river! My *kotik* has drowned! She has been carried away by the current!'

Her face was dark and suffused, a mask of fury. She shook her forefinger at Antonia. 'It was you! You showed her the way to the river! It is your fault! I saw you take my *kotik* down to the river. You killed her!'

At that point Lady Mortlock had gone back to the house and phoned the police.

When she went to bed that night, Antonia lay for quite a while unable to sleep, going over in her mind what she had read. Though there had been no witnesses, it was assumed that Sonya had left the house, wandered out into the garden and down to the river bank where she had slipped and tumbled into the river. The body had never been recovered but that wasn't such an uncommon occurrence. The verdict had been one of tragic accident. It had been an open and shut case. The Dufrettes had been reprimanded for not providing their daughter with adequate care.

Reading her account had had a therapeutic effect on Antonia. It felt like a curtain lifting. She saw how preposterous it had been for her to feel guilty over Sonya's death. Lena had been looking for scapegoats. First she had turned on Antonia, then on the Mortlocks. Lena had suggested that it had been their fault too – why hadn't they put up any river-bank defences? Why wasn't there protective netting? Lena had gone so far as to suggest she might take the Mortlocks to court.

Thinking about what she had written, Antonia suddenly experienced an odd feeling of dissatisfaction, a sense of there being something *wrong*, but by now she had started to feel sleepy.

It was interesting that it had all happened at a time when everybody had been inside – glued to the box. The whole of England, or so it had been reported in the papers. Fewer robberies had been committed that day, if statistics were anything to go by. Fewer crimes generally. It was assumed that criminals too had been watching the royal wedding. Conversely, Antonia thought, how easy it would have been to commit a crime on a day like that.

Had there been a crime at Twiston? *The ring – watch out for that signet ring.* That was Miss Pettigrew whispering in her ear. Antonia saw Major Nagle, taking a cigarette from his Asprey's silver case. He said nothing but gave her a wink. A moment later a second voice spoke – it sounded like Lawrence Dufrette's. 'It seems to me, Mrs Rushton, that you lack the creative balance of imagination and reason. *Ergo,* you can never be a truly successful writer.'

Antonia knew she was dreaming now and yet she was filled with misgivings. Questions formed themselves in her mind, but they were the wrong kind of questions.

Would she ever be able to complete her novel? Would she ever be able to write again? *Could* she write at all?

8

Le Goût du Policier

As she arrived at the club the following morning, the reason for her dissatisfaction dawned on her. Her account of what had happened at Twiston was lively and vivid and it contained some good descriptions and entertaining dialogue. It was not her ability to write that was in question. No. There was a different reason for her dissatisfaction. Although she couldn't put her finger on it, she knew that something was wrong – either with the way she had described one or more of the characters in the drama, or with her reporting of what they said. Some illogicality . . . Some discrepancy?

She was sure she wasn't imagining it . . . What *was* it?

Not many people visited the library that morning and she received only one phone call. A good thing, for she was in such an abstracted state of mind that some club member was bound to notice and complain. She performed her chores mechanically, automaton-like, in a kind of daze. At one point she found herself lifting a pile of books from one of the donation boxes and placing them on her desk, then staring down at them in utter incomprehension. She had absolutely no idea what she should do with the books. Yes, she did. Stamp them, write down their titles, put them on the right shelves. She reached out for the library stamp. (In what way was the signet ring important?)

Eventually she heard the clock chime eleven. She took the folder out of her bag. *The Drowning of Sonya Dufrette,* she had written at the top. Well, she knew she wouldn't rest until she found out what was wrong.

Martin brought her a tray with a pot of coffee, a cup and a plate of Lazzaroni biscuits. Pouring herself coffee, she started skimming through the pages once more. Was there any significance in the fact that Sonya and her doll had been dressed in identical dresses? She couldn't see how there could be.

Sonya's body had never been recovered. Sonya had vanished without a trace. That was one fact that was certain. Twenty years had passed but the body hadn't turned up. If it had, she would have heard about it, she was sure. It would have been in the papers – or on TV – or someone would have mentioned it to her. People didn't just *vanish.* They were either dead or assumed new identities or . . . or . . . No, there was nothing else. That was it. What would be the *point* of giving Sonya a new identity? But then, if she was dead, where was her body? Swallowed by some monstrous fish? Could the body have been weighed down and eased into the river? That would mean murder and there wasn't a scrap of evidence pointing that way. On the other hand, the body might not be in the river at all. Sonya might have been killed somewhere else and the body buried.

The other night Antonia had thought in terms of violence. She had dreamt of blood. Now, why had she? She believed there was a reason for it. Something must have suggested violence to her. Something she had seen without realizing its importance at the time – something she had heard? She didn't think the idea had come to her just like that . . . Once more she saw Sonya's face, as it had been when Dufrette had played with her in the garden – shrieking with laughter, her blue eyes very bright . . . No, not blue – *brown.* Her eyes had been brown. Antonia frowned. Was *that* of any importance? How extremely annoying she didn't even know what she was looking for!

'Who lent thee, child, this meditative guise?'

She looked up and her frown disappeared. She smiled at the wiry man with the twinkling blue eyes and greying blond hair. 'Good morning, Major Payne . . . Is that Matthew Arnold?'

'Indeed it is.'

It was Tuesday of course. He always came down to London on Tuesdays. She noted with approval his bottle-green jacket, his clean shirt and highly polished dark cap-toe shoes. Did anyone 'do' for him, now that his wife was dead? Well, army men were perfectly capable of doing for themselves.

'Proofreading, I see.' He pointed to the sheets on the desk.

'No, no such luck. Raking up the past. This is something I wrote twenty years ago.'

'Something you might turn into a novel?'

'No, not really. Though there's a puzzle there all right.'

She found Major Payne – the 'intellectual Major', as her son had dubbed him – gazing at her with such a blend of affection and solemnity that for an absurd moment she had the notion he might propose to her. It came to her as a relief – mingled, ludicrously, with disappointment – when he said, 'I too have a puzzle for you. Shall we swap? I'll tell you mine, you then tell me yours. Is it a deal?'

'It's a deal.' She felt foolish, but what else could she have said? He could be so disarming.

'Here goes. A man dies on 23rd January, yet is buried on 22nd January. How is that possible?'

'Well . . .' Antonia scowled. 'If the man died in Fiji and the body was flown to Western Samoa for burial, the flight would cross the International Date Line from west to east, wouldn't it, so the date would go back one day?'

'Makes perfect sense,' Major Payne said magnanimously. 'This is a trick question, actually, so the simple answer is that he died at sea on the 23rd but his mortal remains weren't recovered until a year later – next January, in fact.

That's when he was buried, on the 22nd. I told it to my aunt and she loved it.'

Antonia sighed. 'I always go for the complicated.'

'Well, your novel manages to combine both, a complicated plot *and* a trick that is wonderfully simple. It was such fun to read. Few people write stories like yours nowadays.'

'Thank you for saying so, but I am sure you are wrong. Lots of people write better than me.'

'I am not wrong. I am fed up with pretentious bores. Baronesses with missions who shall remain nameless.'

Antonia didn't think it right to ask him to elaborate. How he managed to read so much she had no idea. She had imagined that all his energies would be channelled into the management of his Suffolk farm and the indoor cricket school he had established, which, he had told her, attracted teams from all over England to its six-a-side tournaments and other events. Besides, there were the social dos – dinner parties, polo tournaments – she imagined he'd be in great demand – amazing he hadn't been snapped up yet – what had his late wife been like?

He was talking. '. . . and, really, your sentences are a joy to read.'

'Don't be idiotic.'

'Do you know who said, "I like sentences that don't budge though armies cross them"?'

Antonia was aware that he was looking down at her hands and she put them on her lap. 'Monty?' she suggested flippantly.

'Virginia Woolf actually . . . So what's your puzzle about?' Major Payne twisted his head slightly to one side and screwed up his eyes at one of the sheets on the desk. '*Lawrence Dufrette has the reputation of a maverick and is considered something of a loose cannon*. I can read upside down, you see,' he explained. 'They taught us how to do it in the Secret Service. That was a longish while ago, but I haven't yet lost the knack. Wait a minute.' He tapped the sheet with a forefinger. 'I used to know a Lawrence

Dufrette. Must be the same chap. Name like that. Tall and stately – beak of a nose – wild glare. Like Wellington on amphetamines – or Heseltine, *sans le nez*, on speed?'

'Yes.' Antonia laughed.

'Fancy. It's a small world. Well, he's written a book that's totally bizarre. Under a pen name. I read the review in *Fortean Times* first – I do read an awful lot of tosh, mind. The reviewer gave away Dufrette's real name, so I went and got hold of the book. I was curious. Needless to say it wasn't reviewed anywhere else.'

'Why not?'

'Because it is too bizarre.'

'In what way bizarre? What is it about?'

Major Payne stroked his jaw with a forefinger. 'Well, his theory is that the same interconnected bloodlines – the so-called Babylonian brotherhood – have controlled and dominated our planet for thousands of years. The President of the United States and members of the British royal family are part of it – many other world leaders as well. Mind-controlled human robots are used to pass messages between people outside the normal channels. The communications are dictated under a form of hypnosis brought about by means of a high voltage gun, which lowers blood sugar levels and makes the person more open to suggestion. It isn't science fiction, but the history of the world according to Lawrence Dufrette. He claims in the introduction that he has researched the subject extensively.'

'I wonder if he became completely deranged after Sonya's death,' Antonia said thoughtfully. The next moment she cried, 'Oh – he does list the Babylonian brotherhood in *Who's Who* as one of his interests!'

'That was his daughter, wasn't it? Sonya. There was something wrong with her, correct?'

'Yes. They thought she was autistic.'

'She drowned, didn't she?'

'That was the verdict.'

He looked at her. 'How well do you know Dufrette?'

'We stayed at the same house twenty years ago.

I thought I saw him yesterday – *twice*. Once outside White's, then here, in the library. Sounds incredible, doesn't it, but he seems to haunt me. I hope I am not going mad.'

'There is a definite link between madness and creativity,' Payne said in grave tones. 'It's been scientifically proven. Writers are at a particular risk.'

'Oh, thank you for warning me . . . Where did you meet Lawrence Dufrette?'

'We were in the Secret Service together. Different departments. I had just joined. He wasn't at all popular. Had no friends, apart from old Mortlock, who was already on his way out. Mortlock had been to school with Dufrette *père* . . . Lawrence Dufrette was abrasive, contemptuous and critical of everything and everybody. And that wasn't a front concealing any cavernous uncertainties – he did genuinely believe he was better than everybody else.'

'That was very much the impression he gave when I knew him.'

'I do remember the first time I saw him. I went into his office to borrow a file. He was sitting at his desk, very still, staring straight ahead, his patrician profile tilted ever so slightly upward, as if he were listening to celestial harps lesser mortals couldn't hear.' Payne laughed. He looks ten years younger when he laughs, Antonia thought. 'Then he saw me and looked enormously put out. His face twisted demoniacally . . . Apparently he had a great appetite for byzantine dealings and he engaged in elaborate plotting to eliminate his enemies –'

'Do you know a Major Nagle?' Antonia interrupted.

'Nagle? I believe I have heard the name, but no, I don't know him. I think he left the service altogether. I may be wrong . . . In what way is Nagle important?'

'He was one of Dufrette's enemies.'

'Really? How interesting . . . Did *you* get on well with Dufrette? I do hope he was decent to you?'

'As a matter of fact he was. When his daughter disappeared – presumed drowned in the river – his wife Lena became hysterical. She suggested it had been my fault, but he said nothing – nothing at all. When I told him how sorry I was, he shook my hand . . . I was there, you see, when it happened.'

'What's the puzzle exactly?'

'I believe there is something wrong somewhere in my account of the events leading to Sonya's drowning. I can't say what it is but I know it's there . . .'

There was a pause. 'Do you think she was murdered?' he asked.

Antonia blinked. 'I don't know. I have all sorts of ideas. Some really far-fetched ones. My suspicions keep shifting. A moment ago I even thought Lady Mortlock's interest in eugenics might have had something to do with it!'

'Elimination of the mental defectives, eh?'

'That sort of thing, yes. Very silly, really. Out of the question. I don't think Lady Mortlock cared for Sonya, but then she didn't like children. She'd never had any.' Antonia pushed the folder towards him slightly. 'I'd be glad of your opinion. Do you think you could . . .'

Major Payne said with great alacrity that he would be delighted to read what she had written. He had *le goût du policier*, he was terribly clever at noticing things, but he had never before been involved in a real-life mystery. He could start *now*, couldn't he?

'I'll order some coffee for you, shall I?'

'Please do. They make damned good coffee here.' Picking up the folder and without another word, he went up to one of the high-backed armchairs beside the fireplace and sat down. Antonia watched him take out his pipe, a straight-stemmed briar, which he proceeded to fill with tobacco from a leather pouch. He struck a match, puffed away and opened the folder.

The Sherlock Holmes touch. *Le goût du policier*. They both shared it. This is not a game, she reminded herself.

She hoped she was not making a fool of herself.

9

An Awkward Lie

The telephone call she had received at half-past nine that morning had been from Mrs Cathcart, Colonel Haslett's archivist friend, and it concerned the Gresham papers. Mrs Cathcart was going to collect the papers in person; she was coming later in the day, if that would be convenient. She had spoken in a high precise voice. In a *cab*, she had added with an odd emphasis – she might as well have said she was coming in a chariot. Would Miss Darcy be good enough to have the Gresham papers ready for her? Well packed? Antonia had assured her that she would.

The Gresham papers formed a correspondence dating back to the late 1890s, and were contained in two wooden boxes painted periwinkle blue, stashed away under Antonia's table. The letters she had examined lay on a side table in sorted heaps according to sender. The idea had been for her to read gradually through the whole lot and organize and catalogue it, so that the contents could clearly be seen and assessed, and anything of importance noted. Then they could decide what to do with it. Except now it was Mrs Cathcart who was going to decide.

It was fair, Antonia supposed, to give the Gresham papers out for assessment. It wasn't strictly a library matter. The boxes had been found in the club smoking room, of all places, when the building was renovated a couple of years back, and so the librarian had been asked to take care of them. A proper archivist could do a better job in all probability. It was just that it had been very interesting, to read the sort of letters people wrote then, in that more leisured age, in their beautiful copperplate handwriting, and using elaborately correct grammar and punctuation.

Antonia picked up the letters from the side table and began to place them carefully inside one of the boxes. She looked towards Major Payne and saw him produce a pen and draw a vertical line on the page he had been reading. Had he found something? She couldn't tell from his inscrutable expression though she thought he gave a very slight nod over his coffee cup, denoting satisfaction. (Major Nagle – she couldn't get Major Nagle out of her mind now, for some reason – that still, menacing figure at the window.) Discovering she still held one of the letters, she took it out of its envelope and glanced down at it absently.

My dear Gresham, the letter began. What followed was some not particularly amusing anecdote, told in meticulous detail, about a social evening the writer had spent with some acquaintances known also to the letter's recipient. There was the mention of somebody called Hollingbourne and of a Mrs Duppa, who told fortunes 'rather inaccurately'. Vague scandals were referred to. At one point the writer enquired after the health of Lady Gresham, who, it appeared, had been indisposed for quite a while, and expressed optimism about the invalid's progress. There were bits that were unintentionally funny, Antonia reflected, in a *Diary of a Nobody* kind of way.

As she replaced the letter inside its envelope and back in the box, her mind registered the word 'Nepal'. It had been written in pencil across another envelope in big block capitals. NEPAL. It didn't seem likely that the letters contained correspondence from Nepal, though perhaps someone had travelled there and written to Gresham about it. I'll just have a quick look, Antonia thought. It might contain some interesting traveller's story, and she could tell her last enquirer about it, the old boy who had reminded her of Lawrence Dufrette, if he put in another appearance, that was.

She opened the envelope.

My dear Gresham, the letter began as before. This time the writing was in pencil, and seemed less assured somehow. *I have something to tell you, which I believe to be of great importance, but I hardly know where to commence . . .*

No, no more mysteries. I have enough on my plate already, she thought decisively and, resisting her curiosity, put the letter back into the envelope and replaced it in the box.

'Well, I believe I've got it,' she heard Major Payne say. She turned round. He had left the armchair and was walking towards her. 'You are absolutely right,' he went on. 'There's something, or rather two things that are wrong.'

Antonia felt her pulse quicken. 'What things?'

He leant across the desk towards her, his hand lightly touching hers. She smelled his aftershave, a blend of citrus, cedar wood and tobacco, but the latter could be coming from his pipe. Funny that she had objected strongly to her former husband smoking cigarettes, but she didn't mind a pipe one bit.

'When you first hear of Lena Dufrette, it is from Lady Mortlock. This is what you say.' He cleared his throat. *'Then in 1960 Dufrette married for the second time, an exiled Russian countess or, as Lady Mortlock had put it, "a woman who claimed to be one"*. This rather suggests, doesn't it, that Lady Mortlock only met Lena *after* she married Lawrence Dufrette? She talked of Lena as of a stranger, right?'

'Yes. That was the impression she gave. I remember our conversation very well.'

'Indeed. Yet you, clearly without realizing it, also provide unequivocal evidence to the contrary, namely that Lady Mortlock had known Lena *before* her marriage to Dufrette. This is what Lena tells you when the two of you meet in the garden. *I have been bad, oh so bad, you can't imagine how bad. Ask Hermione Mortlock. She knows me well*

– better than anybody. She will tell you. She has no illusions about me.'

'Better than anybody . . .'

'She might have been lying, mind – or imagining things, if she had been "cranked up", as Veronica Vorodin suggested.'

'No, she didn't lie.' Antonia's eyes were suddenly very bright. 'Something else happened. I never wrote it down, but I've suddenly remembered. Soon after the Dufrettes arrived on the 28th, we had tea in the drawing room, and somebody mentioned a play they had seen. Lena started giggling and she turned to Lady Mortlock and said, 'Do you remember when we went to see the first night of –' She mentioned some title, which no one seemed to have heard of – can't remember what it was, but Lena's tone suggested that it had been something . . . I don't know. She gave a quick lift of her eyebrows –'

'Outré? Naughty? Scandalous?'

'That was what I thought, yes. To which Lady Mortlock replied rather crossly that she didn't know what Lena was talking about. She then said, "I'm sure you are mistaken. The play we went to see was *The Reluctant Debutante*."'

Major Payne cocked an eyebrow. 'A perfectly innocent drawing-room comedy by William Douglas-Home. One of the big West End hits of the mid-fifties . . . *First night*, eh?'

'Yes. I didn't notice the implications at the time, but it does indicate that Lady Mortlock had known Lena in the mid-fifties – well before her marriage to Lawrence Dufrette in 1960. They went to see a play together. Lady Mortlock did give herself away . . . Now let me see. In the mid-fifties Lena was a young girl of seventeen or eighteen . . . How curious. I wonder if –'

'I suggest we don't delve too deeply into that one yet. Let's look at contradiction number two. It's to do with Miss Haywood, the Dufrette nanny, and, again, as it happens, with Lady Mortlock. This is what you wrote on first meeting the nanny on 28th July. *Miss Haywood struck me as extremely tense and preoccupied-looking. Lady Mortlock later told me that her mother was gravely ill, in hospital. Lady Mortlock said she had great admiration for the poor girl, whom she described as "having the patience of a saint – wonderfully suited to the care of a backward child."*

'However!' Major Payne put up his forefinger. 'Only a few pages later you report the servant who brought you your early morning tea on the 29th as telling you that Miss Haywood's mother had been rushed to the hospital with suspected kidney failure and what a shock it had been to the poor girl. *They phoned her from the hospital. Came as a shock to the poor girl. Apparently her mother was fit as a fiddle the last time she saw her. Today of all days. Terrible!*'

Antonia drew in her breath. 'The two don't tally. Of course. Stupid of me not to notice. Either the mother was gravely ill, as Lady Mortlock had said, and Miss Haywood was worried about her, or the mother's sudden hospitalization came as a shock . . . So the mother's illness was fabricated?'

'I do believe it was, yes, but the conspirators didn't do the job properly. They didn't think it through. It wasn't sufficiently rehearsed – or else there were two different versions and they thought they had agreed which one they were doing, only the nanny got it wrong – or the other party got it wrong. Does that make sense?'

'Yes. The nanny was got out of the way on the morning on which Sonya Dufrette disappeared.'

'That's what the evidence suggests. Yes. The nanny was got out of the way and Sonya allowed to go into the garden unattended –'

'Lena. Lena was there, in the hall, when I brought Sonya back to the house.'

'If Miss Haywood had stayed and her charge had disappeared, she'd have got the blame for it. It seems to me,' Major Payne said thoughtfully, 'that someone was showing great consideration for the nanny. I also suspect that the day itself was chosen very carefully – whoever's behind this outrage knew that there'd be no witnesses since everybody would be indoors watching the royal wedding on the box.'

'That's what I thought . . . My God. The cold calculation of it.'

'You say the nanny looked tense and anxious the day before the disappearance. She was clearly playing a part – the loving daughter worried to death about her mother and so on. On the other hand, the anxiety might have been genuine. Perhaps Miss H. had had second thoughts about what she had agreed to and was getting cold feet, but was nevertheless going along with it. Which suggests that money was probably involved.'

Antonia shook her head. 'I can't believe it. What did they want with an autistic child? What did they do to Sonya? She's dead – must be. We are dealing with a monster. What kind of monster though? Child killer – somebody who gets kicks out of it? Paedophile? Or did they want her for her blood and organs? No – that's too far-fetched.'

Payne stroked his jaw with his forefinger. 'It might have been more complicated than that.'

'I can't believe Lady Mortlock's got anything to do with it. I can't!'

'I know we mustn't jump to conclusions, but it does seem that Lady Mortlock is indicated. She is the common factor in the two discrepancies in your account. She lied not only once but twice. *And* she had a great admiration for the nanny. From what you have written, Lady Mortlock strikes me as the kind of woman who would lie only if she had a very good reason for it . . . Is she still alive, do you know?'

10

Sleuths on the Scent

About an hour and a half later they were sitting at a table inside the club dining room. Major Payne had insisted that they continue over lunch. Antonia rarely had lunch at the club. She usually went to a café in Piccadilly.

For a while they found it impossible to talk. The place was full. Quite a few of the club members seemed to be entertaining visitors. There were at least six women wearing smart hats and laughing a lot. The table next to theirs was occupied by two extremely distinguished-looking elderly gentlemen, one sporting a white carnation in his buttonhole, both rather portly and flushed with the wine they had been drinking, also rather deaf, for they were talking at the tops of their voices.

'Suez did destroy his health, you are absolutely right,' one was saying as Antonia and Major Payne sat down. 'That and his amorous indiscretions.' He winked at Antonia and nodded at Payne conspiratorially.

'He was never the same man after Suez. I was with him when he went on that cruise, you know.'

'Really? Part of Eden's entourage, eh? When was that? '56?'

''57. As a matter of fact I was one of his secretaries. We sailed to New Zealand. The RMS *Rangitata*. Lady Eden's idea. It was meant to be recuperative, though Eden found the heat hard to bear. He kept getting these terrible giddy spells.'

Soon after they finished their lunch and left, allowing Payne and Antonia to resume their conversation.

'Is your Egg Florentine all right?' Major Payne asked, pausing with his spoon filled with carrot-and-ginger soup in mid-air. 'I can eat eggs only for breakfast . . . You sure you don't want any wine? We could have a bottle between us –'

'Yes, quite sure, thank you. I've got things to do in the afternoon.'

'Keep forgetting you are still at work. Sorry. Won't do for old Haslett to smell wine on your breath. Better keep our heads clear anyhow. So you say you haven't seen Lady Mortlock since 1981?'

'That's right. I did ring her up a couple of days later, at the beginning of August, and she sounded polite, but extremely distant. She had suddenly turned into a stranger. She said Sir Michael was not at all well and that they'd probably be leaving for Malta quite soon. They had a holiday villa there. I hadn't completed the job I had been doing for her – the Jourdain family history – so I asked when we were going to resume it. She said she feared the family history would have to be put on hold for a while. There were more important things than one's family history. She sounded extremely tight-lipped. She'd contact me when they came back, she said. Well, she never did contact me.'

'Why was that, do you think?'

'I thought at the time that it was because she didn't want any reminders of what had happened. I believed she wanted to isolate the whole distressing event in her mind and avoid anything – anyone – that might recall it. I then realized that I'd left some things at Twiston – an attaché case, a portable typewriter, some books – which I needed. When I phoned again only a couple of days later, the Mortlocks had gone. It was a Mrs Linley, the housekeeper, who answered the phone. We arranged a date for me to go and collect my stuff, but then David was ill, and I rang again to make another arrangement, but nobody answered the phone. I tried several more times, but it wasn't till mid-September that I managed to speak to somebody. As it happened, it was Mrs Maloney, the servant who had informed me about Miss Haywood's departure. She told me that the Mortlocks were still in Malta, but I was welcome to go to Twiston, I only had to say when – she'd be there.'

'You went?'

'Yes. The gardens had been tended beautifully. I didn't care much for the oak. It was the colour of mud. It looked mummified. I suddenly saw it the way Lena had. From a distance it did look like a hideous face distorted in rage.' Antonia smiled and shook her head. 'For some reason it made me think of Major Nagle . . . I bumped into a gardener. I congratulated him on the state of the gardens and he said he was receiving instructions from the Mortlocks' son, who had come back from America.'

'I thought the Mortlocks were childless.'

'They were. George Mortlock is Sir Michael's son from a previous marriage. He is Lady Mortlock's stepson.'

'Did you get to meet him?'

'No. He hadn't moved into the house or anything like that. He lived somewhere else, not far, and only came twice a week, to make sure the housekeeper and the servants kept everything in order.' She paused. 'It was a warm day, the day I went. The house was very quiet. It looked serene. There was nothing to suggest a tragedy had taken place there so recently. The windows had been left open and the curtains were blowing in the wind. I had the oddest feeling that – that Sonya was there, inside the house.' Antonia frowned. 'That she would suddenly appear from behind some curtain and cry, "Boo!" Somehow, at that moment, I felt absolutely sure she wasn't dead. I remember standing in the middle of the hall – listening, waiting. I convinced myself I heard a child's laughter but I am sure that was only my imagination.

When a door opened, I jumped. Only it was Mrs Maloney. The spell was broken. She gave me a cup of tea. She was very friendly. She chatted away. She told me that the Mortlocks had no immediate intention of coming back to England. Sir Michael was still rather poorly. It was his nerves, she said. That's what she had heard from the son.'

'Nervous breakdown?'

'That was the impression I got. Yes. He was extremely upset when Sonya disappeared. More than I thought possible. I saw him dabbing at his eyes. He was the only one who went up to Lena and put his arm around her shoulders. I remember wondering whether he might not have been in love with her.'

Payne smiled. 'He might have been. He was known for his penchant for "chubby chicks". That's how somebody in the department put it.'

'He had a Rubens in his study . . . Well, Sir Michael died the following year – or was it the year after?'

'He died in 1982,' Major Payne said. 'I remember reading his obituary and talking to someone in the department who had known him well. It was exactly thirty years since he had started working at MI5.'

'I too read his obituary . . . There was something funny in it – something I thought odd. What was it? Can't remember now. I did write to Lady Mortlock expressing my condolences. She never wrote back. She sold Twiston a few years later. In 1987, I think. There was an article about it in one of the papers. With pictures.'

'Who bought it? The National Trust?'

'A private buyer, I think.'

Major Payne observed that it must have cost a packet.

'A couple of million or so. A fortune in the eighties . . . Where Lady Mortlock went to live after that, I have no idea, but it shouldn't be too hard to find out.' Antonia paused. 'I suppose I could phone Twiston and ask if they have a contact number or address.'

'You've written the number here,' Major Payne said, tapping the last page of Antonia's typescript.

'So I have. Twiston 207452. They may have changed it of course. I'll check. Lady Mortlock may still be abroad. That would complicate matters.'

'How old did you say she was? Eighty-seven? You sure she is still alive?'

'I'd have heard if she'd died. There'd have been obituaries, even if she'd died abroad . . . I wonder if she'd agree to see me. Or if she did, whether she'd be willing to talk about the past,' Antonia said thoughtfully.

'She might not be, if she had something to hide,' Payne pointed out.

Antonia shook her head. 'I can't believe Lady Mortlock had anything to do with Sonya's disappearance. I can't. It makes no sense . . . Even if she did hate the idea of a mentally deficient child being under her roof, she wouldn't kill her. The idea's absurd. Unless she was mad – which I don't think she was.'

Payne leant across the table. 'She told lies twice. Of course the lies might be unrelated to the disappearance. Still, it's strange, you must admit.'

'Oh it *is* strange. I won't rest until I know the reason. I must see her.'

'That's where we start then.'

There was a pause, then Antonia said, 'She never left the drawing room that morning. She couldn't have done anything to Sonya. She couldn't have phoned the nanny either.'

'Why not? She could have done it from some extension. Don't tell me there were no extensions at Twiston.'

'Well, there were. But Lady Mortlock's voice would have been instantly recognized by the servant who took the call – Mrs Maloney – even if she had tried to disguise it.'

'Perhaps Mrs Maloney was in it too? Squared – her silence bought? Or maybe the caller was somebody else – an accomplice. Maybe Lady Mortlock was just the brains behind it. The mastermind. You look unconvinced . . . The other lead is of course the nanny. I can follow up that one. Find where she is, contrive to meet her, then try to trick her into some sort of confession. I'll have to think of the best way to set about it,' Payne mused aloud. 'Miss Haywood . . . Where is she? What happened to her? If we are right and she did receive a fortune in hush money, she became one very rich young lady in the days that followed the royal wedding. I wonder if she suffers pangs of guilty conscience . . . You thought she looked anxious, didn't you?'

'I wonder if she was a Catholic,' Antonia said suddenly. 'She wore a crucifix round her neck.'

'Might have been just a fashion fad,' Payne said. 'The nanny wasn't pretty, was she?'

'No. Not at all. Plain, actually. Poor complexion. Earnest-looking. Her hair had been dyed blonde and she had one of those unfortunate fringes girls in the early eighties sported in the hope it would make them look like the future Princess of Wales. It didn't suit her at all.'

'A Diana fringe suggests a romantic streak – or an idolatrous one.'

'Or that she wasn't happy in her own skin and wished to be someone else. The simple explanation of course would be that she was trying to be fashionable.'

'What was her first name?'

'I have no idea. Wait. It was something unusual and un-English, I think.'

'That's interesting. Don't tell me *la* Haywood was Russian too. Lena's Russian, isn't she, also that other woman, her cousin? Could there be some *Russian* connection?'

'No, not Russian – Greek. Yes. The nanny was Greek. Half Greek, actually. English father, Greek mother. I remember Lena talking about it. Something to the effect that Greek women made the most motherly of mothers but that they were also very crafty. I can't remember the context . . . What *was* her first name now? I am sure it was mentioned . . .'

'Ariadne? Cassandra?'

'No . . .'

'Pandora? Pandora would be particularly appropriate since by leaving Twiston the nanny opened the box of all evil.'

'You are making it worse.'

'Penelope? Sorry. Melina?'

'It was something rather unusual. It made me think of butterflies, for some reason . . . No, I can't remember.'

'An exotic first name will certainly help if I have to choose between, say, twenty Haywoods in the directory. Though she might have changed it, got married and assumed her husband's name or gone ex-directory in the manner of the rich and famous. But don't let's waste any more time in idle speculation. Let's get our teeth into something more definite first, shall we?' He reached out and touched Antonia's hand. 'Let's plan our respective campaigns and have another get-together later on, so that we can compare notes. How about tonight?' Major Payne added casually. 'Perhaps we could dine together and –'

'No, not tonight.' Antonia pulled out her hand. 'I am baby-sitting tonight. My son and daughter-in-law are going to the theatre and leaving my granddaughter with me.'

'*Granddaughter*? You are joking, aren't you? You haven't got a granddaughter?'

'I have. Her name is Emma and she is three.'

'I would never have believed it.' He had opened his eyes wide. Antonia knew he was overdoing it, yet she couldn't help feeling flattered, foolish woman that she was. 'Never mind. Tomorrow then. Let's get busy today, get down to brass tacks, and we'll compare notes tomorrow at eleven at headquarters. I mean the library. Is that all right?'

Antonia agreed and, as she did, experienced a sense of unreality. Partners in crime? A detective duo? An investigating tandem? Sleuths on the scent? Great fun in detective fiction, but did it work in real life? Well, they were going to find out.

Another thought occurred to her. Was Major Payne really as enthusiastic about it as he looked, or was he doing it because he was intent on spending as much time with her as was decently possible?

11

A Change of Ownership

That afternoon, at half past two exactly, Mrs Cathcart arrived. Antonia had expected someone tall, imperious and galleon-like, that was what her voice had suggested. But Mrs Cathcart turned out to be just the opposite – short, inclined to plumpness and rather untidy in a long cardigan. Her first words to Antonia were about the cab. It was waiting outside the club, she said a little breathlessly, and she didn't want to be long for she would be charged extra. Did Miss Darcy have the Gresham papers ready? Answering in the affirmative, Antonia called Martin and asked him to carry the two wooden boxes out to the cab.

It was at that point that Colonel Haslett appeared, a racing paper sticking out of his pocket, and shook hands with Mrs Cathcart, whom he addressed as 'Penny dear'. He told her she seemed in good form. Was everything under control? Shipshape and Bristol fashion? Capital! She was coming on Friday night for a spot of bridge as per usual, wasn't she, with her lord and master? Splendid!

'You wouldn't believe it, Miss D.,' he said when Mrs Cathcart and the Gresham papers had departed, 'but the woman's a lethal bridge player, positively lethal. We lost a fortune the other night, m'wife and I. We always partner each other. No point otherwise, is there, winning each other's money!' He chuckled. 'Stayed up till four ack-emma, would you believe? Poor Derek Cathcart had to be revived with black coffee at around three. We have to do that every time, but Penny wouldn't hear of calling it a day. Derek finds it jolly hard keeping up with her, I must say. When she starts playing bridge, she's unstoppable. Saw you chewing the fat with young Payne earlier on. In the dining room.' He nodded approvingly. 'Good lunch?'

'Yes. I enjoyed it very much.' Antonia took a surreptitious look at her watch.

'So did I. Top-notch nosh, but then that's how it should be. Poached the chappie from the Savoy Grill. I mean the chef . . . Good company too. My niece and her young man. Dentist. Made me laugh, the things he said. Can't remember what they were, but damned funny. As a matter of fact I knew young Payne's father jolly well at one time. Alex Payne. What was young Payne's name now?' Colonel Haslett tugged at his moustache and looked at her.

'Hugh, I think.' Antonia tried to sound as casual as possible. She felt loath to give grounds for tittle-tattle by showing that anything remotely approaching intimacy might have developed between the club librarian and one of the club members.

'Alex was a crack polo player. In his first season in 1939, I think it was, before the war anyhow, he won the junior regimental tournament in Poona. Marvellous chap. Then we got stationed in the Sudan together. I don't suppose you've been to the Sudan?'

'I am afraid not. Sorry, Colonel Haslett, but I am afraid I'll have to –'

'What upset me most about the Sudan, Miss D., was seeing a model colony turn into a complete and utter shambles through the inefficiency, sloth and the sheer inertia of the inhabitants who took over. I know people are jolly careful these days, saying things like that, but there it is. Decent chap, young Payne. His father worried that he always had his nose in a book and didn't care enough about horses. You wouldn't believe this, but apparently, when young Payne was a boy, he called his dachshund puppy Apollo and his kitten Daphne. When he was asked why, said because dog always chased cat. Got the idea from some poem or other, that's what he said. His father *was* worried about him.'

Antonia suddenly laughed. 'Marvell.'

Colonel Haslett cupped his ear. 'What's that?'

'Apollo hunted Daphne so Only that she might laurel grow,' she quoted.

'So there *was* a poem about it? Ah, that's why I suppose he wants to talk to you!' Colonel Haslett's face lit up. 'I mean young Payne. Have bookish conversations and all that? You seem to fit like hand in glove. Perfect match. Hear you've written a novel?'

As usual, she was overcome with shyness. 'Yes.'

'A mystery, that correct? Well done. Hate mysteries. All that business of fair play. It's never fair, if you ask me. Conjurors' tricks, that's what detective stories are. The moment a clue is dangled before you, hey presto, your attention is distracted by something that's *made* to look like clue, but isn't. Call that fair? Who wants to read stuff like that? Shall I tell you what my favourite book of all time is? *The Wind* . . . um . . .'

'The Wind in the Willows?'

'Gone with the Wind. That's it. Skipped an awful lot of course. Only read the bits where Scarlett puts in an appearance. That Civil War was a bore, don't you think? But Scarlett – what a girl! Oh well. You shouldn't keep me talking, Miss D.!' Colonel Haslett chided her. 'Pleasure of course but must go now. Awful lot to do. You too. The Gresham papers are off your hands now and I'm sure you can concentrate on your filing system without any more distractions.' He gave her arm the usual bracing pat and walked out of the library.

But Antonia wasn't going to work on her filing system today. In fact she didn't feel like working at all. The bug of the hunt had got into her. She sat down at her desk and reached out for the telephone.

* * *

Her call was answered almost at once. 'Twiston House. Mrs Ralston-Scott's secretary speaking,' a woman's voice said.

Ralston-Scott. Must be the new owners.

'My name is Antonia Darcy. I do apologize for bothering you, but, you see, I used to know the people who lived at Twiston before you –'

'You knew Mr and Mrs Sandys?'

'No, no. Sir Michael and Lady Mortlock. That was back in 1981.'

'Oh yes?' the friendly voice continued after a pause. Had a note of caution crept into it or was Antonia imagining it?

'I was wondering whether you had any contact number for Lady Mortlock or for her stepson? It's Lady Mortlock with whom I'd like to get in touch. It is a bit urgent, so I'd be extremely grateful if –'

'I believe I have a number for Mr Mortlock – Mr George Mortlock. He pays us occasional visits. I have never met Lady Mortlock, but let me see – yes, I have a number for her too. It is – have you got a pen?' The secretary read out the number.

'Thank you very much . . . That's central London.'

'Belgravia, I think.'

Not far from the club, Antonia reflected. She could walk. 'Thank you very much indeed,' she said. 'I used to know the Mortlocks very well at one time. I had no idea Twiston had changed hands twice since,' she prattled on. Sometimes, she reflected, important information springs from the most unlikely sources. 'How long have your employers – Mr and Mrs Ralston-Scott, did you say? – been at Twiston?'

'There is only Mrs Ralston-Scott. She has been at Twiston a year. Would that be all, Miss . . .?'

'Darcy. Antonia Darcy . . . So Mrs Ralston-Scott bought Twiston from Mr and Mr Sandys?'

'Yes. They left for Kenya. I believe they are still there. Well, if that's all –'

A click was heard and a muffled woman's voice said, 'Sorry. Are you talking to someone, Laura?'

'Yes, Mrs Ralston-Scott. A Miss Darcy. She wanted Lady Mortlock's phone number.'

Antonia spoke. 'Hello. I am still here.'

'Oh hello. Are you a friend of Lady Mortlock's?' Mrs Ralston-Scott asked. 'You *were*? I see.' It was a pleasant voice. Warm and musical, its upper-class cadences played down. Antonia wondered whether she was a singer. 'Terribly hard keeping in touch with people, isn't it? Especially if one's been abroad. You haven't been abroad, have you? You can go, Laura, thank you.'

'I used to work for Lady Mortlock. Twenty years ago,' Antonia explained.

'I lived abroad until last year. Did a lot of sailing.' Mrs Ralston-Scott clearly wanted to chat. Rich woman at a loose end. Bored and lonely, Antonia imagined. 'Sailed all the way from Monte Carlo down the Italian coast and around the Greek islands to Istanbul, then back . . . I am in port now and like it more than I thought possible! You are familiar with Twiston then?'

'Oh yes. It's a lovely place.'

'That's putting it mildly. There's something magical about it. I can't get enough of it. A Grade 1 listed house. So very English. As a matter of fact there's a lot of repair work going on here at the moment. It's real pandemonium. I am having parts of the gardens redesigned too and I am at my wits' end what to do about that ghastly tree. It seems I have to ask special permission to have it cut down, can you imagine? On top of all my other problems. I am talking about the oak. The one with the horrid hollow.'

'Oh yes. I remember the oak.'

'It gives me the creeps each time I look at it. I always think there's some malignant presence lurking inside. I imagine something unspeakable is about to crawl out! There's a *smell* – I am sure I am not imagining it.'

'Sir Michael was very keen on preserving the oak.'

'I'm sure he was . . . What was your name, did you say? I wonder if perhaps we have met?'

'Antonia. Antonia Darcy. Twenty years ago it used to be Rushton.'

'No – I don't think we've met.'

'The oak has had a glorious history – a noble pedigree.'

'I don't give a damn about its noble pedigree – I want it gone.' A whimpering sound was heard and Mrs Ralston-Scott, speaking away from the receiver, said, 'Yes, darling, Mummy's coming . . . It's my dog. One of my dogs. *Such* a nuisance . . .'

A note of exasperation entered her voice as the whimpering was repeated. 'Doesn't like me spending too much time on the phone. Jealous, silly thing.' Mrs Ralston-Scott gave a musical laugh and again she spoke away from the receiver. 'Laura, put on the record, would you? The one that calms her down . . . No, the *other* one. Yes.' She was speaking into the phone once more. 'I am a slave to my dogs! I must go now. I hope you find Hermione Mortlock on one of her good days. She is not entirely *compos*, you know, so you should be prepared.'

'Really?'

'Yes. She's transcended the milder lunacies of senescence, that's what George Mortlock said. Pathological rather than eccentric. George *does* have a way with words. I too knew her many years ago, but I don't suppose she'll remember me.'

The sweet sounds of a familiar old-fashioned song were heard somewhere in the background. The whimpering stopped. Mrs Ralston-Scott went on, 'Lady Mortlock's been a recluse ever since her husband died. Now she lives with a companion and a nurse. I don't think they encourage visitors but you can try. Good luck.'

Antonia put down the receiver. For several moments she remained deep in thought. She had the vague feeling that something important had been said in the course of the conversation, only she couldn't think what it was.

12

Atonement

He hadn't thought it would be that effortless. There were eighteen Haywoods in the book, but only one woman whose first name was Greek, or what he thought was Greek. Major Payne could hardly contain his satisfaction as he wrote down the address and the telephone number for Andrula Haywood, who lived in Ravenscraig Road, Arnos Grove, London N11.

Was it too much to hope that this was the nanny?

What should he do? Phone first – or simply turn up on the doorstep and take it from there? Play it by ear, eh? Yes, why not. Much better, in fact, when dealing with guilty parties. Receivers could be slammed down only too easily, in fear or in anger, and that would be that, while the vis-à-vis approach had a lot to recommend it if one was playing the detection game. He would be able to observe the eyes, the mouth, the tensing of hands and facial muscles. Watch out for any telltale signs. At this point he had very little to go on. Nothing but guesswork and speculation. The misguided romantic – the lapsed Catholic. Andrula might be neither of these . . . She had been considered a most conscientious nanny until someone (Lady M.?) had offered her a lot of money to abandon her charge on the morning of 29th July 1981.

What he was going to say to her when they met, Major Payne had no idea, but inspiration, he felt sure, would come. He was a quick thinker, had a sympathetic manner. He wasn't a bad hand at drawing people out of themselves. He wasn't easily thwarted or abashed either. People took to him, women in particular – most women.

Women found him charming, reliable, funny, non-threatening. Women frequently made him their confidant – not a role he always relished – it could be a bore. On a number of occasions women had become infatuated with him, which had been a terrible bore. Once an unmarried titled lady had developed quite an obsession with him. She had bought him a Bentley and, when he sent it back, had threatened to shoot a senior member of the Danish royal family, whom she had been entertaining at her country seat; she had finally tried to hang herself in her private chapel but made a botch of it. She had continued writing him notes on perfumed paper from her hospital bed. Now *that* had been scary. That was the kind of insane thing that happened to celibate priests and popular actors, his late wife had joked – he should have been one or the other.

It was three o'clock in the afternoon when he walked through St James's to Green Park underground station and got on the Piccadilly line. It took him thirty minutes to get to Arnos Grove, a pleasant enough residential area, if not a particularly leafy one. It was most certainly not what one would associate with plutocratic excess of any sort. Well, the nanny didn't seem to conform to the popular idea of the newly rich. He had left his *A–Z* behind, consequently he got a cab outside the station.

Suburban semi-detached houses. Miss Haywood couldn't have had an extravagant bone in her body. She hadn't allowed her sudden riches to go to her head. Or could her ill-gained fortune have run out? Or had she felt so guilty about what she had done that she hadn't taken full advantage of the hush money –

'This is it, boss,' the cab driver said. 'There's the church.'

Startled, Payne blinked. 'Church? What church?'

'Ravenscraig Road, you said, didn't you? This address is a church.'

'It can't be.'

But of course it was. It didn't look like a church from the outside, though it said so above the door. *Church of the Tenderness of the Mother of God*. Underneath an inscription in Greek conveyed the same information. The door was open and he could smell incense.

Greek Orthodox, not Catholic. Crucifixes as well as incense were among the trappings of both religions. He stood in the doorway somewhat disconcerted, tugging at his tie, trying to rearrange his ideas. Andrula Haywood had given this as her address, though she couldn't *live* here, surely? Or could she? The church encompassed two semi-detached houses that had been knocked into one.

He walked through the door and was at once enveloped in a mist of sorts. He felt a wave of warm air – a smell of tapers was added to the incense. His impression was that there were hundreds of little lights, flickering like fireflies; thin wax candles sticking out of candelabras that had been positioned at various points around the spacious room. There were curtains or blinds across the narrow windows, so it was difficult to see things clearly, though he did make out an iconostasis and a heavy curtain at one end, also icons in gilded frames on the walls. But for him, the place seemed to be empty.

Then he saw her: a smallish woman dressed all in black, kneeling in front of a large icon. This showed a bearded saint who, judging by his expression, couldn't make up his mind whether to look stern or benevolent. (I mustn't be flippant, Payne reminded himself. Causing offence won't open the gates of confession.)

He stood very still, watching her profile. He rubbed his eyes, which had started smarting. Despite the inadequate lighting, he recognized her at once from Antonia's description – the sallow complexion, the slightly crooked nose, the chunky golden crucifix on a chain around her throat. The hair was no longer blonde and done in a fringe, but dark, streaked with grey, parted in the middle and pulled back. Though she couldn't be more than in her middle forties, she looked older, much older. The face was lined, haggard, and there were dark circles around her eyes, which were shut. Her lips were pressed tightly together. She looked at least fifty-seven or eight, if not older. She had aged prematurely, that much was clear.

Payne stroked his jaw with a forefinger. Had her conscience been troubling her? Was that the reason for the way she looked? Worn out – with care or with guilt. She was leaning forward, her hands clasped in front of her. She hadn't opened her eyes. Her brow was furrowed in concentration. The thin lips had parted and were moving silently. Praying. Payne wondered whether it was for the soul of little Sonya Dufrette – or for forgiveness . . . He saw tears rolling down the withered cheeks.

He stepped back quietly, waiting for her to finish. Interrupting her prayer wouldn't do. If she was aware of his presence, she didn't give any sign. He backed further and leant against the wall. He saw he was standing beside an icon that showed another saint, much younger and more vigorous than the one Andrula Haywood was praying to, though of a somewhat androgynous aspect. He – Major Payne was sure it was a 'he' – was in the process of pulling a devil from the turbulent sea with his left hand, while in his other hand he brandished a hammer.

Eventually Andrula Haywood opened her eyes, crossed herself and started to rise. Payne made a movement towards her, but the next moment three more people entered the church. Two women and an elderly man on crutches. Andrula quickly walked up to them and kissed each one in turn, placing her hands on their shoulders. Payne remained standing beside the wall, watching them. They talked in an animated manner but their conversation was conducted in demotic Greek.

He had done Greek at school, but that had been classical Greek. There had been no classes in colloquial Greek . . . What a grammatical inferno Greek tragedy had been! As for doing Greek composition, he had thought of it as brutal bludgeoning – not so much different from the fate that awaited the devil in the icon, in fact.

He saw the elderly man with the crutches kneel. Andrula laid her hand on his shoulder and shut her eyes once more. Her lips started moving but this time she spoke the words aloud – Greek again. She spoke with fervour. The two women who had come with the man also reached out and placed their hands on his arm and they too spoke aloud. The man bowed his head. They were praying for his healing, Payne felt sure and, though he didn't understand a word of it, he felt touched.

He was reminded of the words of Achilles' ghost to Ulysses: *I would rather be a slave at another's plough, one who is poor with little means of livelihood, than rule all the dead and departed*. Well, Andrula had chosen a life devoted to serving people in need . . . It didn't seem she had got married either . . . Her conscience had prevented her from finding happiness of the more conventional kind.

Glancing at his watch, he saw that nearly twenty-five minutes had passed since he had arrived. He remembered his grandfather saying that a true gentleman's concerns weren't supposed to include the passage of time. He must have been no more than eleven or twelve at the time. Funny, how some memories stuck in the mind –

He caught a movement. The tableau had broken up and the man, supported by the two women, went to light candles. Andrula Haywood turned round and seemed to notice him for the first time. 'Oh, hello,' she said, smiling, and crossed through the swirls of incense, proffering both her hands. 'Welcome. I have never seen you here before, but I hope you will find what you are looking for.' She spoke with a slight Greek accent. Her eyes were kind, but full of pain. (He was sure he wasn't imagining it.)

'As a matter of fact I was looking for you, Miss Haywood. Could I have a word?'

There was a pause. He hoped he didn't sound too intimidating – like a plain clothes policeman.

'You want to talk to me? Of course. Let us go to my

office. There will be a baptism here soon and we will be in the way.'

As though on cue, there entered a tall priest. He was youngish, in his thirties, with a trimmed dark beard and wearing a festive black cassock and the tall cylindrical black hat that went with it. 'Sister Andrula,' he said in English.

She bowed down and kissed his hand. 'Father,' she said.

'God is good. Is everything ready?'

'Yes, Father,' she answered and pointed her hand towards a screen, which presumably concealed the baptismal font.

'I am a little early but I want to pray.' He had given Payne an amiable nod.

'Yes, Father. I won't be long. This gentleman has come to see me.' She then led the way across the room, past the iconostasis, which she described as 'one of the finest products of the nineteenth-century School of Debar', whatever that was. 'I had it sent from Smyrna, my home town. That's where I spent my childhood. It was a lovely place in the mid-fifties. I understand it's somewhat spoilt now. Through here . . .'

She pulled aside a heavy brocade curtain, pushed open a door and they entered a small, cell-like room with plain walls. There wasn't much in it, apart from a small bookcase, a metal safe, a desk with a computer on it and two wooden chairs. 'Please, sit down,' she said. 'I'm not offering you coffee because I'm in a hurry. I am a bit worried about the baptism.' She took the seat on the other side of the desk.

He cast a glance round. 'Do you live here?'

'Yes. I have two rooms and a shower at the back.' She pointed towards a second door in the wall behind him. 'That's all I need.'

'And you – you actually run this church?'

'I run it, yes. I am the owner as well as the manager. Or do you say "proprietor"? It's not that difficult, if one has faith. I get a lot of help from my brothers and sisters – there are fifty-three of us.'

She must mean that in a spiritual rather than filial sense, Payne reflected. 'It doesn't look like a church from the outside – no cupola, no dome.'

Suddenly, something she had just said jarred. The mid-fifties? He must have misheard . . .

'No. It used to be my old house. My neighbours happened to be moving out, so I bought their house as well. What's your interest in the church? You aren't thinking of making me an offer, are you?' She smiled.

It was then that Payne had his happy inspiration. He cleared his throat. 'You had the church built twenty years ago, didn't you?'

She looked at him with a little frown. 'That's correct.'

He leant slightly forward. 'You had a windfall. A big sum of money, but you weren't happy because of the way the money had been acquired.' His eyes never for a moment left her face. 'So, to appease your conscience, you built a church. It was a form of – atonement.'

There was a pause. Her face had gone pale, the lines running down from her nostrils to the ends of her mouth deepened, but she remained composed. 'As a matter of fact you are right, in every detail. How do you know all this? Have you come here to tell me my fortune? This is remarkable, but you must know that I do not approve of fortune-telling.' Her dark eyes fixed on his regimental tie and she smiled once more, a faint smile. 'You don't look like a fortune-teller. Who are you?'

'You don't know me. My name is Payne.'

She drew in her breath. '*Pain*? Well, if you must know, that's what I've been feeling all these years – here.' She touched her heart. Her eyes filled with tears. 'Pain. That's what I've had to live with. Sorry . . .' She shook her head and wiped her eyes.

'I'd like to know what exactly happened on 29th July 1981.' Major Payne delivered this boldly, in measured tones, watching for her reaction. He felt sorry for her but he didn't want to lose the momentum. 'Who was it that paid you to pretend your mother was ill and leave Twiston in the morning? Who telephoned you?'

'*Twiston*?' She frowned, a look of utter incomprehension on her face. 'What is Twiston?'

(Was she pretending? She must be.)

'What did they do with little Sonya Dufrette?'

'*Sonya* –?' She broke off and he saw her expression start changing. It was very peculiar. Her mouth opened slightly. Her eyes stared back at him. She looked startled – shocked. She looked as though she had had some sort of revelation, one that had confirmed her worst fears, that was how Payne was to describe it later to Antonia. He couldn't understand.

She whispered, 'Is – is that what happened? Someone phoned her in the morning and – and said I was ill? Is that what happened?'

What was the woman playing at? 'Miss Haywood, it was *you* somebody phoned –'

This time she corrected him. '*Mrs* Haywood.'

It was only then that realization dawned on him. Smyrna in the mid-fifties – the accent – her age. (She looked in her early sixties because, well, because she *was* in her early sixties.) It all made perfect sense now. He had been an ass.

'Good Lord,' Major Payne said. 'What an absurd misunderstanding. You are her mother.'

13

Mothers and Daughters

Reaching the end of Elizabeth Street, the main shopping quarter of Belgravia, Antonia stopped and took stock of her surroundings. The blocks of mansion flats off Eaton Square were solid in nature, giving evidence of having been built to last, though their Georgian façades were extremely pleasing to the eye too. Wasn't it somewhere here that Lord Lucan had had a flat? Antonia found Coburg Court Mansions soon enough and she entered a rather magnificent hall with a mosaic floor, potted palms, geometrical lights and sun-ray pattern mirrors on the walls. A man who looked like a Field Marshal, but who was actually a commissionaire, greeted her portentously. 'Lady Mortlock? Third floor, flat number five. Does Miss Garnett know you are paying them a visit? She does?' He opened the lift door for her with a dignified gesture.

Antonia navigated a maze of carpeted corridors, went up a flight of stairs, before she eventually stood uncertainly outside Lady Mortlock's flat.

Her heart thumped in her chest. She didn't know quite what to expect. When she rang to arrange the visit, the telephone had been answered by an energetic voice, a Miss Garnett, the companion, as it became clear. Emboldened by her amiable tone, Antonia explained that she had been a good friend of the Mortlocks once, adding for good measure that she had been writing Lady Mortlock's family history.

'But of course,' Miss Garnett breathed. '*The Jourdains of Twiston*. I have read it, all one hundred and five pages. Wonderful stuff. Pity you never managed to complete it. I'd be delighted to meet you. I love chronicles of old dynastic families. I've just finished reading *Knole and the Sackvilles*.'

Antonia murmured humbly, something to the effect that her book could hardly be compared to Vita Sackville-West's, but Miss Garnett would have none of it. Antonia, she said, wrote superbly. The Sackville-Wests, she went on in vehement tones, didn't really deserve a book – they were mediocre spendthrifts and selfish incompetents while the Jourdains were a highly talented clan who had given the world inventors, thinkers, polymaths, intellectuals and educationalists. Pausing, Miss Garnett continued on a more mundane note, 'Hermione seems to be in tolerably good spirits today, and she's been quite alert. She may even recognize you, though there's no guarantee. She's taking a bath at the moment, but if you could come at four, or four thirty, I'd be happy to give you tea. One more thing – isn't your name Rushton?'

'It was. That's my husband's name,' explained Antonia. 'I am divorced now.'

'*That* accounts for it,' said Miss Garnett cheerfully.

Replaying the conversation in her head, Antonia decided she rather liked the sound of Miss Garnett and that she had nothing to fear. The front door was made of solid mahogany and it bore the old-fashioned notice *Please Knock and Ring*. Antonia did both and as she rang the bell, a light came on over the door. Nothing happened though. Several moments passed and she rang again. What was keeping Miss Garnett from opening the door? Antonia suddenly panicked. Why had she come? What was she hoping to find out? Lady Mortlock was a very old woman, bedridden and incapacitated, whose once first-class brain had all but gone. Did she really believe she could expose

Lady Mortlock as a liar, as the mastermind behind the abduction and killing of a child?

Antonia took a step backwards and was on the point of turning round and leaving when she heard a flurry of footsteps followed by a rattling of a door-chain and locks. The door opened.

'Miss Darcy? So sorry to keep you waiting! I am Bea Garnett. How do you do?' Lady Mortlock's companion sounded a bit out of breath, but she held out her hand and shook Antonia's vigorously.

'How do you do,' Antonia said.

Early sixties, stoutish, a round, remarkably smooth face, apple cheeks, at the moment extremely flushed, horn-rimmed glasses halfway down her nose, grey hair done up in a neat bun, pearl earrings and two strings of pearls around her neck. She wore a crêpe de Chine dress of floral pattern.

'Do come in. We've had a bit of a – I suppose you'd call it a rumpus.' Miss Garnett was looking down at her left hand. She had a handkerchief wrapped around it.

'Is everything all right?' Antonia saw that the handkerchief was stained deep red.

'I've cut myself. It's nothing. Just a scratch. Some damned piece of glass. So treacherous. We've had a bit of an upset, that's all. Norah's got it all well under control now. I wouldn't have been able to cope on my own. Too old. I suppose I *am* a bit shaken up . . . Don't you believe it if somebody told you octogenarian ladies are frail and gentle. This one's a devil.' Miss Garnett gave a mirthless laugh and pushed the glasses up her nose.

'Do you mean Lady Mortlock?'

'Who else? I don't know what's got into her, I really don't. She was perfectly calm only a few minutes ago.' They were standing in the hall and she turned to Antonia. 'I wonder if she heard me speaking to you on the phone, whether it had something to do with you? Sometimes Hermione gets agitated about the oddest things. I have given up trying to fathom out the way her mind works, what's left of it. Do let me take you to the sitting room. You must pretend not to see the mess. This way. As I said, she was perfectly fine, calm and sensible. She was telling me about a dream she had had last night . . .'

The sitting room was light and spacious, but overheated and in a state of some disarray.

'It was something about going down in a sinking ship. A ship that had been torpedoed – sometimes Hermione comes up with the most extraordinary details. She saw herself shut inside a small compartment behind a water-tight door, slowly being overcome by a high-pressure gush through a shell-hole.'

'How terrible,' Antonia said.

'I suppose it is. She dreams a lot. She can't sleep at all well, but when she does, dreams a lot. Nightmares, mainly, poor soul. Sometimes she wakes up screaming . . . Look at the mess, just look at it. She does have tantrums, mind – fits of rage – but never before on such a scale. I can't think what –' Miss Garnett broke off again. 'I'm not dripping blood, am I? No. Good. That's Norah,' she said as a voice was heard somewhere in the background. Although the words were blurred and indistinct, the voice sounded as though it were addressing a child.

Antonia smiled. 'She sounds extremely competent.'

Miss Garnett's lips tightened slightly. 'Norah can be trying sometimes. She does take liberties, but, yes, I must say she is fully qualified to deal with difficult cases. She has worked both at an old people's home and at a psychiatric hospital. Hermione attacked her the other day – scratched her arm badly – reminded me her nails needed trimming. We hardly get any visitors these days, and I am not really surprised. Hermione is so unpredictable. Most of her friends are dead anyhow. Do sit down.' Miss Garnett motioned Antonia towards a high primrose-yellow leather-upholstered sofa. 'Hermione's in bed now. She isn't normally, not at this hour, but that's where we take her when she's been a bad girl. Teach her a lesson. She needs to understand that's *not* the way to behave.'

'Plato and Nietzsche.' Antonia picked up two books from the floor.

'She aimed them at Norah's head but missed,' Miss Garnett explained. 'No one would have thought she used to read Plato's Dialogues, if they'd been able to see her earlier on! Nor *Thus Spake Zarathustra* . . . She read them in Greek and in German, respectively, you know. Oh, if you had seen her earlier on – clawing and hissing and kicking and scratching! A proper beldame straight out of *Macbeth*! Knocking things over – throwing them around. Anything she could lay her hands on . . .'

An embroidered stool had been overturned. The floor was littered with more books, bric-a-brac, some of it reduced to smithereens. A vase too had been smashed and the flowers that had been inside it, large crimson roses, strewed the carpet like splashes of blood.

'No, don't touch it. I'll do it . . . It took the two of us to restrain her.' Miss Garnett picked up the roses. 'It's most unfortunate that she should have got like this just when you were expected. I'll go and make the tea now. I could do with a break. I have made some smoked salmon sandwiches; there are meringues and a date-and-walnut cake. Would that be all right?'

'Sounds wonderful. Thank you.'

'I won't be a jiffy.' Miss Garnett went out.

Antonia gazed round the room. From the urn and scrolls she deduced the fireplace to be Adam. There was a small but very beautiful writing desk of the Davenport kind. There were two armchairs, primrose yellow, like the sofa. Three striking period chairs, Hepplewhite, which she felt sure she had seen at Twiston, were ranged against the wall. Some good pictures, one possibly a Sargent. There was a pencil drawing of a triumphant-looking phoenix rising from the flames, with a motto underneath. Antonia expected it to be something on the lines of 'Sorrows Pass and Hope Abides' but, disconcertingly, it turned out to be 'Survival of the Fittest'.

It was only then that she noticed the photographs, which

was surprising given that almost every surface in the room was filled with them. The mantelpiece, the bookcase, the two small tables, the window sills . . . Two photographs lay on the floor amidst shards of glass. They were all black and white.

Leaning over, Antonia picked up one of the photographs gingerly and looked at it.

A girl . . . She thought the face was familiar somehow . . . Perhaps she was mistaken . . . No, it couldn't be . . .

Her heart started beating fast. Rising to her feet, she started examining the rest of the framed photographs. Each and every one of them showed the same beautiful girl with short dark hair and a carefree smile, who looked no more than twenty. The photographs had been taken against the backdrop of Venice's gondolas, canals and churches. The girl's rather chic clothes suggested the late 1950s . . .

Antonia examined the girl's face closely. No, she thought – it can't be.

'Oh, that's so sad.' Miss Garnett's voice was heard from the doorway. 'That's Hermione's daughter. Venice 1958. The last holiday they had together.'

'But –' Antonia bit her lip. Turning round, she watched Miss Garnett place a laden tea tray on the low table in front of the sofa.

'Hermione's daughter died tragically young. Hermione adored her. She never got over it. Oh, but I am sure you know all that.' Miss Garnett picked up the teapot. 'Shall I be mother?'

Andrula Haywood's eyes were full of tears. She wiped them with the back of her hand. 'Yes, I am Chrissie's mother. You thought I was Chrissie?'

'Chrissie?' Major Payne echoed.

'She was christened Chrisothemis, but she never liked her name. It's a beautiful name but she was embarrassed by it. She was very self-conscious about being Greek. She wanted to be English, like her father. I don't know why since he wasn't much good. He left us when Chrissie was four. I don't know where he is. Sorry – I don't know why I am telling you this.'

'Butterflies . . . Of course . . . Sorry, Mrs Haywood.' *Chrysalis*. That was what Antonia must have been thinking about. 'Do go on.'

Her hand went up to her forehead and she looked at him as though she doubted he was quite real. 'Who *are* you? Is your name really Pain?'

'It is. With a Y and an E at the end . . . Major Payne.'

'You are a soldier?'

'Well, yes. In a manner of speaking. I mean I've never done any proper soldiering – plenty of administrative jobs – intelligence service and so on. My son is a soldier. He is in the Guards.'

'Keith, my husband, was a soldier. He was stationed in Cyprus. In 1960. That's where we met. I was very young. I was a hospital nurse. I fell in love with him. I was very much in love with him, but it was a mistake to marry him.'

'Where is your daughter?' Payne asked after a pause.

She bowed her head. 'I don't know. The last time I heard from Chrissie, she was in Australia. That was four months ago. She was in New Zealand before that. She is restless. She is not happy. She keeps moving. She can't settle down. She has money – she's made some wise investments, I think – but she is not happy. She hasn't married. She doesn't keep in touch.' Andrula Haywood sighed. 'Twiston . . . Was that what the house was called? Were you there when it happened? I mean when – when that poor child drowned?'

'No. A friend of mine was. She wants to get to the bottom of it, you see. She wants to find out what really happened. She is worried about – um – some aspects of the affair. There are things that don't quite tally. I am helping her. She is a very good friend.'

'Is she your girlfriend? Sorry. I shouldn't be asking you such questions.'

'No, that's all right. Well, she isn't my girlfriend – not yet at any rate, but I very much hope she'll agree to marry me one day in the not too distant future.' Golly, Major Payne thought. That's the first time I've ever said it aloud.

'I hope you will be very happy. You look like a good and decent man.'

'Thank you. Now then. What was it your daughter told you? I mean about the money, how she got it. Did she explain?'

'She said she had won it at the pools. It was a lot of money. An incredible amount. I couldn't believe it when she told me. I – I didn't like the way she said it. I knew something wasn't right. It happened soon after that child – the child Chrissie had been in charge of – died. The little girl . . .'

'Sonya. Sonya Dufrette.'

'Sonya . . . Yes . . . I never made the connection between the two, I honestly didn't – I mean between Sonya and the money. I did wonder later on, though of course it didn't make any sense, so I dismissed it altogether from my mind. I can always tell when Chrissie tells a lie. She isn't good at it. She isn't a bad girl, but she does do stupid things and then suffers for it.' Andrula paused. 'So. Let me get this clear. She said I was very ill and that she had to come and see me? That she had to leave the house? Is that right?'

'Yes. Somebody put her up to it. It was part of a plan. We don't think it was her idea, if that's any comfort to you. Somebody planned Sonya's disappearance, somebody rich and influential – we don't know who that person is, though we have our suspicions. We have no idea what the reason for it might be either. This person paid your daughter a large amount of money for her to leave the house on the morning of the 29th –'

'That was the day of the royal wedding, wasn't it?'

'It was. We think the royal wedding was pivotal to the

scheme. No witnesses – everybody inside, watching TV. We are talking serious business. Whoever planned Sonya's disappearance meant it to work with oiled precision.'

'My God! That's wicked – evil!' Andrula cried. 'What did they want with a young child like that?'

'That's the question we keep asking ourselves, Mrs Haywood . . . You don't have any idea who it might have been?' Payne asked gently.

She covered her face with her hands. She sat very still. He wondered if she was praying, or simply trying to concentrate. Eventually she spoke. 'Chrissie gave me half of her "winnings", that's what she called it. I did accept it, although, as I said, I wasn't happy about it. I had a funny feeling. We were in Margate. I had a boyfriend then. We were having such a good time, but then I got the paper and read about Sonya's disappearance. "Presumed drowned", it said there. I recognized the name at once. Sonya Dufrette – yes. Chrissie had told me about her position with the Dufrettes – that they were really posh and very eccentric.' Andrula pressed her handkerchief against her lips. 'She liked that little girl, Major Payne.'

'I am sure she did.'

'She felt sorry for her. She did talk about her. She told me Sonya had something wrong with her. Sonya was young for her age. She was seven but she acted like she was five . . . I met them once, actually. Mr and Mrs Dufrette and little Sonya –'

'You met the Dufrettes?'

'Yes. They were going somewhere in the car – a very big car but very old. Anthos – my boyfriend – said it was a Daimler. 1950s model. Anthos knew about cars. They were going to stay with some friends of theirs, somewhere in the country. Chrissie needed to collect something from the house, so they stopped outside. Mrs Dufrette – Lena – came out and said hello to me. She was very friendly. She was a bit drunk, too, I think. She had this amazing hat on. A Stetson and she wore cowboy boots with spurs and she had a red kerchief tied round her neck. Her face was very painted – her lips and cheeks – and she had henna-dyed hair. She was very – colourful.'

'You are too kind. "Garish" is the word I'd choose.'

'Anthos said, "Here comes the circus." Lena asked me whether I could dance *sirtaki* and was it true that Greeks broke plates when they got excited at parties. She said she really liked that – that she liked breaking plates herself, whenever and wherever she got the chance. She was joking of course.'

'Don't be too sure,' Payne murmured. 'Did you get to speak to Dufrette?'

'Mr Dufrette? No. He stayed in the car. He was scribbling something in a notebook. Lena said he was writing a new history of the world. I could see his lips moving – he was talking to himself. All right, I did think them very odd. The little girl didn't say much – she came out too but she just stood there smiling.'

'I see . . . Mind if I smoke?' Payne had produced his pipe.

'Please do. I used to smoke myself but gave up.'

'Did your daughter ever mention a woman called Hermione Mortlock? Lady Mortlock?'

'No, never. At least, not that I remember.'

'Where did your daughter go after she left the Dufrettes' employment?'

'Well, she moved in with us for a bit . . . in this house . . . She didn't like it much. She didn't get on with Anthos.' Andrula sighed.

'Did she receive any visitors – any phone calls? Do you remember?'

'I don't think Chrissie had any visitors, but there were several phone calls for her . . . Two from Lena, actually. Mrs Dufrette.'

Major Payne took his pipe out of his mouth and leant forward. 'Lena phoned your daughter? And it was *after* Sonya's disappearance? You sure?'

'Yes. Twice . . . The first time Chrissie wasn't at home.

I answered the phone. Lena said, could Chrissie get back to her as soon as possible as it was extremely important.'

'How did Lena sound? Anything unusual strike you?'

Andrula frowned. 'Funny you should ask that. She didn't sound like someone who had lost a child. It was the week after the tragedy, you see. I expressed my condolences – I was close to tears, but Lena – Mrs Dufrette – kept making jokes and laughing and acting all comical. I was stunned. Then I thought it was the shock, that she had gone slightly mad, or that she was on medication or something. Anti-depressants can make you high, can't they?'

'I suppose they can. I believe they call Prozac "bottled sunshine".'

'I gave Chrissie the message when she came back. Chrissie went all pale. She looked – well, frightened. She couldn't hide it. She's not very good at hiding her feelings. She then closed herself in the lounge and told us not to go in while she was making the call. She sounded very tense. I could see she was very upset. Afterwards she went straight up to her room. She refused to eat anything. Later I heard her crying, but didn't dare ask her what it was about. I knew then for certain that there was something very wrong, only I couldn't think what it was.'

'You said Lena called a second time?'

'Yes. The very next day. This time Chrissie was at home and again she closed herself in the lounge and screamed at us not to spy on her. With some justification.' Andrula swallowed. 'You see, Anthos did listen in. He ran into the kitchen and got on to the extension. I went after him – told him not to do it, but he pushed me away. He knew something was going on. He wasn't a fool. I am afraid he didn't like Chrissie. He thought she was stuck up – made fun of her hair-do because it was like Princess Diana's – called her a snob. He kept calling her "Her Highness". They were forever snapping at each other.'

'Did he tell you what he had heard?'

'He did. I don't think he made it up. Lena's exact words

were, *You'd better keep your mouth shut, my girl, or they will kill us both.'*

'Really?' Payne sat very still. 'Who's "they"?'

Andrula shrugged. 'I don't know. He didn't hear anything else. The extension went dead; there was something wrong with it. Anthos was convinced that it was something to do with spying, Lena being Russian and all that. I thought he was talking rubbish. I didn't really let it worry me. I decided that Lena had probably gone mad with grief, that she didn't know what she was talking about . . . But Chrissie did look terrible when I saw her later. I asked her what the matter was but she just shook her head.'

There was a pause. 'How long after that did she win the pools?' Payne asked.

'That same week. After she got the money, Chrissie changed and for a while at least she seemed happy. She kept hugging me – kissing me – laughing and crying – tears of joy, she said. She apologized for behaving badly and then said she wanted to share her fortune with me –' Andrula broke off. 'It couldn't have been Lena who gave her the money, could it? I don't think the Dufrettes were really rich, Chrissie said they weren't. So, if she didn't win the pools, who gave her the money?'

'Who indeed?' Payne relit his pipe. '"They"? Who's "they"? The same "they" who had threatened to kill Lena and her? Interesting.'

'What's all this about? That poor child – merciful God, what did they do to the child? What was that other name you mentioned? You asked me if she had phoned? Lady Mortlock? You don't think it was she who was behind it? Whatever that was?'

'The idea did cross our minds. Well, it was Lady Mortlock who lied about you being very ill, in hospital,' Payne said thoughtfully. 'I wonder now . . . I very much wonder.'

14

The Monocled Countess

'Miss Darcy, are you all right?' Miss Garnett touched her arm.

'Yes – I'm fine. Sorry.'

'Would you like a slice of cake, or would you prefer a sandwich?' Miss Garnett had already poured two cups of tea.

'A sandwich – thank you very much.'

Antonia made an effort to concentrate as Miss Garnett talked about illustrious old families like the Actons, the Astors, the Mitfords, the Tennants and indeed the Jourdains – but her thoughts were elsewhere.

Lady Mortlock had never had a daughter. She had never had any children. She had never given birth. She had told a lie. Another lie. Three lies in total.

All the photographs in the room, each and every one of them, were of Lena Dufrette. Lena Sugarev-Drushinski, as she had been back in 1958. Lena and Lady Mortlock had been to see a play together, a play that had been outré if not scandalous. Lady Mortlock had gone out of her way to distance herself from Lena. She had pretended they were strangers –

There was a knock on the door and a youngish woman with a square face and the physique of a prize fighter appeared. Her arms, Antonia observed, were the size of small tree trunks. Two plasters had been stuck on her left arm where presumably Lady Mortlock had scratched her. She wore a smart uniform that looked a little bit too tight for her and trainers whose laces had been left undone. Norah, the nurse.

'I am sorry to interrupt your repast, ladies, but there's an important message from HQ,' she said in tones of comic gravity.

'Oh dear,' Miss Garnett said. 'Not another crisis, I hope?'

'Nope. All's quiet on the Western Front. Her Ladyship's compliments and would Mrs Antonia Rushton care to go and see her now?'

'Would Mrs Rushton . . .?' Miss Garnett pushed her glasses up her nose. 'Hermione actually *said* that?'

'Yep. She wants to see her. *Now.*'

'So Lady Mortlock knows I am here?' Antonia put down her cup.

'Oh yes. She knows all right. She recognized your voice and everything. She told me all about you, actually.'

Antonia blinked. 'Really?'

'She told me how you used to kill stoats.' Norah laughed exuberantly. 'Only kidding. In my kind of job, if one doesn't crack jokes, one would go mad,' she explained. 'You agree, don't you, Miss G.?'

'That would be enough, Norah,' Miss Garnett said and she turned to Antonia. 'What do you think? You'd be quite safe, I am sure. Norah will be outside the door. On the other hand –'

'Hurry up, Miss G. I suggest Mrs Rushton goes at once, otherwise Her Ladyship may change her mind. She may go back to where she was earlier on and *that*, I must tell you, wasn't a good place.'

'Don't call her "Her Ladyship", Norah.'

Antonia rose. 'I'll go. After all, that's why I came.'

As they walked down the corridor, Norah popped a piece of chewing gum into her mouth and said, 'These old bags are driving me mad. In some ways Miss G. is worse than Lady M. There it is. The lair of the beast.' She opened a door. 'I'll be here.' She pointed to a chair. 'Give me a shout if she turns nasty. You've written your last will and testament of course? You're insured? Only kidding.'

The bedroom was as large as the sitting room, its walls covered in wallpaper of Delft blue. The pattern was of snow-white cranes in vertiginous flight. There were no pictures on the walls, only a magnificent mirror encrusted with bees in ormolu. In the middle of the room stood a four-poster bed made of rosewood. Lady Mortlock sat bolt upright, propped up by satin pillows, clutching a pair of rimless reading glasses over what looked like a small black prayer book. Antonia was surprised – Lady Mortlock had always been scornful of religion. Well, people mellowed with age and last minute conversions were not unknown.

Lady Mortlock was still recognizable as the imperious woman whose family history Antonia had been writing twenty years earlier, but only just. Her frame in a cream-coloured nightdress was shrunken, her face emaciated, the parchment-like skin stretched across the skull, the lips wasted and grey. Her eyes were like bullet-holes, almost invisible in their orbits, rimmed with startlingly vivid red. The eyelashes were gone, though she still had her brows. Her hair was white and wispy and it was covered with an old-fashioned black net. Lady Mortlock's Roman nose seemed more prominent now – the only prominent thing about her. The hands that clutched at the book were brown with liver spots and claw-like.

Antonia had expected the dazed-sheep look of the gaga old, but Lady Mortlock's eyes were unnervingly alert. She looked a cross between a mummy that had been reanimated by some mad scientist and an ancient bird of prey.

'No doubt you disapprove? You always disapproved of them, didn't you? You never said anything but I could see you disapproved.'

'Good afternoon, Lady Mortlock,' Antonia said brightly, reminding herself that her work at the club had equipped her for dealing with the non sequiturs of old people. She felt sudden horror at the thought of shaking hands with Lady Mortlock. She imagined Lady Mortlock's hand to feel like a loose set of bones tied inside a very dry suede bag. Mercifully, the old woman's hands remained on her lap.

'I mean my father's books. This is one of them.' Lady Mortlock tapped her glasses against the book on her lap. Her voice, surprisingly, was very much as Antonia remembered it – deep and autocratic, though there was a somewhat hollow ring to it now. 'I saw you looking at it a minute ago. *The Future of Eugenics*. It was written in 1928. I don't suppose many books are written on the subject nowadays, are they?'

'I don't know. I don't think so.'

'What *is* the future of eugenics? Never mind. Come and sit here, Antonia. Beside me.' She pointed to a small armchair upholstered in maroon velvet. 'Bea says it's extremely comfortable and about such things Bea is usually right. That's where she sits when I ask her to read to me. I am no good in the evenings. I go blind. Let me look at you,' she said as Antonia sat down beside her. 'Well, neither of us is getting any younger. You are far from repellent, but you have put on weight. You need to take more exercise. Have a massage once a month. Have your hair dyed blonde, now why don't you? It would suit you, I think. I never did any of these things, mind. Despised women who did. Despised the flesh, rather refused to recognize it – with one notable exception.' She paused. 'You were in the sitting room, weren't you?'

'Yes.' Antonia shifted slightly in her chair.

'You recognized her, didn't you? Don't deny it. Now she – *she* – has changed beyond recognition. She came to see me some time ago . . . Change and decay . . . Change and decay everywhere I see! You know Elizabeth Street?' Lady Mortlock pointed a skeletal finger towards the window. 'I bet you didn't know it started as Eliza Street? Duchesses do their shopping there now but one hundred years ago it was a terribly disreputable place, with tarts plying their trade and earning a few pence from the river traffic. Now, *that's* one change for the better, but I can't think of many others.'

'How are you?' Antonia asked.

'The mind goes first. Every minute, every second, brings me closer to the grave. I am constantly made aware of it. When I turned eighty –' Lady Mortlock broke off with a frown. 'How old am I now?'

'Eighty-seven.'

'When I turned eighty, I suddenly became extremely self-conscious about my age and the decline in my powers. I realized that intellectually I had started slipping. In consequence I tried to learn even more things than usual by heart, partly to prove to myself that I could do it, partly to ensure that I didn't bore or irritate my visitors. I also insisted that I be given a course of vitamin B12 injections. Well, I have fewer visitors now and I no longer remember things. The injections continue, but I don't think they have any effect, apart from making me feel rather sore and a bit nauseous. The very distant past sometimes comes back, crystal-clear, to taunt me mainly, but what I did ten minutes ago is lost in a fog. It's no mere loss of memory. I believe I have *fugues*. Was it me who scratched the nurse woman? We don't keep cats, so it must have been me.'

'I don't know. I don't think so.'

'You don't want to upset me. You think I might get a heart attack or something if you do.' Lady Mortlock paused. 'You did see the photographs in the sitting room, of course?'

'I did.' Antonia decided she might as well take the bull by the horns. 'You knew Lena before she married Lawrence Dufrette.'

'Was it ever suggested otherwise?'

'Yes. You said that you had first met her when Lawrence introduced her as his young bride.'

'Really? I believe you are right. I did. Lena came to see

me, you know. I don't remember when. Was it last year? Two years ago? It might have been last month. It doesn't matter. She told me all manner of useless things. That she and Lawrence had separated, that she had had a fortune which she had frittered away and was now destitute, that Lawrence had been *quite* unable to keep his hands off that girl of theirs and how her mother's heart had been broken, how much she missed Baltic herring on buttered brown bread, how ungrateful and mean someone called Vivian was –'

Antonia frowned. 'Sorry to interrupt you –'

'Lena seemed to believe I would be *interested*. She looked dreadful. She's got really fat. Her hair was sickly orange and she reeked of brandy. She kept snivelling, bemoaning her fate. She tried to hold my hand. She even attempted to kiss me. It all made me so grievously ill that Bea thought the end had come. Bea had no idea of course that my visitor and the girl in the photographs were in fact the same person. Well, in a manner of speaking they weren't . . . Do you dream, Antonia?'

'I do.'

'I had a very peculiar dream the other night. The wake of a *battu*. Dead boars, at least fifty of them, all very young, laid out on the drive leading up to the house. Some of them still twitching. The house, I am sure, was Twiston. All lit by *flambeaux* held by beaters – while men in letter-box red outfits were cutting out the boars' livers. It has to be done at the moment of death, you see, that's when it becomes a delicacy. One of the men was Michael and he was extremely busy cutting away with an enormous carving knife. His hands were covered in blood . . . He looked different from the others. He was got up in white robes, like some high priest . . . Funny how badly Michael took it when that little girl drowned. One would have thought she was his daughter!'

'Miss Garnett thinks the girl in the photographs is your daughter.'

'Well, that was a fiction which was started by George.

Michael's son. In the name of decency and propriety, I imagine. George had guessed my secret, you see. George is the master of polite fictions. He used to be in the diplomatic corps. Insufferable prig. Can't stand him. When he is here, I always put on a show. I act as though I were really demented.' Lady Mortlock laughed – it came out as a cackle.

'Was Lena one of your pupils?'

'Most perceptive of you. Yes, she was one of my pupils. She was at Ashcroft from 1951 till 1956, I think. She was not the brightest of girls, but one of the prettiest. No – "pretty" is not right. Lena had a certain quality, I can't quite explain it . . . I taught her German. I allowed myself to become extremely fond of her. In academic terms she was little better than "satisfactory". Do you know how I define "satisfactory"? "Neither laudable nor culpable." None of it matters now. Long time ago.' Lady Mortlock paused. 'What else do you want to know? You are after something, aren't you? You didn't just wake up this morning and say to yourself, high time I looked up Hermione Mortlock, did you? You must have a good reason. Out with it.'

Antonia began, 'Yesterday was twenty years since Sonya's disappearance –'

'Whose disappearance?'

'Sonya's. Sonya Dufrette – Lena's daughter.'

'Oh yes. Lena's daughter. I remember her. Shrimp of a girl.' Lady Mortlock yawned, displaying dazzling white teeth of preternatural regularity, clearly the result of superior dentistry. 'She drowned, didn't she? She had some form of mental deficiency. She was damaged goods. Hardly surprising. Bad heredity on both sides. If she'd been allowed to grow up, she'd have been one of those slobbering child-like idiots.'

'What do you mean "allowed"?'

'That's only a figure of speech, Antonia. I'd be extremely grateful if you refrained from snapping at me,' Lady Mortlock said grandly. 'I did tell Lena to reconsider when she told me she was pregnant – we were still on speaking terms then – and she promised she would, but didn't. She said afterwards she had forgotten – that it would have been too much trouble, having an abortion. I wanted her to have an abortion. Among other things, that would have made her marriage to Lawrence less real . . . Oh she was hopeless – hopeless!'

Antonia opened her mouth but then decided against saying anything. Better let her speak on, she decided.

'I did warn her of the possible consequences. Lawrence suffered from pathological folie de grandeur while hers was an addictive, irresponsible, rather reckless personality – and of course she was a Yusupov on the distaff side. It was a recipe for disaster. The marriage itself should never have taken place . . . Sonya drowned, didn't she? Michael cried his eyes out, the old fool. He kept calling out her name in his sleep . . . In my opinion that was the best thing that could have happened in the circumstances. What good would it have been to anyone if the girl had lived on – if she had grown up? So much time and energy, not to mention money, are spent nowadays on the care of idiot children. It's like growing weeds in a garden. That poor young woman, I remember, Sonya's nanny, didn't have time to breathe. What good was Sonya to anyone?'

'Her father loved her.'

'A little bit too well, perhaps? No, don't ask me what I mean – *please* – too tedious for words! A bee in Lena's bonnet, that's all. I shouldn't have mentioned it at all. Lolita love. Still, to be fair to her, Lena had to put up with an awful lot. Not only married to a madman, but with an idiot child. Small wonder she became so fat and took to drink . . . Do you know? Every now and then I'd remember the sunny girl with skin as smooth and pale as pearls, the radiant smile and lithe limbs, and I'd feel warm – *here*.' Lady Mortlock touched her shrivelled bosom. 'Lena, you see, was the love of my life. My one folly. My only taste of the forbidden fruit. Lena made me happy in a way I'd never been happy before – or since.'

'Didn't Sir Michael suspect anything?'

'About my *vicio nifando*? No. Nothing at all. Poor Michael. He who trained spies for a living wasn't particularly perceptive in his private life. I took good care not to be discovered of course. Oh I hated the secrecy, the subterfuge, the pretence, but it was necessary. Duty and discipline, that was my motto. It wouldn't have done for anyone to know. Remember that I was an extremely successful professional woman. It was under my headship that Ashcroft became a byword for academic excellence at a time when many other supposedly good schools were reeling under the pressures of post-war inflation and social change. There was Michael's career to consider too. Dear me. It was so difficult. I remember reading Radclyffe Hall and feeling absolutely terrified. Are you familiar with *The Well of Loneliness*?'

'I know what it's about, but I haven't read it.'

'You needn't sound so defensive . . . Look at this. You might as well.' Lady Mortlock took a folded sheet of paper from inside the book on her lap and handed it over to Antonia. 'Read it. Read it aloud.'

Antonia obeyed. The paper was yellow and brittle with age. *'Dear Mine, my darling Mine –'*

'Hermione – Mione – Mine. It's the name Lena had for me. I loved it when she said it. Go on, go on, don't stop. Why did you stop?'

'I do love you and want you and want to spend my life with you – more than anything in the world, and by this, I mean anything.' Antonia looked up. 'It's unsigned.'

'Lena wrote it. I let Bea think it's one of Michael's love letters. Well, Michael never wrote me any love letters. Michael was never interested in me in that way. Mercifully, he turned out to be what is known as "under-sexed". I wouldn't have survived the marriage otherwise!' She cackled. 'We did our own things. Sometimes, at weekends, he disappeared completely. He went bird-watching. Anyhow. Lena kept writing notes like that, reckless creature. She loved me too. I think she was sincere. At one point she did want us to move in together, but of course that was out of the question. It was the fifties. I could never have contemplated setting up house with another woman and leading the life of a social outcast. Never. Besides, it wouldn't have worked. I loved Lena but I also saw how she would deteriorate with age. The seeds were already there . . . By the way, it was *she* who seduced me, not the other way round. She was extremely knowledgeable about that sort of thing. You see, before I met her, she had been with both men *and* women. I was thirty-seven. Nothing like it had ever happened to me before. As a matter of fact, I rather despised women of that ilk. I remember when we went to see that play –'

'Not *The Reluctant Debutante*?'

'No. Of course not. Whatever gave you the idea? It was an underground play called *The Monocled Countess*. It had been inspired by Wedekind's *Lulu*. The main protagonist was this tortured gentlewoman. A pathetic, tragic-comic sort of creature who sits at a rather louche cabaret and drowns her frustrated lusts in absinthe as she ogles the naked girlies who prance around her. We see her sitting at a table, on her own, with a carefully poised, long cigarette holder, a monocle and a mannish bob. That is how the play opens. After her heart is broken by a heartless little minx, she starts visiting Sapphic brothels. All of that was considered extremely risqué at the time. I don't suppose anyone would bat an eyelid nowadays?'

'No.'

'The performance took place in a cellar of sorts. Lena screamed with laughter throughout – she thought it all hilarious. I on the other hand could hardly contain my tears. Well, that was when I saw how different we were. The first cracks, as they say, had started appearing. Lena then introduced me to these two other women who lived together. Philippa and Diane. Philippa was the vanilla one; she had immaculately curled golden hair, tippety-tappety shoes, little white gloves and a skirt you could twirl yourself to death in. Diane was remarkably butch. Stocky, with a crew-cut, *extremely* baggy trousers and a striped blazer, with a sharkskin waistcoat underneath. She smoked untipped cigarettes and took snuff, I think. She took a wild fancy to me. She claimed I looked like the central figure in Jean Dupas's picture *Les Perruches*. You know the tall, dark woman with the Roman nose who's holding two rose bouquets?'

Antonia frowned. 'She is surrounded by nudes, isn't she?'

'Indeed she is – while she herself is wearing a long black, rather puritanical-looking dress. I thought it quite flattering, actually. Philippa on the other hand tried to teach me *polari*, the dyke argot. It's all very different now, isn't it? I mean women do whatever they please. They are already vicars and they hope to become bishops, and they have male strippers at their hen parties. As you can see, I've been keeping up with the Zeitgeist. Well, Antonia, it was good seeing you. Would you like to go now? I am very tired.'

Antonia looked at her in desperation. 'The day before Sonya disappeared you told me that Miss Haywood's mother was very ill, in hospital,' she said. 'That was a lie. What was the purpose of it?'

'Miss Haywood's mother? What are you talking about?'

Antonia persisted. 'It happened the day before Sonya disappeared –'

Suddenly Lady Mortlock gave a nod. 'Oh yes. Yes. As a matter of fact I do remember our conversation. I did tell you that Miss Haywood's mother was rushed to hospital. That's correct.'

Antonia wondered if Lady Mortlock had started playing some game with her. She leant forward. 'She wasn't. That was a lie.'

Lady Mortlock shrugged. 'Well, my dear Antonia, if it was, I had no idea. That was what I was told by Lena.'

'I don't believe you. I think the lie originated with you,'

Antonia suggested boldly. I have nothing to lose, she thought.

There was a moment's pause. Lady Mortlock sat staring at her. 'Are you by any chance thinking what I believe you are thinking? That I killed Sonya on account of her mental deficiency, because of my obsession with eugenics? That I ordered her to be drowned in the river, like some unwanted kitten? That perhaps I paid someone to do it?'

'Well, did you?'

'I can't believe we are having this conversation. That's the kind of thing that happens in detective stories of the more far-fetched kind. This is rather entertaining actually. Perhaps Guedalla was right when he said that detective stories are the normal recreation of noble minds. I am glad you didn't leave when I told you to. I do feel better. Let's see. I never left the drawing room that morning, not for a moment. Plenty of witnesses, including you. Consequently, it couldn't have been me in person. Now then, could I have done it by proxy? Could I have commissioned one of my gardeners? Or perhaps that Major?' She cackled. 'What was his name? Eagle? Some such name. He was the only one without an alibi that morning – and he detested Lawrence.'

'His name was Nagle.'

'One of those seemingly unlikely murderous partnerships. *Lady Mortlock and Major Nagle*. You saw him kiss my hand when he arrived at Twiston for that party of course? You were in the hall at the time. Don't you remember? Major Nagle raised my hand to his lips and held it there. It was an anachronistic, theatrical, rather foreign kind of gesture – Rudolph Valentino became famous for that sort of thing – *not* what one would associate with an English officer and gentleman. Why do you think Major Nagle did that? Didn't it occur to you that he might be reassuring me that he'd carry out his pledge to me? That he wouldn't fail me?'

'No – no, I don't remember.'

'Perhaps the Major and I were members of some crazy

neo-Nazi cult? Perhaps we were at the centre of some *Herrenvolk* plot to purge the world of its imbecile infants?'

Actually that is not such a bad idea for a story, Antonia thought. It could certainly be made to work. If people could believe that Diana and Dodi were alive, having faked their deaths, they could believe *anything*.

Lady Mortlock might have read her mind because she sighed and said, 'Well, I credited you with greater intelligence than that, Antonia. I am disappointed in you.'

15

'They'

'Well, Antonia – I hope you don't mind me calling you Antonia?' Major Payne said. 'Miss Darcy sounds forbidding somehow, don't you think?'

'I don't see why it should.'

'Shades of *Pride and Prejudice* and that pompous ass Darcy, whom I never managed to like, not even after his transformation. And wasn't there a Miss Darcy – a snobbish sister, who was even worse?'

'No. That was Bingley's sister. Miss Darcy was rather nice,' Antonia said. 'If I remember correctly, she is described as having "no equal for beauty, elegance and accomplishments".'

'Oh yes. *And* for the affection she inspires.' He looked at her in a way which made it clear he considered that an attribute she herself possessed in abundance.

It was half past eleven the following morning and they were in the club library, comparing notes over coffee. At least they had been comparing notes before they went off at a tangent. Antonia wasn't sure whether she should feel annoyed or flattered by his attentions which seemed to be becoming more ardent. She blamed herself for encouraging him, by first telling him of the rather annoying phone call she had received from her former husband the night before, then teasing him about the dog Apollo and the cat Daphne. Major Payne had got hold of her hand and said he wouldn't let go of it unless she told him how she had learnt about it.

Antonia could have named Colonel Haslett as her informant at once, but had delayed for at least a quarter of a minute, during which time her hand had remained in his. She had made several futile attempts to pull it from his grip, which had only led to him tightening it. She hadn't tried hard enough. She had enjoyed the experience and now had a ridiculously guilty feeling about it. That, she told herself, was *not* how responsible people in their fifties behaved. They had acted like silly teenagers. What would have happened if somebody had come in and seen them, engaged in a playful skirmish across her desk? Dallying in the library!

Antonia felt hot and a little faint. She found she was panicking. She wasn't ready for a relationship, let alone marriage. It is too soon to allow another man into my life, she thought.

The day was warm and the library windows were open. From outside there came the smell of freshly mown grass – which, again, forcibly, reminded her of that fateful day at Twiston – also the sounds of Radio 4. The gardener was a young university student and he had his transistor radio on. As it happened, he was listening to a programme called *Hopes and Desires*, the first of a series of comedies about unconscious yearnings.

'Well, if you are not happy with Miss Darcy, you can address me as Mrs Rushton.' Which, Antonia pointed out with greater severity than she intended, happened to be her married name.

He sighed. 'I'd rather call you Antonia and I hope you will call me Hugh one day. Well, we are making progress. The moving finger,' he went on quickly, unless that be misconstrued, 'is now firmly fixed on Lena . . . Lena didn't really care about her daughter. Lena fed Lady Mortlock the canard about Miss Haywood's mother being ill in hospital. Lena phoned the nanny – shortly after Sonya disappeared. She didn't sound at all like a mother mourning the death of her child. She warned the nanny against talking. Her exact words were, *You'd better keep your mouth shut, my girl, or they will kill us both.* We do assume, don't we, that Lena was part of whatever conspiracy there was? That she knew exactly what happened?'

'We do.'

'But we don't believe Lady Mortlock was the mastermind behind the conspiracy?'

'No. I don't really think Lady Mortlock had anything to do with Sonya's disappearance. The only reason she told lies was because she didn't want it to be known that she had had an affair with Lena.'

'You don't think that she and Major Nagle –'

'No. The *Herrenvolk* conspiracy was not meant to be taken seriously. She was making fun of me.'

'Was she though?'

'Of course she was.'

'It might have been one of those double bluffs,' Payne reflected. 'Maybe there *was* a conspiracy but she named Major Nagle because it made it all seem so absurd? Maybe she wanted you to dismiss the idea out of hand – which you did. What if she *was* telling the truth? *Wait*. What if her real partner was somebody else – somebody who was very close to her? What if her partner was her husband – or should I say her *so-called husband*?'

'Sir Michael?'

'Sir Michael. Why did the Mortlocks stay together? From what Lady M. told you, theirs was clearly a marriage in name only – a *mariage blanc*. What if they were together exclusively for ideological reasons? What if they were confederates? No one would have thought it of Sir Michael, but he was actually a Freemason and apparently he belonged to a number of other esoteric societies, somebody in the department told me once.'

'His obituary mentioned it too,' she murmured, remembering.

'There you are. He might have been a bad blood nut as well – he might even have been more fanatical than her!'

Payne paused. 'Are you sure Sir Michael didn't leave the room that morning while you were all watching the royal wedding?'

'No . . . Actually, he did. Yes. I forgot to mention it in my account, I know. But he wasn't the only one. People did go out – the Falconers, Mrs Lynch-Marquis – for no more than a couple of minutes at a time and by themselves. The usual. There were two downstairs lavatories. Sir Michael couldn't have been out for more than five minutes, I think. He went to the kitchen to have a word with the men who were providing the oak with a base. He had remembered something. It seemed to be urgent.'

'How can you be sure he went to the kitchen? No, of course you aren't sure. It's not as though you followed him.'

'Five minutes wouldn't have been enough for him to go down to the river and drown Sonya.'

'Who says Sonya drowned? He might have killed her somewhere else and hidden the body.'

Antonia smiled. 'I could just about get away with it if I were to put this in a book –'

'All right – but, my dear girl, the fact remains that some sort of conspiracy *was* at work. We know for a fact that somebody – the mysterious and rather sinister "they" – did buy the nanny's silence.'

'And not only the nanny's,' Antonia said, her eyes suddenly bright. She went on slowly, 'Lady Mortlock said that Lena had had a fortune, but that *she had frittered it away.* Lena told her about it when she went to see her.'

'Did she now? How very interesting.' Payne stroked his jaw with a forefinger. 'And Lena wasn't talking about the Yusupov millions?'

'No. The Yusupov millions are the stuff of legends, but they had been spent by the time Lena was born.'

'It might have been a fantasy of course – a figment of Lena's drunken dreaming.'

'What if it wasn't?'

'If it wasn't . . . Well, then it would mean that in the not too distant past, say in the last twenty years, Lena had been in possession of a lot of money.' Payne paused. 'Where did the money come from? Who gave it to her?'

'The obvious answer is, the mysterious and rather sinister "they". The same person – or persons – who paid Sonya's nanny, paid Sonya's mother as well.'

'A deal, eh?'

Antonia said, 'It is Lena who holds the key to the mystery. Lena knows what happened to her daughter. Lena knows who "they" are.'

'The Mortlocks. My money's on the Mortlocks.'

'We must go and talk to Lena.'

'It shouldn't be too difficult to track her down, should it?'

'I already have,' Antonia said. 'Before I took my leave of Miss Garnett, I asked if Mrs Dufrette had left a contact number or address when she called, and it turned out that she had. Lena left both a number *and* an address.'

'Where does she live?'

'A hotel named the Elsnor. It's in Bayswater. Rather a run-down sort of place.'

'That's appropriate. Isn't Lena a ruin herself?'

'Miss Garnett knows the hotel. She was taken to tea there as a girl, but the place now is apparently unrecognizable, gone to the dogs completely. Miss Garnett referred to it as a "hell-hole".'

There was a pause. 'I don't think we should bother to phone. We are going to pay Lena a blitz visit,' Major Payne said.

'Who's going? Me or you?'

'This time . . . I think we should go together. We can pretend to be a married couple.'

Antonia bristled. 'I don't see why we should want to do that.'

'Lena would feel less threatened if she were to be approached by a nice middle-aged couple,' Major Payne explained. 'The idea is to stage a casual encounter, buy her a drink, set a trap and trick her into some sort of confession.'

'Since she appears to be an alcoholic *and* penniless, it's unlikely she'd feel threatened if a giant lizard went along and offered to buy her a drink,' Antonia pointed out. A married couple, she thought. Really. Hugh was forgetting himself. She meant Major Payne. Earlier on he had addressed her as 'my dear girl' – how dared he!

'The bar. That's where we'll probably find her. We must visit the Elsnor at the cocktail hour.'

'No such thing as the "cocktail hour" any longer exists.'

'The Elsnor, did you say? Are you sure it's not the Els*inore*? Would be so much more suitable a place for conjuring up ghosts from the past –'

'Stop showing off,' Antonia said.

16

'She was never in the river . . .'

The Elsnor was a private hotel in Bayswater that occupied two corner houses in a noisy region east of Queen's Road. It had been grand and ugly once, in the best manner of hotels built in the late Victorian era, but, having fallen on bad times, was merely ugly now.

'It has the air of neglected mystery about it,' Major Payne declared. *'Sacré bleu, Prince Omelette! C'est le spectre de ton père,'* he sang out suddenly. That, he explained, came from a particularly witless French opera based on *Hamlet*, which he had seen at Covent Garden a while ago. No, it hadn't been a *buffo opera* – it hadn't been *meant* to be funny.

It was seven o'clock that same evening.

They entered the hotel through the revolving doors. An acrid smell hung on the air, suggesting some sort of conflagration had taken place. Antonia looked round nervously. A short circuit? Surely not a *gun*? Major Payne drew her attention to the fact that the two receptionists were under fire. One was being accused of having lost the passport belonging to a Japanese tourist, while the other was trying to convince a group of extremely tense-looking German tourists that no booking had been made in their name and that they had come to the wrong hotel. 'But this is not possible,' the leader of the group was saying. 'I made the reservations myself. I want to see the manager at once.' The manager, he was told, was away.

They started crossing the hall and passed by a sunken sofa. They saw a fearfully made-up girl in a miniskirt, black fishnet stockings and knee-length boots, who couldn't have been more than fifteen, sitting on the lap of a bald stout man who looked like a commercial traveller of the more prosperous variety, gazing earnestly into his eyes. Antonia shot Major Payne an eloquent look.

'Don't jump to conclusions. She may be his daughter. She may be upset about something,' Payne murmured. That was only a moment before the commercial traveller brought his face close to the girl's and ran his tongue across her lips and chin.

Placing his hand at Antonia's elbow in a protective manner, Payne propelled her briskly through the hall.

They were following the sign pointing in the direction of the bar. 'I bet it leads to the saunas,' Antonia said. 'It seems to be that sort of place. '

However, the arrow did not lie and soon they found themselves entering the Elsnor bar. Beside the door there stood an ancient stuffed bear with eyes of coloured glass. Its right paw was raised in greeting, the left one was missing. Inside the bar it reeked of stale smoke and some exotic, rather sickening, scent, which, Major Payne insisted, was actually formaldehyde. It was a dark cavern of a room with vaulted ceilings, empty and very quiet. They could hear water dripping dolorously somewhere.

'Doesn't it put you in mind of the Blitz? What will you have?' Payne asked her. His hand was still at her elbow.

'Gin and tonic. Why are you whispering?'

'I feel like a neat whisky . . . There's a speck of soot on your cheek. Do let me.' He took out a starched handkerchief. Who did his ironing? Antonia wondered. 'Don't move . . . Are your eyes actually blue? Do they change colour? Don't move. It's gone . . . No waiters . . . Why isn't she here?' He looked round at the empty tables.

'She might be dead,' Antonia suggested. 'Alcoholics and

junkies have notoriously short lifespans. They might be carrying her coffin down the back stairs at this very moment.' Was she seeking refuge in morbid flippancy, as a form of defence against his flirtatiousness?

'Let's find the barman,' he said.

But there was no barman. It was only as they approached the bar counter that they noticed the barmaid. A bull-shouldered woman with orange hair and the lurid lips of a Land Girl, who sat slumped on a stool. So focused was she on her own drink, a tall glass filled with vermouth the colour of old blood, which she was sucking through a green straw, that she took no notice of them.

They halted and Payne said, 'Good Lord.'

'Yes, it's her,' Antonia whispered. 'It's Lena . . . In charge of the drinks.'

'Asking Mistress Fox to feed the chickens, eh?'

'Yes. It can only happen at a place like this.'

'Big, loose and picturesque . . . Dracula's daughter . . . The fantastical hausfrau . . .'

'She looks like an inflated Zandra Rhodes doll. She still rims her eyes with kohl.'

'Let's go and beard this phantom bride in her bibulous bower!'

'Be *quiet*, Hugh.'

'We'll play it by ear,' Major Payne explained *sotto voce*, privately noting with some satisfaction that she had called him Hugh. 'The main thing is to act as though we have no idea who she is.'

'She's not likely to recognize me, is she?' Antonia sounded anxious.

'Fear not. I am sure you haven't changed one little bit,' he said gallantly. 'It's only that she looks pickled. Observe the catatonic stare. Leave it to me. I'll start, you follow my cues. We'll concoct our plot as we go along.'

As they approached the curve of the bar, Lena looked up and regarded them out of puffy eyes. 'Hello,' she said amiably. 'Such a hot day, isn't it? There used to be a fan, but someone stole it.' She no longer spoke with a Russian accent but slurred some of her words a bit. She smacked her lips. 'Disgraceful. What would you two love birds like?'

She was wearing a faded maroon-coloured velvet gown that seemed to have seen better days and heavy costume jewellery. Her ear lobes were weighed down by enormous pendant earrings made of sparkling Swarowski crystals set in bronze frames. Her face was the shape of a full moon and plastered with pancake make-up. 'A gin and tonic for my wife and a scotch for me, please,' Payne ordered. 'Neat.'

On the counter in front of her, there lay a half-eaten bar of chocolate, a lipstick, a powder compact, four large tablets with a purplish coating and a sheet of pale mauve paper – it looked like a letter, Antonia thought.

'We don't get many married couples here,' Lena observed. 'Only foreigners bring their wives.'

'We lit on the Elsnor by a trick of fate. Charming place,' Major Payne said. 'Have you got Famous Grouse?'

'Are you a soldier?' Lena asked. She popped one of the purple pills into her mouth, washed it down with vermouth, then busied herself with bottles and glasses. She was painfully slow and clumsy. 'You certainly have that air. My papa served with the Imperial Cossacks for a while. He was aide-de-camp to the Tsar's brother. You *are* a soldier, aren't you?'

'Spot on, dear lady. Major Payne at your service.' Antonia had never heard him put on this voice before. He made himself sound ridiculously Blimpish.

'Can you read that letter?' Antonia whispered when Lena turned round to get a bottle of tonic. 'I think it's a letter. *It's upside down.*'

Payne rose to the challenge at once. 'I'll try.' She saw him tilting his head to one side and squinting.

'All the ice's melted, I can't understand why,' Lena said. 'There's plenty of lemon. Have you been abroad?' She was peering into Antonia's face now. 'You have a lovely tan. You look a simpatico sort of person. You've been abroad, haven't you?' Antonia's heart missed a beat, but Lena showed no flicker of recognition.

'Spot on again,' Payne said. 'Kenya, actually. Got off the plane three hours ago. We'd been visiting friends. Name of Sandys,' he added casually and he gave Antonia a wink. Sandys, she had told him, were the couple who had bought Twiston from the Mortlocks and then sold it to Mrs Ralston-Scott before leaving for Kenya. She thought she could guess the kind of game he had started playing. He had managed to establish a connection with Twiston without arousing Lena's suspicions. What next? she wondered, fascinated.

'Kenya, eh? Lovely place.' Lena nodded approvingly. 'Or so I've been told. Safaris and moonlit picnics and sundowners till sunrise? Lovely place to be. No matter how much you drink, you never get drunk. It's the air that does it, apparently. So fresh and pure. My papa got to know the White Valley. He became a tremendously popular figure at the Muthaiga Club. He got on famously with the crowd. He was in Kenya in 1940-something.'

'That's jolly interesting,' Major Payne said in a hearty manner. 'He must have been there when Lord Erroll was murdered?'

'Yes, I believe so. Here you are, your drinkies . . . *Prosit*.' She picked up her own glass. 'You don't mind if I continue?'

'No, of course not, dear lady. Perhaps you will allow me to order you a refill when you finish?'

'That's all right,' Lena said. 'I can have as much as I want.' She waved her hand at the range of bottles behind her. 'I can have anything I like whenever I like. Bliss.' She picked up her glass. 'Your good health.'

'*Nazdarovye*,' Payne responded in part. Antonia shook her head at him frantically – they weren't supposed to know she was Russian!

'What I'd really like now is an Egyptian cigarette that has been dipped lightly in cognac, but I am not allowed.' Lena sighed. 'Doctor's orders. The merest puff will kill me, apparently. I shall never launch merrily down the path of sin again. Doomed from here to eternity . . . Oh well, *c'est la vie*. How did you know I was Russian?'

'Oh – you said your papa was aide-de-camp to the Tsar's brother. You meant the Tsar of Russia, correct?' Payne said coolly. 'I don't know many other tsars. *And* you mentioned Cossacks.'

'Quite the little detective, aren't you?' Lena laughed in a flirtatious manner.

There was a pause as they occupied themselves with their drinks. It was Antonia who broke the silence. 'Do you know, they still talk about the Erroll murder. They keep arguing about it. I mean in Kenya. Everybody seems to be an expert on the subject.' She laughed. 'I *adore* unsolved mysteries, don't you?' She delivered this effusively, in her best memsahib voice, and received a nod of approval from Payne.

For a moment Lena said nothing. She went on sucking vermouth through her straw. She appeared not to have heard. Then she said, 'They wrote a book about it, didn't they? They thought it was the husband who did it.'

'Sir Jock Delves Broughton. That's still open to debate,' Payne said. 'As so often happens with such cases. I find they never die down, not quite. Old Sandys told me about another one. Murder that took place twenty years ago – at the very house he bought! Pile of a place on the river. Outside Richmond.' He paused, but there was no reaction from Lena. 'Called – what was it, my love?' He turned towards Antonia.

'Twiston. We are thinking of paying it a visit, actually,' Antonia said. 'There's always an – *atmosphere* – at places like that. And this place, it seems, is really special.'

They were looking at Lena, but she hadn't stirred. She was staring down into her drink, her podgy hands clutching at the glass as though she feared somebody might snatch it away from her.

'Twiston, that's correct.' Payne slapped his forehead with the palm of his hand. 'The old cerebellum's not functioning properly. Jetlag. Forget my own name next. Never been good on planes. Murder happened at the time of the previous owners. Couple called Mortlock. It was a young girl who got killed. Terrible tragedy.' He was gratified to see Lena look up slowly.

Antonia said in a low voice, 'The funny thing is – now you wouldn't believe this, but the place seems to be haunted!' It was Hugh's reference to Elsinore that had given her the idea.

'What d'you mean – haunted?' Lena ran her tongue across her lips.

'It's the ghost of the little girl that got murdered. She appears in the garden.' Major Payne took out his pipe. 'Always from the direction of the river.'

'What fucking nonsense is that?' Lena spoke thickly. She was scowling. 'What the fuck are you talking about?' Suddenly all her amiability had evaporated.

'Name of Sonya, I think? Sandys says he's seen her, several times. Others have seen her too,' Payne went on improvising. 'A very tiny girl – flaxen hair – white dress with little bells at the waist –'

They heard Lena gasp. 'Your friend Sandys is a liar!' she cried and she brought her fist down. Her double chin quivered.

There was a moment's silence, then Major Payne spluttered, 'I assure you, dear lady, Sandys is a fellow of great integrity – not the least bit fanciful either!'

'Sorry, but I can't allow this. You've got it all wrong. In the first place, there was no murder.' Lena was clearly making a monumental effort to appear calm. 'You don't know the story. A little girl did drown in the river, true, but that was an accident, *not* murder. That was an accident, a fucking accident. Sonya – the little girl – drowned. She fell into the river –'

'Oh, you know about it?' Antonia breathed. 'You weren't by any chance there when it happened?'

Lena considered the point and seemed to come to a decision. 'As a matter of fact I *was* there. It was all most upsetting. I was staying at the house. I – um – I knew the girl's parents. We were fellow guests. Actually, I was great friends with the mother.'

'What was she like?' Payne asked slyly. He put a match to his pipe.

'Oh, wonderful woman. Big-hearted. Giving. She'd had a very hard life. She'd never known true love, not for long. Only one man had ever loved her – and one woman. They had both worshipped her.' Lena dabbed at her eyes with the sleeve of her gown. 'Oh, she was a sweet-tempered, sensitive creature. One of the very best. The same, alas, can't be said about the father, but I mustn't gossip. Hate gossip. What I mean is, I know perfectly well what I am talking about.'

'Remarkable,' Payne said.

'Do tell us more!' Antonia gushed.

'There is nothing to tell. Why are people such ghouls? Sonya – I mean the little girl – fell into the river and drowned, that's all there is to it. She was young for her age. Backward. Terribly difficult, taking care of a child like that. I couldn't – I mean the *mother* couldn't call her time her own! They found her doll floating on the river, but of the girl there was no sign. Her body was never recovered, see? It was an accident. So next time you see your friend Sandys, kindly inform him that he's got the wrong end of the stick altogether. Tell him to be very careful. It's actually a crime spreading malicious rumours. If he's not careful, your friend Sandys may find himself in court.'

'Dear lady!' Major Payne protested. 'I assure you –'

'You too.' Lena shook her forefinger at him. Her mountainous bosom rose and fell. She picked up her glass and, not bothering with the straw, downed the rest of the vermouth. 'You too may land in real hot water if you go about telling people Sonya was killed. Murder indeed! Nonsense. Your friend Sandys needs to have his head examined if he's seeing ghosts. Anyone who is seeing ghosts needs to have their head examined.' She licked her lips. 'It's all wrong anyhow. Sonya couldn't have been coming from the direction of the river for the simple reason that . . .'

'Yes?' Antonia leaned forward.

'Nothing,' Lena said. 'Nothing at all. She couldn't have, that's all. There are no ghosts anyhow . . . I need a drinkie. Mamma needs a drinkie. Badly.'

She had started wheezing like an ancient concertina. Her face under the make-up had become suffused. Her eyes were bloodshot. Her mouth, fish-like, kept opening and shutting. All of a sudden she looked dangerously on the verge of collapse.

'Are you all right?' Antonia said. 'Perhaps some water –'

'No, not water. A proper drinkie. Mamma needs a brandy.'

'Shall I pour you one?' In the most casual manner imaginable, Major Payne walked round the bar and stood beside Lena. 'Brandy, did you say?'

'Yes. Brandy, my friend. That's the best gut-rot there is. Armagnac, that's lovely. Lovely smooth taste. Oh, Mamma's so thirsty. Mamma loves it when someone else does the pouring . . . That's how things *used* to be at my father's house. We were served by hussars. Bowing and clicking their heels. Not a single crease in their uniforms. Such style, such poise. Everything as it should be. Ah, glorious days. Thank you, kind sir.' She almost snatched the glass from Major Payne's hand and started drinking. Her hand shook and some brandy got spilled. She made several gasping noises. She drank the whole of the brandy, to the last drop, as though it had been water. 'More,' she ordered imperiously. '*More*. Another brandy – quick! Mamma's still unwell. Mamma needs her medicine.'

Payne picked up the bottle.

Antonia looked horrified. 'Hugh, you mustn't – it'd kill her,' she whispered.

He shook his head and mouthed, *It won't*.

'I used to live at the Dorchester, you know, but I was downgraded,' Lena said presently. Her glass, her second, was empty and she was holding it up. Payne obliged her. 'Vivian's so – so *mean*. After everything I did,' she slurred. 'I don't like my room here at all, but I was told I'd been given enough. I was told I was greedy . . . *Prosit* . . . Mamma feels better now. Not good – Mamma will never feel good, not as long as she's in this world, but Mamma feels better.' She took a sip. 'What were we talking about? Oh yes, that Twiston business. Well, it proved to be most unsettling, more than I ever imagined. Lawrence became quite impossible. Lawrence, you see, is the kind of man who would perpetrate evil for the betterment of evil,' she said, sounding oddly like the headmaster of his old school, Payne thought.

Lena smacked her lips. 'He kept blaming me. Said it had been my fault. If he knew what I had done – really done – ah, if he only knew! – he would have killed me. He'd have strangled me. Cut me into little pieces. I have no doubt about it.'

'What *did* you do?' Antonia asked boldly.

'In a way that was my revenge – taking away from him the one thing he adored. But let me tell you first what *he* did. I mean, when it was all over. You know Lawrence, of course? He kept kissing Sonya's toys – kissing her photo – her little shoes. He blubbed all over that giraffe. Disgusting. I never liked the way he kissed *her*, you see. That was *before* – before she left us. The way he crooned that song to her. *If you love me, Dilly, Dilly, I will love you*. Gives me the creeps, just remembering.' Lena's speech was becoming slushier. 'Like someone serenading their lover! My poor *kotik*. That's why I did it. Whatever *else* anyone may say . . . *Sans reproche, c'est moi*.'

'What was it you did exactly?' Payne asked.

Lena took another sip of brandy and smacked her lips. 'Well,' she said conversationally, 'I'm sure there'd be those who'd say what an absolutely foul thing for a mother to do, but I acted out of the best motives. You don't think I should have said no to the money, do you?'

'No, of course not. The money must have been jolly useful,' Payne said.

'It was. Only it ran out. Don't you just hate it, when money runs out?'

'Great bore. I know the feeling too well.' Payne sighed.

This was surreal, Antonia thought.

Lena slurred on. 'Did you say you'd been staying at Twiston?'

'Yes.'

'Hermione and Michael no longer live there.' Lena took another sip of brandy. 'No . . . Poor Michael's dead anyway . . . *They* couldn't have been talking . . . Nobody could have . . .'

'Who's "they"?'

Lena started shaking her head. 'No, no, *no*. Out of the question . . . Out of the fucking question . . . They knew they'd be sent to the clink if they did talk about it . . . They are no fools . . . I mean she – *she* is no fool.' Lena reached out and tapped the letter that lay before her. 'He is dead. Well out of it.'

'*Were* the Mortlocks behind it?' Antonia asked. She saw Payne frowning down at the letter, which, she was sure, he could now read without any difficulty.

'The Mortlocks . . . Hermione was discreet . . . Always very discreet . . . He was a passionate man. No one would have thought it.' Lena shook her head. 'Hermione feared scandal more than the Devil. I never feared the Devil myself – never! Do you realize? *I actually lived with him.*'

They had to strain to make out what she was saying now, the slurring had become so bad. Her eyes were almost entirely out of focus. She couldn't last much longer, Payne knew. Besides he had heard someone enter the bar.

He asked, 'Why did you say Sonya's ghost couldn't have been coming from the direction of the river?' Antonia saw him reach out towards the letter.

''Strordinary question. Because –' Lena put up her forefinger – 'she was never in the river in the first place. That's why.'

'Where is she? Where's the body?'

Antonia was to think later that had Lena answered the question, their quest would have been over, there and then, anticlimactically, rather flatly, in fact, beside the bar at the Elsnor hotel. She would never have gone to Twiston – and then the murder would never have been discovered.

Only Lena didn't answer the question. As she emitted a gurgling sound and her heavy shoulders started heaving, Payne quickly walked away from her and joined Antonia. Lena's eyes nearly popped out of her head and her mouth opened wide. The retching noises, when they came, were quite appalling. Lena's head wobbled up and down. Suddenly lurching to the left she was violently sick. Then again – and again. Mercifully the bar stood between her and them.

'Badmouthing as usual – in more ways than one,' a voice said behind them. 'How unfortunate that it should have happened now, but then that's Lena for you. Unpredictable, to say the least.'

They turned round. A tall elderly man with very light blue eyes, a high-bridged nose and a mane of silvery white hair brushed back stood in front of them. He was clad very correctly in a blue-and-white striped serge suit and was holding a Panama hat in his right hand and a black Malacca cane in his left. There was something of the *grand seigneur* about him. At the moment his long face was cadaverously pale and twisted in a squeamish grimace. He raised his neck as if his shirt collar was too tight and he looked away from the bar.

Antonia drew in her breath. This was the man who had visited her at the club library the other day, and asked about books on the Himalayas. The man she had taken for –

'Dufrette!' Major Payne exclaimed.

17

The Sanity of Lawrence Dufrette

Lawrence Dufrette addressed himself to Antonia exclusively. 'Odd thing, bumping into you again, or maybe not so odd?' He dabbed at his brow with the silk handkerchief from his breast pocket. The handkerchief bore the initials L.D., embroidered in blue silk, so there was no doubt it was him. 'Mrs Rushton, isn't it? Antonia Rushton? At the Military Club the other day they told me to ask for Miss Darcy.'

She nodded. 'My maiden name.'

'I see. Divorced? Then we do have something in common.' He gave a Mephistophelean grin and patted his pocket. 'My decree absolute. That was the purpose of my visit, to tell Lena in person, lest there be any misunderstanding. Communicating with Lena has always been a nightmare. She never answers any letters or faxes. Not even when they are from my solicitor. *Especially* when they are from my solicitor. She pretends she has never received anything. It is invariably a long and laborious process getting her on the phone and when I do manage to speak to her, she is either too drunk or too hung-over to make any sense.'

They had turned their backs on the dreadful scene in the bar and were walking briskly through the hall towards the exit. 'Just a moment,' Antonia said. They saw her walk up to the reception desk.

'As a matter of fact we've met before. I used to work in the department that was next to yours,' Payne said. 'You've probably forgotten.'

'I am afraid so. I am cursed with an appalling memory.'

'My name is Payne. Major Payne.'

At the word 'Major', Lawrence Dufrette gave a little histrionic shudder. 'I can't say I remember your name. Not at all.' He dabbed at his brow. 'So hot, so damnably hot . . . Oh there you are, Mrs Rushton. Is anything the matter?'

'No. I told the receptionists that their barmaid was feeling rather unwell and would they see if she needed any assistance.'

'You are too kind. What Lena needs is a – No, I won't say it. You don't deserve to be shocked. You are a good woman, Mrs Rushton. I remember how sweet you were to Sonya.'

'Have you been to the Elsnor before?'

'Unfortunately, yes. Once . . . Lena wasn't always like that, you know. There was a time when she was beautiful – spirited – exciting – *fun*. I was mad about her. We were that jousting couple, Benedick and Beatrice. I adored her. I couldn't bear to be parted from her. I never for a moment imagined that my marriage would end up with the lethal conspiracies of – of –' He broke off unable to find another theatrical metaphor.

'Edward Albee's Martha and George?' Major Payne suggested.

Dufrette shot him a sidelong glance. They were now standing outside the hotel. It was a balmy evening. 'I'd like to offer you a drink,' Dufrette told Antonia and he took her arm. 'May I? We need to talk. Somehow I don't think your presence at the Elsnor was entirely accidental. Something is going on, isn't it?'

'You may put it that way,' Antonia said. 'By the way, Major Payne is a friend of mine. I understand you used to work together –'

'That Italian bar over there isn't too bad.' Dufrette

pointed with his cane. The place was called Papa Rodari. 'We need to talk, Mrs Rushton.'

They walked across the road and entered the bar. There weren't many people. They sat at a table beside the window. Payne had tagged along. As far as Dufrette was concerned, he might not have existed, but although he hadn't been included in Dufrette's invitation, he hadn't been excluded either.

'What will you have?' Dufrette asked Antonia.

Again she plumped for a gin and tonic. For himself Dufrette ordered a vermouth. So he and Lena did have at least *one* taste in common, Antonia thought, amused. Major Payne told the waiter he wanted a scotch with lots of ice. After the waiter had gone, Dufrette turned to Antonia. 'Now then. Why did you look terrified when I spoke to you in the library?'

'It was the anniversary of Sonya's death.' Antonia decided to be as truthful as possible. After all, he had been behaving impeccably towards her. 'I envisaged some unpleasant confrontation. I thought you had sought me out –'

'I hadn't the least notion that you would turn out to be the librarian! It was one of those extraordinary coincidences.'

'I thought you might blame me for Sonya's death.'

His brows went up. 'Blame you for Sonya's death? My good woman. How could you think such a thing? That's absolutely terrible.'

Antonia smiled faintly. 'I was in a highly neurotic state. I wasn't thinking rationally –'

'I felt so sorry for you that day on the river bank,' Dufrette said. 'Lena making a scene, screaming at you. I should have intervened – put an end to her mendacious caterwauling – told her to shut up. I *wanted* to, but I couldn't move. I couldn't speak. I couldn't think of anything but Sonya. What she would look like when the body was eventually fished out of the water. In a way I was glad that it was never found . . . I loved her so!'

'I know.' Antonia touched his arm.

The words of 'Lavender's Blue' floated into her head. *If you love me, Dilly, Dilly, I will love you . . .* She remembered the heavy hints Lena had dropped. *I didn't like the way he kissed her.* Was there anything in that? Could Lena be trusted? Antonia decided not. *Like serenading a lover,* Lena had said. *Lolita love.* That had been Lady Mortlock's way of putting it.

The next moment Antonia recalled that she had heard 'Lavender's Blue' not such a long time ago – only where? She frowned. She had the feeling that it was extremely important that she should remember. When she did remember the place where she had heard the song, she told herself, she would know *why* it had been important . . . Was she being irrational again?

She said, 'I believe I can understand how terrible it was for you. My son was almost the same age as Sonya, you see.'

'I do remember you mentioning your little boy. How is he? What was his name? Jonathan?'

'David.'

'Doing well, I hope?'

'Yes. Not so little any more. He is fine. He is twenty-six. Married – with a child of his own. A daughter.'

'Good to hear that. I am delighted. So you have a granddaughter! How old is she?'

He sounds so *normal,* Antonia thought. 'Three and a half.'

'Splendid. I would have loved to have grandchildren – read Belloc's *Cautionary Tales* to them – I can do the voices perfectly.' He gave a wistful smile. 'Sadly, it wasn't to be . . . It was absolutely dreadful, that day, when it happened. And the following day was worse – the day we left Twiston and drove to London . . . 30th July. The heat. The Union Jacks, as we drove through London. The hordes of delirious fools still walking in the streets, singing, gawping outside Buckingham Palace, shouting, "Diana, Diana." The silly goose wasn't even there . . . I told you that marriage wouldn't last, didn't I? I was right! Thank you.'

Their drinks had arrived. He took a sip of vermouth. 'That journey and its aftermath were the stuff of nightmares. Lena got drunk. The grieving mamma, don't you know. I wanted to cry but couldn't. I went into the nursery. Everything was exactly as we had left it. I took out all of Sonya's toys and arranged them on the floor. The one she loved best was a giraffe called Curzon. I had given him the name. One of Curzon's ears still bore an imprint of Sonya's teeth, where she had bitten him. I took Curzon to my room and put him on my bedside table. Then, ten days later, something very odd happened. Curzon disappeared.'

'Disappeared?'

'Yes. He vanished. Nobody seemed to know where he had gone. We searched everywhere, but couldn't find him. For some reason I was profoundly upset by that second disappearance. I cried *then*.' Dufrette's hand went up to his mouth. 'Buckets. Couldn't stop myself. I know it sounds ridiculous . . .'

'No, it doesn't,' Antonia said.

'Was he ever found?' Major Payne asked over his scotch. 'I mean Curzon?'

'No. He wasn't.' Dufrette turned towards Antonia. 'I wanted to talk to you in the library the other day, but didn't after I saw the expression on your face. You looked terrified.'

Antonia blushed. 'I am sorry. Are you a member of the Military Club? I've never seen you there before.'

'I am a member, yes, but it was ages since I'd been there. I know old Haslett and so on, but I am afraid I rather detest it there, so I never visit it. I am a member of several other clubs. Terrible places, but then I am not your typical kind of clubman.' Compressing his lips slightly, Dufrette shot a pointed glance at Payne as though to imply that he thought him precisely that – the typical clubman, a type he unequivocally despised.

'So you really needed a book on the Himalayas? For your nephew?'

'No, that was only an excuse. I had to think of something. I'd been making a round of all my clubs, promoting my book in my own peculiar way – since nobody else would.'

'Promoting your book?'

'Yes. Self-publicity of a particularly furtive kind, I hate to admit, but it is an extremely important book. A warning to mankind.' He paused. 'What I do is enter the library, distract the librarian with some query and then place a copy of my book somewhere handy. Clubs are good because members leave donations all the time, isn't that right?'

'They do.' Antonia gave a little sigh. 'All the time.' She paused. '*The Greatest Secret*. You left it in one of my boxes, didn't you?'

'Frightfully *infra dig*.' Dufrette took another sip of vermouth. 'I get no profit whatsoever, but it's terribly important that people should read my book, that's why I have been going to such lengths . . . The threat is imminent . . . I don't expect you to have read it, but I do believe you should. Time may be very short now.'

'I have read your book,' Payne said.

Dufrette's face remained blank. 'Really?'

'Yes. I found it fascinating.'

'You did?' Dufrette said in a flat voice.

'Absolutely. It's quite amazing.'

'It's the truth. There isn't a single word in my book which doesn't reflect the truth.' Dufrette delivered this with great gravity. 'Are you sure we are talking about the same book? I wrote it pseudonymously.'

'The Babylonian brotherhood – race of interbreeding bloodlines,' Payne said. 'They established institutions like religions in an attempt to imprison the masses mentally and emotionally – so far they have operated in secret but they are preparing to reveal themselves and take over.'

Dufrette looked at him again. 'Well, the danger is

imminent. They were behind Diana's murder. Of course most of the royal family are brotherhood members. You see, she *knew*. She was foolish but remarkably intuitive. Why hasn't it occurred to anyone that the Pont d'Alma tunnel is *not* the way to Dodi al Fayed's flat? It takes you *away* from that area. I checked personally. I went to Paris and walked the route the Mercedes had taken that night. There are thirty pillars in that tunnel and the Mercedes hit the thirteenth because it was meant to.'

'The Babylonian brotherhood throughout the centuries has had an obsession with the number thirteen,' Major Payne explained to Antonia with a deadpan expression. She managed a grave nod.

'That's absolutely correct. Diana, on the other hand, had an aversion to it, and she would not allow a thirteenth lot in her dress auction at Christie's the June before she died. Well, Henri Paul was *directed* to pick out the thirteenth pillar at the highest speed imaginable. It was inevitable that he should. His subconscious had been programmed.' Dufrette took a sip of vermouth.

Payne cleared his throat. 'Your research was impressive, the details you provide fascinating.' Dufrette remained silent and continued sipping his drink, but it was clear he was listening carefully. He's buttering him up, Antonia thought. Suddenly she saw them as Humours: Vanity exploited by Cunning.

'I found the chapter entitled "Knights of the Black Sun" of particular interest. Although the information you communicate is of the kind that stretches one's sense of reality to breaking point,' Major Payne continued, 'you treat your readers with tremendous respect.'

'I do?'

'Yes. You must be one of the very few possessors of this truly astonishing data – yet you do not for a moment patronize the reader, rather you leave them to edit the information for themselves. Besides, you are brave enough to stick to your guns while you make it abundantly clear that you expect great opposition to your ideas.'

'Well, I have been described as a raving lunatic – as a "highly dangerous nutcase" – and so on,' Dufrette said with an indulgent smile. 'I am perfectly aware of the fact. Still, even if one is in a minority of one, the truth is the truth.'

'Is that Gandhi?'

Dufrette cast him another glance. 'An intellectual Major, eh? What an oxymoron that is. Like – like "premeditated spontaneity", or *Nature Morte Vivante*.' He gave an unexpected whinny of a laugh. 'What did you say your name was?'

'Payne . . . That's a Dali, isn't it?'

'What? Oh, the painting! Still life moving. Yes . . . You are showing off now, Payne. Still, better an intellectual braggadocio than a philistine ignoramus. Incidentally, do you know where "braggadocio" comes from?'

'Marlowe? No – Spenser. *Faerie Queen*. A boastful character who –'

'Yes, yes. Stop showing off. You seem to be quite different, Payne. Generals are pompous asses, the colonel's a bore – but majors, majors I abhor,' Dufrette recited gleefully. 'Either rogues, bumbling fools or cads – or downright crooks.'

'In fiction, certainly.'

'No, not only in fiction. There's Diana's awful love rat . . . And the one who fathered the fat duchess – he has a penchant for massage parlours, hasn't he? I personally knew a Major Yeats Brown, who was an occultist and a numerologist. He drank himself to death. He favoured the kind of Cyprus brandy that could take the shell off an egg. Then of course there was Nagle who as good as killed his wife. He was a sadist.' Dufrette turned to Antonia. 'Do you remember friend Nagle?'

She said she did. Once more she saw the stock-still figure at the window, looking down at her and Sonya.

Dufrette's eyes remained on her. 'What exactly brought you to the Elsnor?'

'We wanted to talk to Lena . . . I hope this won't cause

you too much distress, but we have reason to believe that Sonya did not just wander down to the river and drown that day.'

'You have been – *investigating*?' Dufrette looked from Antonia to Payne.

'Well, we've been visiting people – asking questions.'

'And have you reached any conclusions?'

'Yes.' Antonia took a deep breath. 'We have. There is still a lot we don't know, but – we don't think Sonya drowned. She never went anywhere near the river that day. Her nanny was paid to leave her unattended. Your – Sonya's mother too was paid a large sum of money.'

'Go on.' Antonia saw Dufrette's eyes narrow.

'We believe that there was some sort of conspiracy involving more than one person. We believe it might have been the Mortlocks. Well, Sonya was – taken. We have no idea for what reason. If she *was* murdered . . .' Antonia paused but Dufrette's expression didn't change. '. . . we think her body is somewhere other than the river. The day was chosen carefully – the royal wedding would have made sure there were not many people around. Sonya was allowed to leave the house –'

'*Lena*,' Dufrette said harshly. 'That bitch . . . Michael actually *liked* her. I don't think he or Hermione had anything to do with it, though.'

'Well, we believe Lena cooperated fully with whoever it was. We believe she was paid a lot of money. The plan was to make it look as though Sonya had drowned. A false trail was laid – Sonya's daisy chain and bracelet beside the path – her doll in the river . . . Lena gave herself away. She as good as admitted her part in the plot. She never actually said the Mortlocks were behind it, but that was the impression we got.'

'Interesting,' Dufrette said thoughtfully. 'A lot of money, did you say? Well, that would explain Lena's sudden shopping sprees. Of course. *Of course*. The things she bought – all the extravagant, exorbitantly priced useless *objets!* Manolo Blahnik shoes and alligator skin pumps –

the most ridiculous-looking Ascot-y hats – bottles of Louis Roederer Brut Premier – jars of expensive face creams . . . I knew she didn't have that kind of money, so I wondered whether she might have been shoplifting, but then she bought herself the latest BMW. Well, she might have taken a rich lover. Not as unlikely as you might think. Some men's tastes incline towards the – shall we say, the *recherché* if not the downright bizarre?'

'When did her spending sprees start?' Major Payne asked.

'A fortnight after Sonya drowned . . . We were leading separate lives, so I wasn't really interested, but I did ask her where she got the money. She said it had come from Russia. Some rigmarole concerning property that had belonged to her family before the Revolution. Dachas – land – and so on. It had all been nationalized when the Communists took over but now it was all being returned to her family, of which she was the only surviving member . . . I knew that couldn't be right. The Communists still ruled in Russia – it was still the Soviet Union – Brezhnev hadn't died yet. Anyway, I didn't care. Soon after I moved out . . . No, I don't think the Mortlocks had anything to do with it. For one thing, they weren't *rich*. Extremely well-off, yes, but I don't think they had that kind of money –'

'Who's Vivian?' Antonia asked suddenly. 'Lena referred to someone called Vivian. She said that Vivian had been rather mean – that she had loved living at the Dorchester but been "downgraded". She mentioned Vivian to Lady Mortlock too and again she complained of his meanness and ingratitude . . . Could that be the person who took Sonya?'

'Vivian?' Dufrette's expression changed. 'No, not Vivian,' he said slowly, running his tongue across his lips.

'Well, it might have been a woman – Viv*ienne*,' Major Payne pointed out.

'Do you know this person?' Antonia asked Dufrette.

He remained silent. He produced a pair of reading

glasses and put them on his nose. 'The letter. Let's take a look at the letter first.' Dufrette's pale blue eyes, above the half moons, fixed on Major Payne. 'I saw you take a letter from the counter, Payne. It was the moment before Lena's hideous heavings started. Unless my eyes deceived me, it was a sheet of thick writing paper, pale mauve in colour, with gold edges? I believe I've seen that paper before. Two letters written on that same paper arrived for Lena in the days after Sonya drowned . . . D'you mind showing me the letter, Payne?'

18

B.B.

Major Payne remained unperturbed. 'It occurred to me it might be important,' he said with an easy smile. Pushing his hand inside his jacket, he produced the letter. 'I couldn't read it because it is in Russian. *Nazdarovye*. That's the only Russian word I know. I am not familiar with the Cyrillic alphabet.' He unfolded the sheet and laid it down on the table. 'Thick paper, pale mauve with gold edges – you are absolutely correct, Dufrette. I meant to ask someone to translate it – someone who knows Russian.'

Dufrette touched the letter with his long pale forefinger.

'Do you know Russian?' Payne asked.

'No. I meant to learn it when I married Lena, but never got round to it. It wasn't necessary, really. When she was a child Lena had an English nanny, and then of course she was sent to a school in England.'

'Ashcroft,' Antonia said.

'Yes. That was Hermione's school. One of the best in the land, though you wouldn't have believed it if you judged it by Lena.'

Did he know about Lena and Lady Mortlock? Antonia wondered but decided not to say anything. Why cloud the issue? She looked down at the letter. 'No address. 17th March 2001. That's four months ago.'

'You believe it's a letter from someone who also wrote to

Lena twenty years ago?' Major Payne addressed Dufrette. 'Do you know who?'

'No . . . Not at the time.'

'Weren't you ever curious to discover who was writing to your wife? Didn't you ever ask her?'

'I was never curious.'

'There's no name at the bottom – only initials,' Antonia went on. 'B.B.'

Major Payne picked up the letter, sniffed at it, then held it up to the light. He's doing his Sherlock Holmes trick, Antonia thought. 'Ink the colour of burnt sugar . . . A loping scrawl – it suggests a no-nonsense personality . . . Very expensive . . . Water sign. *Maison de la Roche, Paris* . . . So B.B. might be living in France –'

'No, not B.B. In Russian that's V.V. B in Cyrillic is actually V in the Roman alphabet,' Dufrette explained, turning towards Antonia. 'Don't you see? She said V.V. – not Vivian.'

'V.V.? Well, she spoke rather indistinctly. She was slurring a lot. Lady Mortlock too thought it was Vivian. So Lena was referring to the person by their initials.'

'What did she say exactly?' Dufrette asked.

'She complained about V.V.'s meanness. V.V. had given her money but was reluctant to give her any more . . . Do you know who that might be?'

'As a matter of fact,' Dufrette said slowly, 'I do.' He removed his reading glasses. 'The funny thing was that it did occur to me at the time that there might have been an abduction and that our nanny might have been involved. But I was thinking of the wrong kind of abduction. Chrissie was Greek, had a Greek mother, and I knew there was a trade to supply childless couples with children in rural parts of Greece. It's an open secret out there, apparently. I did imagine that Chrissie might have been in touch with child traffickers . . . Blond, blue-eyed children fetch the highest price on the black market. I had read an article about it –'

'She hated Greeks. That's what her mother said,' Payne put in.

'I know. That's why I decided in the end that a Greek conspiracy was unlikely. Besides, it is boys mainly who are in demand. No Greek family would have had any use for a retarded girl . . . Well, an abduction did take place,' Dufrette said, 'but it was what you'd call an "inside job" . . . I should have guessed it was them at once, only I didn't.' He started counting on his fingers. 'They were childless. They adored children. They doted on Sonya. They always gave her presents. They paid us regular visits, but after she "drowned" they vanished from our lives.'

'My God,' Antonia whispered as realization dawned on her.

'They sent me a letter of condolence. It was an exceptionally nice letter. It moved me to tears. It was signed by both of them but I am sure it was she who wrote it . . . It was something to the effect that I shouldn't grieve – that I should have no doubt in my mind that Sonya was in paradise – that she was well and happy . . . In a funny kind of way, she must have been telling the truth. One of their holiday homes was on the Seychelles. It was the kind of place tourist brochures tend to describe as a "paradise island".'

Antonia saw it in her mind's eye. Clear blue-green water that caught the sun and dazzled in a thousand brilliant points like molten silver – unbroken horizons on a vast disc of paler blue sparkling with sunlight – a green belt of palm trees with wooded hills rising beyond them . . . Antonia heard Sonya's delighted laughter – the splashing of water – Veronica Vorodin's voice saying, 'Don't go too far in, darling. Stay close to Mummy.'

Major Payne cleared his throat. 'You are talking about the Vorodins, right? The mega-rich Russian couple that turned out not to be the type that howls for pearls and caviar? They had been staying at Twiston, but left early on the morning of the 29th.' He tapped the letter. 'V.V. That's Veronica Vorodin, isn't it?'

'Yes. Veronica engineered the whole thing. It was her. I am sure of it,' Dufrette said. 'She had brains as well as beauty. Anatole was a decent sort of chap but not particularly bright.'

'Veronica held the belief that a mentally disabled child was a gift from God,' Antonia said. 'She told me that having a child like that would never let her forget her own humanity, that it would prevent her from getting spoilt by her wealth.' Antonia paused. 'She said she'd love a child like Sonya more than she would a normal one . . . Could she have felt guilty on account of being rich? Could she have been looking for hardships – as some form of atonement?'

Dufrette frowned. 'Lena's mother was like that. All the Yusupovs are a bit mad. Evgenia – Lena's mother – was preposterously pious. She could have lived in Biarritz, but she became a nun instead. She chose to end her days at some slummy Franciscan convent. Apparently she did things she didn't even have to do, like shaving her head and picking nettles with her bare hands.' He paused. 'The Vorodins' letter of condolence was written on plain white paper with black borders – nothing like this one. As I said, it was addressed to me . . . *Only to me*. It didn't register at the time. I was moving in an impenetrable fog of grief. I mean, there was no mention of Lena. That's where Veronica slipped up – do you see?'

'Yes. You were the only one who needed comfort. Lena knew that Sonya wasn't dead.'

Payne said, 'Let's see what happened exactly. Veronica and Anatole took their departure early on the morning of the 29th. They said they had a plane to catch. One of them then phoned Twiston pretending to be the hospital where the nanny's mother had been "rushed".'

'It must have been Veronica. She had been an actress, hadn't she?' Antonia looked at Dufrette.

'Yes. Before she married Anatole. She was wonderful with voices. Could do anyone – Bonnie Tyler, Mrs

Thatcher, Barbara Windsor. Had us in stitches. Joyce Grenfell, Penelope Keith.'

Payne continued, 'The Vorodins left, but came back later, when they knew you'd all be sitting in front of the box. They parked their car outside the gates. They found Sonya in the garden. Lena had made sure of that . . . Sonya would have gone to them straight away, wouldn't she?'

'Oh yes. She knew them. She liked them, though of course she'd have gone to anyone.' Dufrette gave a sad smile. 'She was like a friendly puppy. She lacked any defence mechanism.'

'I wonder if Veronica regarded what they were doing as some sort of rescue operation.' At once Antonia wished she hadn't spoken.

'You mean – rescue Sonya from her pernicious parents? You are probably right. I was not a good father.' Dufrette's lower lip trembled. 'If I had been, I'd have taken better care of Sonya.' Suddenly his hands clenched in fists. 'How could Veronica do a thing like that to me? She knew how much I loved Sonya! To – to make me think that Sonya had drowned. That was – cruel.'

The sound of an ambulance siren came from the street outside. Payne asked, 'Would you have agreed if they had asked you to allow Sonya to be adopted by them?'

'No. Of course not. Out of the question. Never . . . Lena sold our daughter,' Dufrette's voice shook. 'She's got a lot to answer for.'

'They *had* to make it look like drowning,' Antonia said. 'They needed to make everybody believe that Sonya had drowned, that she was dead. If the police thought it was merely an abduction, they would have started a search for her. Sooner or later they'd have got to the truth.'

'Would Sonya have needed a passport? She was seven,' Major Payne mused aloud. 'No. She would have been added to one of the passports of her new parents . . . Where *did* they take her?'

'To paradise,' Dufrette said grimly. 'Some faraway place, where no one knew them – where news of Sonya's disappearance couldn't have penetrated . . . *Lena*. Yes. It all starts and ends with Lena. Lena *knows* . . . She will lead me to them . . . I'll find them. Even if I have to travel to the end of the world, I will find them.' Dufrette gripped his cane and rose slowly from his seat. A vein pulsed in his temple. He looks like an elderly hound of impeccable pedigree, Antonia thought.

Reaching out for the letter, he put it into his pocket. 'My little girl. I want my little girl,' he whispered. 'Lena *must* know . . . A little talk, yes . . . No preliminaries, no deviation from the subject. Just a few straightforward questions. There'll be no cajoling and no entreaties. If I don't get the answers I expect –' He broke off. 'Look what I have here.'

He put his hand inside his jacket, paused dramatically, then produced a gun. He gave a smile, his wolfish smile.

It was a small gun, no more than five inches long, but showy, trimmed in silver and mother of pearl. Antonia supposed it had come from an antique duelling set. It seemed in excellent condition. What was it – a Derringer? (She had done research on firearms for a possible novel not such a long time ago.)

Major Payne too was looking at the gun with interest. 'Is it loaded?'

'Of course it is loaded.' Lawrence Dufrette went on smiling. 'What would be the point of carrying an empty gun?'

He put the gun back into his pocket, paid the bill and started walking towards the exit. He had a preoccupied air about him. He seemed to have forgotten all about them.

They followed him at a distance. Antonia wondered whether they should inform the police. There might be trouble. Unprepossessing as Lena was, Antonia felt it was wrong to allow Lawrence Dufrette to shoot her, which she believed he'd do if Lena refused to cooperate.

'Lena couldn't have recovered yet, could she?' Antonia whispered.

'Highly unlikely. Not even if somebody has managed to force ten Prairie Oysters and an industrial dose of Alka-Seltzer down her throat. No. She's probably comatose. *I* would be, if I'd pumped so much brandy into my veins.'

'She might be sleeping it off.'

But it was much worse than that. As they walked across to the Elsnor, they heard the siren again and saw an ambulance leave. It had been parked outside the hotel. Several moments later they made enquiries at the reception desk and were told that Madame Lena had been taken away. Madame Lena had been found unconscious, lying behind the bar in a pool of her own vomit. She wasn't going to recover soon, no. Her condition had actually been described as 'life-threatening'. There was the likelihood that Madame Lena might not last the night.

19

The End of the Affair?

That same evening they sat at Porter's in Covent Garden, having a late supper. Antonia had allowed herself to be persuaded. She had felt too tired to argue or put up any opposition. Besides, she felt she owed it to Hugh. He had been a good sport. He had indulged her. He had encouraged her. Their 'investigation' was at an end. It was all over. She had got him involved in a wild-goose chase, a quest for a murder that never happened, but he didn't seem to mind one little bit. He was a good sport.

'Cheer up, Antonia,' Major Payne said. After she gave a listless smile, he set her another puzzle. 'A man stands beside a darkened window. He is desperately keen to open it, yet he knows that, if he did, it would kill him. Why?'

'Um – the man suffers from a rare disease – a virtual allergy to sunlight? I believe it's called *xeroderma pigmentosum*. I know it's not that, Hugh. You might as well tell me.'

'Well, the simple answer is that the man is claustrophobic. He is in a submarine. If he opens the window, water will rush in and he'll drown.'

'Why is the window darkened?'

'That's been put in to throw you off the scent . . . More wine?' He picked up the bottle. It was an exceptionally good wine.

'Yes please.' She held up her glass. It was going to be her third.

He gave himself a refill too, then said, '*Tabula rasa*, eh? No murder.' He raised his glass. 'Let's drink to it.'

'Let's.'

They drank, then Antonia began, 'Why do I always go for the complicated? I do it every time. That's why perhaps I can't succeed as a crime writer. I always feel I need to go for complexity – for an abundance of red herrings – for intricate clues – for far-fetched motives – for ingenuity-gone-mad. I suppose I do it out of fear that my denouement, when it comes, would turn out to be too trite. I get myself into a state about the timing of the denouement as well. Is it too soon – too late? Oh, it's agony. I hate myself for it. I lack confidence, that's what it is.'

She paused and took another sip of wine. She was becoming garrulous. She was getting mixed up. Why had she started talking about her writing problems? Well, the wine was at last taking effect. *Good*. High time. That was better than feeling depressed and anticlimactic and empty and futile . . . How idiotically self-indulgent of her to be disappointed that there had been no murder, to feel 'flat' about the absence of a dramatic denouement, to mourn over the lack of a final twist in the tale. This is *not* a tale, she reminded herself.

'Your confidence will go up with every novel you put under your belt,' Major Payne was saying. 'I refuse to believe your new novel is going badly.'

'As a matter of fact it's going nowhere.' Antonia took another sip of wine. 'I haven't yet taken it out of the bottom drawer.'

'Well, that's because you've been busy, running about interviewing autocratic Lady Mortlock, exotic Lena, mad bad Lawrence Dufrette –'

'Do they *exist*? Sometimes I wonder . . . You do make them sound like characters in a book.' She frowned. 'Were we really at a place called the Elsnor today?'

'We were. Twice.'

'True. Yes . . . I did imagine all sorts of deranged and awful things. I even thought Sonya might have been the victim of some sacrificial ritual performed by the Babylonian brotherhood! Do they perform sacrificial rituals?'

'As a matter of fact they do. Young children and virgins, if Dufrette is to be believed, are in particular demand.'

Antonia shook her head. 'All along – all along – the rather obvious solution has been staring me in the face. Neat, bloodless, convincing, not particularly original. Adoption. Pure and simple. All right, not pure and not simple, not this one, but nothing like the gothic horrors I imagined. Why didn't I think that Sonya might have been taken, not for some hideous reason, but because she had been loved and wanted and cherished? I had at my disposal all the clues pointing in the right direction . . . Besides, the Vorodins weren't there when it happened!'

'Ah yes. That should have alerted you at once. That's always highly suspicious, isn't it? The perfect alibi. "Alibi", after all, means "elsewhere".'

'*Doing evil that good may come.* That's in the Bible, I think. That's what Veronica must have believed she was doing . . . I rather liked Veronica. I thought she was genuinely caring, sweet and sensitive. Not at all spoilt by wealth. I am convinced she has been a good mother to Sonya. Better than Lena would ever have been. I hope Dufrette never finds them. He is a dangerous man. He called the Vorodins thieves. He said they stole his daughter.'

'Which, at any rate, is not strictly true. The Vorodins didn't steal Sonya. They paid vast sums for her,' Payne pointed out. 'By their own lights, they did the decent thing.'

'Where do you think they are?'

'In South America, somewhere, surrounded by servants and bodyguards and high-tech surveillance systems and the best resident doctors and nurses money can buy. You shouldn't be depressed, really. This is a happy ending of sorts. There was no murder. That's good news. Let's drink to it.'

They drank to it. 'What's the matter now?' Payne asked as Antonia sighed.

'I've been leading you on a wild-goose chase –'

'What absolute rot.'

'Kind of you to say so, but I *have* wasted your time.' Antonia vaguely wondered whether she wasn't spouting all these negative statements so that he could contradict them and reassure her. If she had to be honest with herself, she rather enjoyed being reassured by him.

'Nothing of the sort. I enjoyed every minute of it.' Major Payne reached out and took her hand. She let him hold it. What the hell, she thought.

He went on, 'The – what shall we call it? The hunt for Sonya Dufrette hasn't been a failure. *Au contraire*. All right, we haven't been able to discover Sonya's whereabouts, but we *did* find out what happened. You had a hunch that there was something wrong and you were proved correct. A crime *was* committed, no matter how noble the motive for it. We did uncover greed, skulduggery, intricate scheming and deception. That's an achievement. Truth has prevailed. That's a cause for celebration and that's what we are having now.' He raised his glass again. 'To Truth.' He looked at her. 'And to Beauty too.'

'You are being silly now. *Very* silly. I am not really happy about it. In fact I wish we'd let sleeping dogs lie.'

He shook his head with exaggerated disapproval. 'I am surprised at you, Antonia. Judging by your book, I was convinced that you were an uncompromising moralist.'

'What I mean is, I am extremely uneasy about Dufrette – about what he might do next. He won't give up until he has tracked down the Vorodins. And he won't wait until Lena recovers – if she ever does – to get Veronica's address. He will find another source of information soon enough. He said it himself. He looked absolutely determined.'

'Yes.' Payne ran a thoughtful forefinger along his jaw. 'Absolutely, uncompromisingly, insanely determined. He looked like a man possessed by the spirit of a wolf hanged for manslaughter. Does that strike you as completely nonsensical? Why do these things sound so much better in one's head? Am I right in thinking that it rather captures the essence of Lawrence?'

'The hour of the wolf,' Antonia said. 'I hope it never comes . . . That's when people die, isn't it?'

'Yes. According to Scandinavian mythology.'

'He has a gun. He is prepared to use it,' Antonia went on. 'He not only wants his daughter back – *he wants revenge*. You did hear him say, "Paytime." Lena, the nanny, Veronica – are they safe from him? I know this sounds wildly melodramatic, but then Dufrette is a melodramatic kind of person.'

'True . . . He does seem to relish the role of the lone vigilante . . . He didn't like it one bit when you suggested that the police should be told. Crikey – he actually *snarled* at you!'

They had been standing inside the Elsnor lobby. Lawrence Dufrette had said he'd be *very* cross if they told the police. He had patted his pocket suggestively. He had expressed the hope that their paths wouldn't cross again. He had said their meddling days were over, that they should make themselves scarce, that from that moment on *he* was in charge, that his hour had come. He had spoken in a low menacing voice. He had directed at Antonia a look full of antagonism and scorn and, yes, he had snarled at her. She had been shocked. She had thought they had been getting on really well. Of all the Dr Jekyll and Mr Hyde transformations!

'Not a word of thanks either,' Major Payne murmured. 'To think that, but for us, he would never have known his daughter was alive.'

'*And* he took that letter. We shouldn't have let him. He will get someone to translate it for him . . . I wonder what was in it.'

'It may be something totally irrelevant. Veronica saying, I took Sonya to Versailles yesterday. She enjoyed herself an awful lot. We wished you were here with us.'

'I can't imagine anyone wishing Lena were with them anywhere . . . Could they be in France?'

'I don't know. V.V. did use French writing paper, but that means nothing . . . Shall we order pudding and coffee? What would you like?'

'A *pêche Melba* with chocolate sauce,' Antonia said recklessly. 'How about informing the police?'

'I don't think it will make much difference.' Payne took out his pipe. He went on, 'You see, don't you, that we can't prove a thing? Dufrette will no doubt deny the existence of any letter point blank and express concern over the state of our respective minds. Miss Haywood *may* break down and confess fully, but there's no guarantee. And I think it highly unlikely that Lena will ever admit to selling her daughter to the Vorodins.'

'What if Lena did tell the truth about Dufrette and Sonya? What if some kind of sexual abuse did take place?'

'Again, nothing that has the remotest chance of standing up in court. It was twenty years ago. A mentally deficient child too. Would Sonya – assuming she were ever tracked down – be able to testify? I rather doubt it.' Payne lit his pipe.

There was another pause.

'We could always report Dufrette for possessing a gun,' Antonia said.

'They are sure to discover that he has a licence for it.'

Antonia sighed.

20

Interlude

The next day Major Payne was called away to his farm in Suffolk, rather urgently, as a sudden crisis had arisen. His manager had been involved in a car crash, not a fatal one, but he was to spend at least a month in hospital, consequently Payne needed to take over the reins. He asked Antonia to go with him and, although she was tempted, she said it would be impossible. She couldn't afford to take any more days off so soon after coming back from her holiday. They agreed to keep in touch either by e-mail or by phone.

'Do let me know if something crops up,' he said.

'Like what?'

'I don't know. Something might. I have a funny feeling . . . Somehow I don't think this is the end of the affair,' he said. 'For one thing we haven't found Sonya Dufrette.'

She let him kiss her goodbye.

As it happened, she was very busy herself. It was the day for her monthly report to the club committee and she discovered she hadn't done it. What with the flurry of recent activities, it had completely slipped her mind. She had only remembered the report as she woke up in the morning, and had jumped out of bed in a panic. She did manage to complete it in less than an hour, though it was far from satisfactory – or so she feared. Her only hope was that it wouldn't be scrutinized too closely. That's what she told Hugh, who phoned her at half-past eleven that same morning to see how she was getting on. He was insouciant about it. 'Bluff your way through. They aren't a particularly efficient bunch, from what I have heard.' He meant the club committee. She agreed – they weren't. 'What's that music?' he asked. 'Are you having a knees-up in the library?'

'It's the gardener's radio. History of flamenco.'

At three o'clock in the afternoon she went up the wide sweep of the staircase. She walked along the corridor, beautifully carpeted and decorated with taste but besmirched by a superfluity of signs and directions. The club was a notorious maze and, without the signs, newcomers would get lost and wander around until rescued by club members or staff. Antonia knew the place like the back of her hand, so the signs only annoyed her.

The committee meetings were invariably held in a huge gilded room with long curtained windows that looked over an enclosed formal garden. The walls were decorated with portraits of Nelson, Wellington and George V in his Sailor King uniform. Above the fireplace there was an obscure painting of the Battle of Balaclava.

Antonia was the first to arrive. It always happened that way. The committee weren't famous for their punctuality. For a couple of moments she amused herself idly, standing beside the portrait of George V, bringing her face very close to it and seeing the intricately, even finickily, rendered blue uniform and perfectly trimmed beard disintegrate into a fuzzy, meaningless blur of brushstrokes. She then headed for the rickety, baize-covered card table, around which were ranged some ill-assorted chairs of good quality. She sat on one of the two Sheratons and, inconsequentially, remembered that last time she had sat on the Louis Quinze.

She opened her folder in front of her. Random thoughts kept revolving inside her head. The true nature and personality of Lawrence Dufrette. (How dangerous was he?) The need for a pair of shoes to go with the dark blue suit she was wearing. (Would Hugh like them?) The possible whereabouts of Veronica and Sonya. (What new names might Sonya have been given?) Hugh's whereabouts at that very moment. (Could he be attending some tea-party organized by one of his numerous well-wishers with the sole purpose of introducing him to some highly eligible local widow? She sincerely hoped not.)

Where had Curzon, the giraffe with the bitten ear, disappeared? The answer to this one suggested itself almost at once: Sonya had missed it and Veronica had contacted Lena and asked her to send it to them, which Lena had done . . . So Lena *did* have a forwarding address . . .

Where was it she had heard 'Lavender's Blue' played? And why did she think it was extremely important that she should remember . . . Had it been on the radio? She felt sure she had been sitting in the library . . . Had Mrs Cathcart hummed it, perhaps? Unlikely. Colonel Haslett? No, she didn't think so. Colonel Haslett often hummed but it was usually some Gilbert and Sullivan tune – or 'Colonel Bogey'.

Antonia shut her eyes. *Watch out for that ring,* Miss Pettigrew had said.

Suddenly she sat up. She had heard the familiar cackling and shuffling noises outside the door, heralding the imminent arrival of the club committee. They didn't come in at once, though, but started a discussion outside, over whether the sign on the door should be changed from *Vacant* to *Meeting in Progress,* or whether doing so would put off any legitimate latecomers. Eventually it was decided to change the sign, and three people entered the room.

Mrs Compton, Mr Reece and Commander Bridges.

They appeared greatly surprised to see Antonia and even more surprised when they heard that she had been waiting since three o'clock. 'Oh dear. We *did* say half-past, didn't we, Douglas?' Mrs Compton said. She was a tall willowy woman of indeterminate years, dressed elegantly in a light green suit with darker green facings, whose immaculate coiffure the unlikely colour of 'Dutch gold' added to her height and sophistication.

Commander Bridges, thus appealed to, went very pink. He attempted to solve the dilemma between his conscience and manners by saying that it had been half-past three *to start with* – and that went back *at least five years* – they must be living in the past! He made it sound like some sort of a joke. He tugged at his intricately tied cravat and beamed and nodded at Antonia. He was clad in a dark blazer and grey trousers. He was seventy-six but looked younger, though sitting down and getting up were a problem. Antonia saw him glance down nervously at the Louis Quinze. He hated being helped either way. Given the option, he would have remained standing.

Mr Reece asked Commander Bridges if he knew the latest cricket score.

'This room needs changing,' Mrs Compton observed, looking around with a critical expression, holding her chin between her thumb and forefinger. 'Don't you think? I don't know what it is. Something – I don't know. Don't you think?'

'We did it only recently, Arabella,' Mr Reece said cheerfully. He was a large, stout man in his early sixties, with a pleasant red face, wearing tweeds. He looked like a gentleman farmer but was in fact a magistrate. 'Can't afford to do it again. The budget –'

'Ah, the budget.' Mrs Compton sounded scornful.

'Afraid so. It's tighter than ever,' Commander Bridges said. 'Heaven knows how we manage.'

'Refreshments coming up,' Mr Reece announced. He rubbed his hands. 'Jolly good.'

A waiter had wheeled in a trolley. Commander Bridges started easing himself into the chair. They all looked away delicately. 'Two messages,' the waiter said. 'One from Mr Beeson, the other from Lady Franks. Apologies, et cetera. They aren't coming, so start without them.'

Mrs Compton waited until he had left the room and said triumphantly, 'This is the *third* time. I detest counting, but it is the *third* time. I do think, Douglas, you should say something. It's not as though we have all the time in the world!'

Commander Bridges harrumphed. 'Yes, yes, of course, Arabella.'

'Muffins. Crumpets.' Mr Reece had started lifting lids. 'Can I tempt you, anyone? Arabella? Antonia?'

Antonia said she would like a cup of tea and a muffin.

'It is too hot for muffins,' Mrs Compton said.

'Sausage rolls. May I tempt you? Douglas? Ladies? The sandwiches look good.'

Mrs Compton said, 'No, nothing to eat. Just some tea.' She sighed. She opened her handbag in a portentous manner which suggested that some life-saving piece of equipment might be inside, but which merely resulted in her producing her reading glasses.

'A muffin, Robert, thank you . . . A cup of tea too, yes. Thank you.'

'It's too hot for muffins,' Mrs Compton said again.

Antonia took a covert glance at her watch.

'Let's start, shall we?' Commander Bridges said, smiling amiably over his cup. 'The librarian's report . . . Antonia, would you like to –'

'The last report was rather inconclusive, I thought,' Mrs Compton interjected. 'Don't you think?'

'It was the *meeting* that was inconclusive,' Mr Reece said.

'I don't understand what you mean, Robert.'

Antonia waited politely. The room was getting warmer by the minute. She could see the sun and the blue sky outside. Also the tree – an elm, not an oak. (She wished she didn't keep seeing the oak at Twiston.) Shouldn't they open one of the windows? Her eyes shut and opened. It wouldn't do for her to doze off! For some reason she found herself thinking of the Vorodins and their plan. That carefully premeditated abduction. All very ingenious, but – plans sometimes went wrong, didn't they? That was an interesting line of thought. What if the Vorodins had arrived and found that Sonya wasn't there? Just imagine that that was what did happen. Now, where *could* Sonya have gone? Well, she had liked hiding –

'Let's start, shall we? Antonia, are you ready?' Commander Bridges said.

'Yes. Sorry.'

Antonia raced through her report. Every now and then she glanced up. Commander Bridges kept beaming at her. Mrs Compton was looking round the room and shaking her head. Mr Reece was eating a sausage roll with a great deal of concentration.

When she finished, Commander Bridges said, 'Well done, Antonia. That was jolly thorough.'

'I have a request,' she said. 'I do need more bookshelves and journal racks.'

'How much money do you want?' Mr Reece asked with a smile, brushing crumbs off his waistcoat with his napkin. 'I think we could rustle up seventy or eighty pounds, can't we, Douglas?'

'Yes, yes. I think we can. Shelves *are* important.'

Mrs Compton heaved another sigh but raised no objection. Antonia felt herself relax.

The letting of the library to non-club members, to *outsiders*, for social functions, such as book readings and small wedding receptions, was discussed next. It was always a controversial point. The general feeling was *against* outsiders. Members, most of them diehard traditionalists, resented intrusions from the outside world intensely. But the fees the club charged were not to be sneezed at, Mr Reece pointed out – they provided them with a goodish income.

As for book donations . . .

'I am totally against book donations. Totally. They are so . . .' Mrs Compton – the widow of a Whitehall official – searched for a word. 'A bit like a *jumble* sale, don't you think? A lot of the books people donate are in an appalling state. No better than second-hand junk, really.'

'No, not all the books –' Antonia began.

'I've seen them! Then there is the *kind* of books some

people leave. Don't you remember when the Gloucesters came – that VE Day? When the Duke picked up a book and it turned out to be –' Mrs Compton broke off. 'Don't you *remember*?'

'Arabella, that was ages ago,' Mr Reece said.

'It was I who had to write a letter of apology afterwards.'

The incident in question had taken place before Antonia's time –

Suddenly she was reminded of that other letter. The letter written in Russian and signed V.V. What had Veronica written about, on her characteristic mauve paper with gilded edges? Would they ever know? Dufrette was unlikely to call them up and tell them what was in it. Dufrette didn't want to have anything to do with them. They shouldn't have let him take the letter, just like that. Could they have stopped him though? Would he have used the gun if they had tried?

But perhaps Hugh was right. Perhaps the letter didn't contain anything of importance.

There, however, Antonia was wrong. The letter did contain important information.

It explained the motive for the murder.

21

A Demon in My View

It was the following Wednesday. Temperatures had been soaring since nine o'clock in the morning, and by midday sweltering heat was coming through the open windows of the library. Air-conditioning would have made life bearable, Antonia reflected, but that had never been an option. The rather tight budget would never have allowed it. Besides, how many such days were there in an average English summer?

She drifted drowsily about the library, fanning herself with an ancient gold-edged dinner-party menu she had found inside a dog-eared copy of Thesiger's *Marsh Arabs*, assembling a pile of stray magazines. Her feet felt heavy as lead. The usual racing papers. *Country Life, National Geographic, Spectator.* The *Salisbury Review,* inside which she had found the latest issue of *Playboy.* Antonia smiled. Well, she had found worse . . .

She remembered the luncheon menu they had had the day Sonya disappeared. Orange cocktails, iced, from a jug. Gulls' eggs (two each). Fried salmon with rich sauce. Poussin with red wine. Charlotte russe. Coffee. Lady Mortlock had seen no reason why luncheon shouldn't have been served. Only Lawrence Dufrette had refused to eat. Lena had got drunk. Major Nagle had had a tray sent up to his room . . .

The gardener's radio was on once more. It was so loud,

it might have been in the room, and she had no other choice but listen to it as she went about her job. She didn't mind. She didn't have the energy to mind anything in this heat.

Two o'clock. The news. She squinted down at her watch. *The hottest day on record.* Just hearing the weather report made her sweat more. Was it as hot as in the marshes of Arabia?

Thesiger had been to the club once. She had seen him: very tall and unbent despite his great age, with a hawk-like nose, wearing his OE tie, a tweed jacket and twill trousers. Afterwards a club member had come up to her. It transpired he had been to prep school with Thesiger. 'He was an odd fellow. We were nine or ten and awfully keen on *Prester John*. We were all identifying with David Crawford, the hero, you know. Only Thesiger identified with Laputa, the Zulu chief. An odd fellow. Wasn't a bit surprised when I heard he had made his home at Maralai and become known to the locals as "Mzee Julu".'

She didn't fancy the idea of life at Maralai at all. Too hot. How I'd like to go north, to the Faroe islands, mist-laden Atlantic wonders, Antonia murmured dreamily. It stays cool up there. What had put the Faroe islands in her head? The *National Geographic* – the picture on the cover. There was an explanation for most things.

Various tasks kept presenting themselves. The cataloguing of the biographies section. An assessment as to what needed purchasing from Hatchards. She needed to phone the book binders as well. However, none of these tasks seemed very important or worthwhile in this weather. She decided to reduce her movements to a minimum and execute only very light chores, of the kind that didn't involve any degree of physical exertion. That morning she had put on a short-sleeved cotton dress, though it didn't seem to help much. It was a certain cool shade of blue, that was why she had chosen it – no, it was *not* lavender blue.

She considered again the matter of the obituary – what

Hugh had told her on the phone earlier on. Anatole Vorodin, it transpired, had died back in 1988. Hugh had found his obituary.

No children.

It was suggestive, certainly. It had given them food for thought. Hugh had said that it might only mean that the *Times* obituary writer hadn't done his research properly – or it might mean that the widow had suppressed certain facts . . . Yes, that was more likely. Cunning vixen, V.V.!

How hot it was. Antonia wished she could concentrate better.

With the exception of *Playboy*, which she intended to dispose of discreetly later on, she laid the magazines out on the mahogany table in the middle of the room, taking great care to line them up neatly.

She watered the wilting aspidistras and rubber plants, then stood beside the window, looking out. Everything was very still. Not a whiff of wind. No birdsong. No buzzing of insects. The sky was a fierce, burning white, the trees ferocious shades of rusty red and sulphur yellow. A mist of sorts hung on the air – a greyish gauze through which there shone the merciless golden globe of the sun. It hurt her eyes to look at it. At the far end of the garden, the student gardener was deadheading the roses. He was in his shirtsleeves, wearing a straw hat and dark glasses and appeared quite unperturbed. He looked up and waved at her. She waved back. Everything seemed to be happening in slow motion. The gardener's transistor radio was on a trestle table underneath the window, which explained why she could hear the transmission so loud and clear.

'No children,' she said aloud. 'They had no children. His wife survives him but they had no children.'

Hugh's phone call had come an hour or so before. He had been on the internet, apparently, looking up entries under 'Vorodin', 'Vorodins', 'Veronica Vorodin' and 'Anatole Vorodin'. There were several entries, he said, but each time he clicked on them, he got a notice saying, 'This file no longer exists,' or 'The page cannot be found.' Or 'The page you are looking for might have been removed, had its name changed or be temporarily unavailable.'

The only exception had been an obituary from *The Times*, announcing the death on 2nd March 1988 in a paragliding accident in the Bahamas of Anatole Vorodin, Veronica's husband.

Born 1943, in Geneva. Of Russian-French extraction. The son of Vladislav Vorodin and Marie-Josephe de Roustang. (Of the de Roustang dentistry equipment dynasty.) Educated privately, at the Sorbonne and Yale. In 1961 produced a single entitled 'Rich Rovers in Rio', now largely forgotten. Played the piano at the Algonquin in New York, and at some Paris jazz clubs, but his musical career never took off. Got a bit part in *Those Magnificent Men in Their Flying Machines*, but never made it as an actor either. Renowned for his and his wife's philanthropic work and children's charities. Hobbies included paragliding, yachting and collecting first editions of *Flash Gordon* comics. It was the obit's last line, Hugh said, that was of possible interest.

He is survived by his wife Veronica. They had no children.

The erasure of Sonya. That was how Hugh had put it. What did Antonia make of it? Well, Veronica could easily have managed to provide imprecise information. She had done it out of caution. She had been afraid she might be discovered, so she had made a decision. Sonya – even if her name had been changed to something else – would receive no mention as their daughter. Had Veronica made sure that every file that mentioned the Vorodin name was removed from the net? Antonia believed it could be done. Still, she felt somewhat disconcerted by the news.

She sat down at her desk. Her swivel chair felt extremely comfortable. Should she ring Martin and ask him to bring her a cup of coffee or a glass of icy lemonade? No. Too much effort. Her hand felt numb. The Radio 4 news bulletin was over and some lively debate about oleanders was now taking place. Oleanders? Had she heard correctly? 'Can you advise me how to make them flower? I've tried everything – even crushed snails, which, we were told, make a wonderful fertilizer.'

How did these people find the energy to muster up so much enthusiasm about crushed snails? 'Oleanders,' the voice went on, 'are like children. They need very special care. Keep them indoors longer in spring . . .'

Like children . . . The silly things people said. Children were much more special, much more precious than oleanders. Even children like Sonya, whom Lady Mortlock had described as 'damaged goods' . . . Sonya should have been kept indoors. Nothing would have happened if she had been kept indoors. Antonia flexed her hand gently, trying to get rid of the pins and needles. Her eyes opened and closed again.

No children . . . Was the selling and subsequent abduction of Sonya Dufrette the only theory that fitted the facts? Well, yes – it was. What other reason could there have been for such large sums of money to be handed out to Lena Dufrette and the nanny? There were also the initials at the bottom of that letter. V.V. Lawrence Dufrette was sure that Veronica had masterminded the taking of Sonya.

No – there was no doubt that Sonya was spirited away from Twiston and adopted by the Vorodins. She was given a new name and a new identity. She was passed off as the Vorodins' daughter and they went to live at some place where no one knew them – the Bahamas, maybe, where Anatole Vorodin was eventually to die in a paragliding accident.

Still, let's assume, Antonia reasoned in her dreamlike state, that 'no children' meant precisely that. That the ultimate happy ending wasn't a happy ending after all. It was possible, wasn't it, that, at some point between the royal wedding on 29th July 1981 and Anatole Vorodin's death on 2nd March 1988, Sonya Dufrette herself died – either as a result of an accident or through illness. But wouldn't the obituary then have said, 'His daughter predeceased him'? Well, not necessarily – not if Veronica

Vorodin had withheld the information that there was a daughter in the first place.

Antonia heard the door open and somebody enter the library. A heavy, lumbering tread. Opening her eyes a fraction she saw the stocky figure of a man in a checked hacking jacket. She watched him take *The Times* and the racing paper from the mahogany table and ease himself into an armchair. Mid-sixties? Sandy hair sleeked back, jowly square face with bulldog features, brick-coloured, a reddish nose, a drinker's nose, she imagined; a small moustache, extremely pouchy eyes of the 'fried-egg' variety. He kept mopping his brow with a large handkerchief. What big hands he had! Enormous pink hands, like hams –

Did he have a ring on? No – she couldn't see a ring. Why was she interested in his ring? Well, it wasn't her who was interested in it but Miss Pettigrew. Miss Pettigrew had an *idée fixe* about a ring. Antonia smiled. *Watch out for the ring*. How ridiculous. If she didn't feel so lethargic, she would laugh aloud. She was allowing bizarre intrusions of irrationality to enter the detection business!

Was she dreaming? No. The man was real. He was there all right. She heard the paper rustle in his hands. She could hear his noisy breathing. She went on observing him from under half-closed eyelids. Striped tie – school or regiment, she couldn't tell. It had been loosened. Small wonder! How did he survive in that jacket? She didn't think she had seen him before. He was an instantly recognizable military type. Not a very nice person, she didn't think. She might be doing him a grave injustice, mind. Appearances could be deceptive . . . His bottom lip protruded like the jaw of some belligerent freshwater fish. He was scowling. Not an attractive face – not by a long chalk. A somewhat haunted look about him – or was she being fanciful again? She saw him drop *The Times* and pick up the racing paper.

He wasn't aware of her presence. Well, she hadn't stirred. She had pushed her chair back and was sitting in the shadow of the arch formed by the staircase where she imagined it felt cooler . . .

The discussion on the radio was still going on, how funny. They had been talking all this time, these indefatigable gardeners. 'I live in Cornwall and this is a piece of my lawn with a brown-headed weed in it. If you'd care to take a look – I have tried a number of weedkillers . . .'

Fancy bringing a weed into the studio! *Gardeners' Question Time*. That was the name of the programme. Of course. She never listened to it, if she could help it, didn't see the point of it, really. She wasn't interested in gardening. Antonia felt her eyelids drooping. It was as though she had been staring at a ticking hypnotist's watch that had been going back and forth. *Click-clack, click-clack* . . . She could hear the watch very clearly now.

Click-clack.

No. That was the sound of the gardener's secateurs coming from the garden. He must be standing somewhere close to the window. Only the other day she had considered that listening to the radio was rather out of place in the club environment, but at that particular moment nothing could be more appropriate. Had the gardener drawn closer, so that he could get some gardening tips? Yes. Tips from the gardening experts. How to kill children – no, *weeds*. She meant weeds of course . . .

Antonia couldn't tell how much time had elapsed. Two minutes – five? She woke up with a start, her heart beating fast, a metallic taste in her mouth. She had dreamt that she was at Twiston once more, walking about the garden in the afternoon glare, shading her eyes with her hand, looking for Sonya, calling out her name, steeling herself for what she might find . . .

Somebody was talking about Twiston at that very moment.

Her eyes opened wide. The man was still there in the chair, but it wasn't him. Of course not. It was a voice on the radio. A woman's voice. Very musical. Familiar somehow . . .

'. . . outside Richmond-on-Thames. We bought it last

year. A splendid place. The kind of place exiles think of when they dream of home, as somebody put it. Lovely gardens – with one exception. There is a tree there. An oak which is extremely ancient – over three hundred years old. It has illustrious origins – planted by James I and all that. It has a plaque on it that says so. It is dead of course. It is ugly. It looks like some malignant growth. It was highly thought of by the previous owners – they provided it with a cement base, if you please. It is entirely hollow inside, you see.'

That was Mrs Ralston-Scott talking. The name came to Antonia at once. She was fully awake now and listening intently. She sat up and was surprised how quickly she had emerged from her stupor. She had spoken to Mrs Ralston-Scott on the phone only the week before, when she rang up to ask for Lady Mortlock's telephone number.

'The hollow seems to hold incredible attraction for all sorts of beasts and they tend to leap inside the tree. Squirrels and stray cats and once I thought I saw a rat as big as a kitten! My own dogs – I have two spaniels – seem to have developed that unfortunate habit too. I have got to detest that damned tree as much as – well, as much as one can detest a tree.' (The audience laughed.) 'There is a *smell* coming from inside the hollow, which makes walking in the garden on a balmy summer's evening not such a pleasant experience after all. The long and the short of it – I don't know whether you dear people are the right ones to consult about it – you'd probably be opposed to the idea, but I want and *mean* to get rid of the tree. I intend to have it sawn down . . .'

Antonia's eye caught a movement. The paper had slipped from the man's hands. His face was turned towards the open window, from where the voice on the radio was coming. He sat completely still, as though suddenly turned to stone. He appeared to be listening intently to Mrs Ralston-Scott's voice. He seemed mesmerized by what he was hearing – or could it be that he was feeling ill? His face looked very odd indeed. It had turned puce. His mouth was open. Antonia wondered whether the heat had got to him at last, whether he might have suffered sunstroke, or was on the verge of some form of cardiac arrest. His eyes were bulging monstrously, bringing to mind the frog Footman in *Alice,* imparting to his face the aspect of someone who's had a shock. Someone in mortal fear or in the thrall of some unimaginable horror. Though, again, Antonia reflected, it might be her imagination playing tricks on her. *Do not rely on fanciful conclusions before you have first validated them with facts.* She had read that somewhere. Yes, quite.

The man seemed to find it hard to breathe. Something was the matter with him.

'So that's my dilemma,' Mrs Ralston-Scott concluded. 'To cut or not to cut. Unless you can suggest . . .'

Antonia didn't hear the rest. The man had given a groan and lurched forward. She saw him rise from his chair. He pushed his hand into his pocket and took out his car keys. His mouth was shut now and he seemed to have managed to get a grip on himself. He started walking towards the door but halted in front of Antonia's desk, quite close by – she could have reached out and touched him. She smelled his aftershave – old-fashioned lavender water. Again, he didn't see her. He shot out his cuffs. As he mopped his forehead with his handkerchief and straightened his tie, Antonia recognized him. Or thought she did. It was the odd juxtaposition of enormous ham-like fists and beautifully tended fingernails that did it. As she told Hugh later, she was forever on the lookout for quirky details.

The last time she had seen him was twenty years ago, on 29th July, to be precise. Then he had been in a state of some considerable agitation caused by the loss of his signet ring.

The man was Major Nagle.

22

The Hollow

It took her several moments to recover from the nightmarish jolt. She waited until he had lumbered out of the door, then, acting on an impulse, got up, walked round her desk and followed him. The heaviness had left her and she suddenly found herself overtaken by a strange, dreamlike lightness. Her head too had cleared.

That Major Nagle should have appeared precisely when he did and given her the chance to observe him was an extraordinary coincidence, she reflected, but then coincidences did happen. The pieces of the puzzle rearranged themselves in her mind. She remembered things which she should have thought of earlier on, but hadn't, though her subconscious had not been inactive. She had after all heard Miss Pettigrew's voice rather early on, urging her to watch out for the ring.

Dufrette's row with Major Nagle and the latter's subsequent humiliation on the fatal morning. The suggestion Dufrette had made that Nagle was something of a sadist and that he had driven his wife to madness and suicide. Nagle's distress and anger. Nagle had wanted to leave at once but Sir Michael had managed to persuade him to stay on. Nagle had then spent the whole morning in his room. He had been the only member of the house party whose movements hadn't been accounted for. Nagle's great agitation over the loss of his signet ring –

In a flash Antonia saw what must have happened. The abduction plan had been concocted all right. The Vorodins paid Lena and the nanny. The date was fixed – 29th July, the day of the royal wedding, when they could be fairly sure there would be no witnesses. All of that *did* happen. The Vorodins left early in the morning. The phone call removing the nanny from the scene was put through. Lena then made sure that Sonya would be in the garden.

Only something took place before the Vorodins came back.

The plan went wrong.

What they hadn't counted on was that Major Nagle would walk out of the house and go into the garden, still simmering with fury, harbouring murderous grudges about Dufrette. Antonia remembered Dufrette's words. *If looks could kill.* Did Nagle mean to kill Sonya? Antonia remembered him staring down at them from his window. She had felt disturbed by that stock-still figure whose face she couldn't see. Well, maybe he did mean to kill. Or maybe not.

Perhaps Nagle went out, needing a walk to calm his jangled nerves, to clear his head and collect his thoughts. As he strode about the garden, he came upon Dufrette's daughter. At this – seeing what he must have regarded as an extension of his foe – all the pent-up resentment burst out of him and he hit her . . .

Or it might have been an accident. Sonya might have stood in the middle of the path and got in his way – proffering him the flowers she had picked as likely as not. Maybe he pushed her roughly aside with his ham-like hand. Thoughts of Dufrette might have made him exercise undue force. Sonya, frail and doll-like, fell back and hit her head against a stone – on one of the decorative rocks? Nagle walked on but after a few steps looked back over his shoulder. Seeing the girl lying immobile, he wheeled round and retraced his steps. He touched her arm or cheek – shook her. She didn't stir. He saw blood oozing out of a wound in her temple or the back of her head. Realizing she was dead, Nagle panicked. He had killed her! Had he been seen? No, no one. What should he do with the body? He couldn't leave it there! His eyes then fell on the tree, the ancient oak with the gaping hollow, on which men in overalls had been working earlier on. He saw the cement mixer beside the tree.

Everybody in the house knew the tree was being provided with a cement base. Nagle had a brainwave. Picking up the tiny body, he carried it to the oak and lowered it inside the hollow, into the still unset cement. Then he got busy, pouring more cement over the body. He succeeded in immuring Sonya inside the hollow – but lost his ring in the process. Nagle's signet ring fell off his finger and remained under the layers of cement, with the body. Nagle realized that only when it was too late. By then the place was swarming with police. Hence his agitation, which Antonia well remembered. And there he was now, twenty years on, hearing the voice of Mrs Ralston-Scott, Twiston's current chatelaine, talking of her intention to have the oak sawn down. The realization that the cutting of the tree would inevitably result in the discovery not only of Sonya's body, but of his signet ring as well, must have hit him hard – which explained his shocked expression.

Walking out of the club, Antonia stood on the steps in the shimmering heat, looking round, trying to locate Major Nagle. The next moment she saw him further down the street, entering his car, a battered Ford. She saw him start the engine. In some desperation she cast round looking for means of transport. There was only one thought in her mind – follow him, don't let him out of your sight.

As luck would have it, a taxi drew up and an elderly gentleman accompanied by a younger one got out. Antonia signalled to the driver and ran up to the taxi. She got into the passenger seat and said in a breathless voice, 'Follow that car. Quick!' Sweat was pouring down her face. Not even in her wildest imagination had she seen herself in a situation like that. The driver stared at her. 'He is my husband – would you please hurry up?' She didn't quite know why she said it was her husband – maybe because it was preferable to saying, 'He is a murderer.'

'Where are we going?' the driver asked.

'Richmond, I think,' Antonia said. Her voice sounded harsh. 'Richmond-on-Thames.'

'You *think*?'

'Richmond, yes. I am pretty sure he's going to Richmond. Place called Twiston. It's a big house outside Richmond. I'll tell you how to get there.'

'I don't want any trouble,' the driver said, starting the engine. He clearly regarded her as a jealous, possibly vengeful, wife in pursuit of her flighty husband. His eyes raked her up and down as though to make absolutely certain she didn't have a gun or any other weapon on her person.

Antonia remained silent. Trouble. Would there be trouble? What was Major Nagle planning to do exactly? Well, drive his car to Twiston – sneak into the garden and make an attempt to get his ring back . . . But that would be impossible, surely? He would have to cut the tree first – the ancient oak. Then there was the twenty-year-old cement base – he would have to smash his way through the cement first. He wouldn't be able to do it. The idea was absurd.

On the other hand, why not? He was a powerfully built man. He might have a tool box in the boot of his car. A hammer. He would need a big hammer, or something equally heavy. Could he do it with a spanner? He would need an axe first and foremost! What about the noise? He couldn't start hacking at the oak or hammering away without being heard. There were dogs at the house – Mrs Ralston-Scott's spaniels. Could he pretend to be a tree surgeon? Could he get away with it? Well, Mrs Ralston-Scott couldn't have left London yet – she was probably still in the radio studio. That was probably his chance – tell whoever was at the house, the secretary Laura or any servants, that he had been hired to saw down the tree. But he didn't *look* like a tree surgeon!

It was evident to her that Major Nagle was acting on a wild impulse. Well, he was a desperate man. He hadn't been able to give the matter any coherent thought. He had looked apoplectic. He knew he was facing exposure – trial – social ruin – years in prison . . . Perhaps he would park his car outside the gates and sit inside and wait until dark? Would that help though? The noise would be much more conspicuous at night.

Antonia glanced at her watch. Three o'clock. They were stopping at traffic lights. In her mind she went back to the fatal day. So what happened after Nagle immured Sonya inside the tree? Well, he went up to the house and returned to his room. He hadn't been seen. Soon after, the Vorodins arrived, as arranged. Maybe he watched them from his window, which overlooked that part of the garden. The Vorodins didn't see Sonya but assumed she would appear at any moment. They found her doll, daisy chain and bracelet and laid the false trail to the river, suggesting she had drowned. Unwittingly they had helped Nagle! They had drawn attention away from the tree and focused it on the river. Antonia imagined Nagle nodding approvingly from behind the window curtain. Then the Vorodins waited a bit longer, but still Sonya did not appear. Eventually they went away, afraid that they might be seen. They were, after all, supposed to be on a plane bound for the USA. They must have suspected there was something wrong. Then of course they saw the news on the TV or read about Sonya's disappearance and presumed drowning in the papers. What did they feel? Shock – regret – great sadness – guilt – remorse? That they were good and decent people Antonia had no doubt. They must have let Lena and the nanny keep the money . . .

So *They had no children* in Anatole Vorodin's obituary meant precisely that. The Vorodins had never had any children, natural or adopted.

What about Veronica's letter to Lena then? Well, it might have nothing to do with Sonya. They might have simply kept in touch, the way cousins did –

'I lost him,' she heard the driver say. 'Your husband. I don't know where he went.'

'Never mind, drive to Richmond,' Antonia said. He would be there. Perhaps he had gone to buy a hammer – or an axe. She was certain he would wind up at Twiston.

They arrived at Richmond some minutes before five o'clock. Antonia was amazed at herself for remembering the way to Twiston so well after twenty years. She told the driver to stop outside the wrought-iron gates. She realized then that she didn't have any money on her. She had left her handbag in the library. She felt the merciless sun rays upon her and was aware of the rivulets of sweat coursing down her face. She didn't even have a handkerchief to wipe her face!

'I am sorry. Please, come to the club tomorrow morning,' she said. 'I'll pay you then.'

She must have presented a pathetic sight for the driver did not make a scene. He looked at her, shook his head and handed her a bundle of tissues. He then started the engine. Antonia stood watching the phantom of her distorted reflection receding in the curve of the dark glass, and as the cab disappeared in the distance, she dabbed at her brow and cheeks. Her nostrils caught a faint tang of wood smoke. She walked up to the gates and found them locked, but there was a smaller door further down the wall, which was open.

She went in.

23

The Edwardian Game Larder

Crunch-crunch, went the gravel under her feet, astonishingly loud, as she walked along the avenue in the ever-scorching sun. She hoped she wouldn't encounter any of Mrs Ralston-Scott's gardeners or dogs.

A sound that conveys ownership and ease. The words of Sir Michael Mortlock came back to her incongruously. Sir Michael, it occurred to her, had been the sanest person at Twiston on that fatal day, also the nicest. He hadn't contributed to any of the gossip-mongering. He had tried to pour oil on troubled waters. He had done his best to keep everybody happy. She thought she could smell his cigar – Partagas, that was the Cuban brand he had smoked. (The silly things one remembered!) She expected to see him sitting on the rustic seat under the oak, clad in a light flannel suit and sporting a straw boater with a pink ribbon, engrossed in Geoffrey Household's *Rogue Male*, which he must be reading for the tenth time. He would look up from the book at her approach, rise to his feet and take off his hat with old-fashioned courtesy, his pink wrinkled face creasing into a smile, his faded brown eyes twinkling. 'Ah, Antonia. It was so much better in those days, when you knew who your enemy was, don't you think?' She then remembered that Sir Michael was long gone, dead – had been dead for nearly twenty years.

She recalled reading Sir Michael's obituary in *The Times*.

It had come to her as a great surprise that he had been a Freemason as well as a member of various other esoteric-sounding societies. No one would have associated him with that sort of thing. Sir Michael had always struck her as the most down-to-earth of men, unaffected, placid, amiable and more than a little vague – not at all the kind that would go in for dressing up in strange robes and executing equally strange handshakes with his fellow Masons.

Hugh had suggested that Sir Michael might have been a member of some kind of *Herrenvolk* cult. Impossible – ridiculous. What next? A member of the Babylonian brotherhood? There had been a chapter in Dufrette's book entitled 'Knights of the Dark Sun'. The Dark Knights practised the sacrifice of children and virgins, or so Dufrette had claimed. Sir Michael had been seen outside Twiston with his hands covered in blood. He had been holding a knife. Well, he had been cutting the liver out of a young boar. No – that was a dream Lady Mortlock had had. But didn't dreams reflect reality in a distorted kind of way?

Antonia rubbed her temples. *Could* one discipline one's thoughts? Although the proximity of the river and the trees in the garden made the atmosphere here less sultry, she continued to feel rather light-headed. Every now and then luminous spots that were dark around the edges flashed before her eyes.

Sir Michael was the only person who had been nice to Lena . . . He had *liked* Lena, Dufrette had said. Sir Michael had had a penchant for large ladies . . . He had kept inviting the Dufrettes to Twiston despite his wife's disapproval of them . . . Antonia saw him once more, this time beside the river, putting an arm around Lena . . . No one else had tried to comfort Lena . . . Sir Michael had disappeared at weekends – Lady Mortlock said so . . . He had said he was going bird-watching . . .

Crunch-crunch. Antonia's progress was slow, deliberately so. She had to be careful . . . An adagio prelude to a furious overture? She hoped not. She walked with her head bowed, straining her ears for the sounds of a hammer striking against cement, though she knew that would be unlikely. Other noises kept coming to her ears: rustling of leaves, whispering, distant footfalls, dogs' muffled barking, the splashing of the river, even the sweet old-fashioned sounds of 'Lavender's Blue'! She couldn't be sure about any of them. For one thing the river couldn't be heard from here. On a quiet day like this, there wasn't likely to be a single ripple on it. She was imagining things. If she didn't get a grip on herself, she'd be seeing Sonya's ghost coming from the direction of the river next! The thought sent a slight shiver down her spine.

There was no sign of Major Nagle. He hadn't arrived yet, or could he be approaching the oak by a different route?

A rogue male. Was he dangerous? Was he likely to turn nasty? Well, yes. If he saw that she suspected – nay, *knew* what he had done. He would have brought a hammer with him. All he needed to do was raise the hammer in his ham-like hand and bring it down on her head. Would he dare? The odd thing was that she didn't feel in the least afraid. She had been brought to Twiston by a twist of fate, by a strange concatenation of chance and circumstance. She was on the track of a child-killer. She didn't feel anxious, excited or thrilled either. This, Antonia thought, is something I've *got* to do. This is journey's end. The denouement. No – the final action-filled sequence *before* the denouement. The chapter she would call 'Rogue Male'. The denouement of course was going to take place in the library at Twiston –

She shook her head. She was mixing fact and fiction again! She was overheated, probably dangerously so.

She imagined her face taking on the characteristics of a hunting creature: brows drawn together, lips pursed tight, nostrils dilating as those of a dog on the scent . . . Shouldn't she have called the police and informed them of her findings? It was only now that the thought occurred to her and she frowned. Well, yes – this *was* a matter for the police. Only, she felt sure, they wouldn't take any of it seriously. They would consider her unhinged – the dehydrated victim of sunstroke. Or – or they might think it was a publicity stunt, that she was doing it to increase the sales of her one detective novel.

What was that, madam? A sadistic Major? A doll-like child immured inside the hollow of a Jacobean oak? A signet ring embedded in the cement? Revelations brought about by *Gardeners' Question Time*? Even if they had been prepared to listen to her story, even if they gave her the benefit of the doubt and accepted that there might be something in it, they wouldn't have rushed to Twiston in hot pursuit of Major Nagle. By the time they did decide to interview Nagle, it would be too late. He would have been able to remove the body and his ring several times over.

Though would he? The whole idea seemed fantastic.

How she needed Hugh's advice! If only he had been with her now.

She had come upon the old-fashioned garden thermometer that marked the highest and lowest temperatures of the day. It was attached to the wall of an octagonal structure with small round windows whose panes were of butter-scotch yellow and a pointed chocolate-coloured roof ending in what looked like a giant humbug, situated under a birch tree. She remembered both, the thermometer and the building, very well indeed. The thermometer, she discovered, stood at eighty-four and a half.

The building had held her entranced when she had first laid eyes on it. It was at once whimsical and vaguely menacing. It had something of the fairy-tale about it (shades of *Hansel and Gretel*?), though it had been a mere game larder in Edwardian times, placed under the birch tree for coolness' sake, and by the time she had first seen it, no longer in use. As far as she could recall, it was only Sir Michael who had come to it to examine the thermometer. Sir Michael had considered converting the larder to a storage place of some kind, she couldn't think exactly for what. As a matter of fact she had observed him carry an ancient lacquered toy-box through the garden and place it inside the larder. It had been – why, it was the day of her departure from Twiston! The day after the tragedy . . .

Her eye fell on an object on the ground. Something that had gleamed in the sun. She picked it up. A metal button, from a man's blazer. Her heart missed a beat. Could Major Nagle be taking cover inside the game larder? The place was large enough – just about. No – the button was quite old, she could see now. It had been on the ground for some time, years maybe. Major Nagle was wearing a hacking jacket which had a completely different set of buttons. Besides, the door was padlocked and rusty and overgrown with some white flowering creeper that seemed quite undisturbed. What was it called? *Polygonum* . . .? One of the experts on the *Gardeners' Question Time* panel would know. The plant, she imagined, was of the kind that grew quickly, smotheringly, and was a menace to anything else that wanted to grow.

Suddenly Antonia had a strange feeling, she couldn't quite explain, and she stood frowning at the small white flowers that covered the larder door. Like a shrine, she thought. She tried to peer inside through one of the small yellow-panelled windows, but could see nothing. Sir Michael had had a nervous breakdown in the wake of Sonya's disappearance and died soon after. That toy-box – like a child's coffin. What if . . . No. *No.*

The heat.

Where *was* the oak? Antonia stood looking round. Was it to the left or the right? Well, directions didn't really matter – the tree was so big, it could easily be seen from anywhere in the garden. Only now she couldn't see it. Not at all. How peculiar . . . She started walking again, followed the path to the left. There was the statue of Pan covered in green moss and the disused pond filled with murky rain water. There was the rustic seat too, where Sir Michael had liked to sit. But the seat used to be *under* the oak! She saw the oak in her mind's eye: dark and lifeless and melancholy, with brittle sharp branches, like a skeletal hand reaching into the sky. The oak should be – out there.

But it wasn't. Not any longer. Taking a few steps, Antonia stood blinking. She gasped as her eyes fell on the stump. It resembled the crater of a mini volcano. The oak was gone. It had been cut – removed – disposed of. The area had been carefully cleaned. There was not a single branch or bough littering the ground. How was that possible? When did it happen? Hadn't Mrs Ralston-Scott been talking about the oak only three hours ago – she had sought advice on national radio. To cut or not to cut, she had said.

Then Antonia saw what had happened. The programme had been a repeat. The radio recording must have been made the week before. Mrs Ralston-Scott hadn't wasted time. She had called the tree surgeon soon after her appearance on *Gardeners' Question Time*, probably the very next day, and requested the removal of the offensive oak. Enough, she must have thought, was enough.

Antonia knelt beside the dun-coloured stump. The tree, she could see now, had been entirely hollow inside. The cement base was still there, but it had been broken up, smashed into several pieces. She ran her hand across one – burrowed her fingers in the cracks. There was nothing there. Nothing at all. Not a single trace of a small skeleton. No child had ever been immured in the hollow. That, she realized, had been her wild imagination at work again. Of all the preposterous propositions!

She felt the blood rushing into her face. She bit her lip. She didn't know whether to laugh or weep. *Watch out for the ring*, Miss Pettigrew had whispered in her ear, but Miss Pettigrew had proved a bad counsellor.

Never trust an imaginary friend, Antonia thought as she rose to her feet.

24

The Hour of the Wolf

But then who was that man – the man she had observed in the club library – and what had it all meant? An expression of shock had been on his brick-red face all right. She didn't think she had been wrong about that. He had been listening to the radio, to *Gardeners' Question Time,* to Mrs Ralston-Scott's voice talking about the proposed sawing down of the ancient oak . . . Though had he?

Antonia sat down on the rustic seat, shut her eyes and replayed in her mind the scene she had observed, slowly, very carefully. The man had been reading the paper and she had seen him drop it as though in sudden agitation. It had been a racing paper. She had assumed that he had received a shock because of something he had heard on the radio, but what if it was something he had *read* in the racing paper that had caused him to look as though he were going to have a heart attack? *The racing results* . . . Yes. He was a betting man. A lethal gambler. He had put a lot of money on the wrong horse and lost. That would account for it. He had lost a fortune, that's why he had looked staggered – so terribly upset. Her imagination had done the rest.

The man hadn't been Major Nagle. It would have been too extraordinary, too fantastic, too serendipitous a coincidence if it had been him. It had been someone else. Another military type. Somebody who had had no intention of coming to Twiston, who had no idea where Twiston was. A stranger. She had been a fool. A crazy overheated fool. She couldn't have misread the situation more completely. Her theory of the body in the hollow, like the uniform of George V in the portrait in the committee room, had seemed so perfect and clear from a distance, but on close inspection it proved to be no more than a fuzzy and meaningless blur. She had acted precipitously. She had ignored reason and allowed her imagination to lead her on a trail of false clues – and there she was now, in her summer frock, sunburnt, hot and grimy, at Twiston.

Full circle, Antonia thought. Things had come full circle. It had all started at Twiston, with a tragedy, followed by a mystery, and it was ending at Twiston with a loose end. That was life, sadly. Only in detective stories were problems resolved neatly on the last page.

She sighed and shook her head. She had been a fool. It would be embarrassing to tell anyone about it, even Hugh! She couldn't blame the heat completely and exclusively – she had to take some responsibility for it herself . . . At least there had been no murder and chances were that Sonya was still alive, leading a happy life with Mrs Vorodin somewhere abroad, near a cobalt-blue sea and golden beaches, under cloudless skies . . .

What now? She had no money on her. How could she get back to London? She couldn't go on depending on the kindness of cab drivers! What a ridiculous situation. Perhaps she could ring David and ask him to come and collect her in his car? Yes. But she didn't have any change for a phone call; she didn't even know where the nearest telephone booth was . . . She did possess a mobile phone but hardly ever used it. She always managed to leave it at home. She had no option but to go up to the house and ask Mrs Ralston-Scott for permission to use the telephone. Rising, Antonia began to walk slowly towards the house.

What explanation for her presence on the grounds of Twiston should she give? Should she tell Mrs Ralston-Scott who she was and remind her of their conversation on the telephone the week before? Perhaps she could say that she was staying at a place not far from Twiston and that she had come to the house to relive memories? No – that wouldn't explain why she needed to make an urgent phone call to her son in London –

Suddenly she stopped. She had come out into a clearing. It was a smallish lawn with a sundial in its centre, surrounded by statuary of the classical kind. It was a secluded spot and she had no recollection of having been in this part of the garden before. It was at the middle of the lawn, at what lay there beside the sundial that she stood staring. She couldn't believe her eyes. The scene had a theatrical, surreal, rather hallucinatory quality about it. Well, she had come thinking of a body, looking for a body, and she seemed to have found it. Only – only it was the wrong body.

This was not the tiny body of a child but that of a grossly fat woman . . .

Antonia felt her legs moving once more. Then she stopped again.

The woman was dressed in a long white dress. She lay on her back, spread-eagled, arms flung out. Her face was bluish in colour, like a discarded rubber mask. Blubber lips. Swollen, sagging flesh – blotched, like a toad's – obscene! Folds of double chin. The light brown eyes were wide open and glazed. Her hair very long, grey and straggly. She brought to mind some grotesque middle-aged Ophelia –

And she was not alone. It was only then, with a start, that Antonia noticed the man who stood beside the woman's body, looking down at it. He was very still. She should have noticed him first, but she hadn't – she had taken him for one of the statues! Her attention had been on the dead body on the ground alone.

The man had an air of detached consideration about him. He was elderly and his great height, mane of silver hair and fastidious expression lent him a patrician distinction.

Then Antonia received her third jolt. The man, she realized, was Lawrence Dufrette and in his hand he was holding a gun.

It was the antique, freakishly small, mother-of-pearl-encrusted Derringer.

Several moments passed. Antonia continued staring, hypnotized, horrified, taking in more details. Her eyes were on the red stain on the woman's temple where blood had oozed and dripped on the white dress, which she imagined was actually a nightgown of some sort. She then noticed the dark bruise on the woman's forehead.

Lawrence Dufrette turned round slowly and looked at her. '*Antonia*? What are you doing here?' He sounded tired. 'I told you to leave it all to me, didn't I? Why don't you listen?' Seeing her eyes fixed on the gun, he gave a smile, the wolfish smile she knew. 'It *is* real, you know. It is loaded.' There was blood on his hand, she noticed – also on his chin.

The woman's blood . . . Who *was* she?

Antonia said nothing. She seemed to have lost the ability to speak. Dufrette was wearing a sand-coloured safari suit. He was thinner than the last time she had seen him, that's why he had struck her as taller. There was a glint in his eye she didn't like. 'What's the matter? The cat got your tongue?' He was looking not at her, but down at his gun.

She said, 'Major Payne will be here at any moment.' Would that deter him? For the first time she felt very frightened.

This seemed to amuse him for he laughed. 'Ah, your sidekick. Or is it the other way round? Who's the Watson?' He laughed again, more shrilly. The whinny – it sent goose-bumps down her back. 'I always found these husband-and-wife duos such flavourless confections, rather annoying, actually, with their constant clever talk, jocular sparrings and synthetic passions. Nick and Norah

Charles . . . Mr and Mrs Paul Temple. Are you familiar with the Temples? Each adventure starts with a mystery of sorts, but it is invariably lost in the action that follows. Someone tries to eliminate them – the car Mrs Temple is in explodes – Paul Temple is shot at – they never die of course, but then that's third-rate fiction for you. Now, if *I* were to pull the trigger I wouldn't miss, I assure you. I have every right to defend myself. You have been stalking me.'

Antonia put up her hand. 'No, that's not true –'

'This, I explained to you, was a private matter. A very private matter. What right have you got to poke your nose into it? I did ask you to stop snooping. I asked you very politely, I remember. I *did* ask you.' His voice rose. The hysterical note was unmistakable. She saw him raise the gun –

Talk. Distract him. Don't panic. Don't stop. She said, 'I am sorry. I didn't know you were here. I had absolutely no idea. I came chasing after someone.' She discovered she was still clutching the blazer button she had found beside the Edwardian game larder. 'I thought I saw Major Nagle. In the club library. I thought he was on his way here, so I followed him. Do you remember Major Nagle?'

'*Nagle*?' Dufrette lowered the gun a little. He scowled. 'Of course I remember Nagle. What about him?'

'I thought I saw him at the club –'

'What are you talking about? You couldn't have. Nagle's gone. He's disappeared completely. Abroad, I expect. Lying low in some obscure location. A guesthouse in Gstaad – a *pension* in Pons?' Dufrette giggled. 'Small surprise. His name was mud after I had finished with him. I met several fellows who said they'd been trying to get on to his spoor but failed. No one knows where he is. I'd have been the first to hear if he was back. I have my spies, you know.'

'I thought it was he who killed Sonya.'

Dufrette lowered the gun further. He stared at her. 'You thought Nagle killed Sonya? You are a fool, Antonia. A greater fool than I imagined.' He paused. 'Sonya, if you must know, is alive, though she seems to be far from well. Actually, I am dreadfully worried about her. I don't quite know what to do.' He was still holding the gun in his right hand, but he pushed his left hand inside his jacket and produced a folded sheet of paper. Pale mauve with gilded edges. She recognized it at once. He frowned down at it thoughtfully.

'The letter,' she said. 'Veronica Vorodin's letter.'

'Yes, the letter. How uncommonly perspicacious of you.'

'Did you have it translated?'

'As a matter of fact I did. This morning. I wanted it done sooner but the fellow was away. It's somebody I was at school with. He read Russian at Cambridge. Was Burgess's *facile princeps* catamite for a while, though that's neither here nor there. Name of Rose. You wouldn't know him.'

'What's in the letter?'

'Ah, wouldn't you like to know!' Dufrette put the letter back into his pocket. His eyes flashed angrily and he waved the gun. 'You *love* asking questions, don't you? Who do you think you are? Oedipus come to consult the Oracle? What's in the letter indeed! Well, none of your bloody business. This is a very private matter. Can't you get it into your thick head? Can't you *understand*?' He raised his voice once again. 'What kind of an impertinent nosy parker are you?'

'I – I am sorry,' she stammered. 'I am afraid I've been obsessed with the mystery of Sonya's disappearance . . .'

She saw him examine the gun and wondered whether he would use it on her. He might – he was mad.

In something of a panic, not knowing what else to say, she blurted out, 'Why did you kill her?'

She immediately wished she hadn't, but the question, rather than send him into a renewed paroxysm of fury, seemed only to puzzle him. 'Kill – who?' His eyes strayed down to the body on the ground. '*Her*? You think I killed her? Well, I didn't.'

'Who is she?'

Dufrette said, 'My good woman, I haven't got the slightest idea. I was taking a short cut, you see. I was on my way to the house. Didn't look where I was going. Plenty on my mind, I must admit.' Suddenly he sounded extremely amiable. 'I stumbled on her, literally. Nearly fell over. Saw she was dead at once. She hadn't been dead long, mind. I checked. She was still warm. I turned her over. That's when I got blood on my hand, I expect.' He took out his handkerchief and wiped his fingers. 'You thought I shot her?'

Antonia pointed to the wound on the woman's temple. 'How – how did she get that?'

'That's not a shot wound,' he said.

It dawned on her then that, incredible as it might appear, he was telling the truth after all. If he had fired his gun, she would have heard it, she reflected. She had been in the garden for at least fifteen minutes. The gun had no silencer. She would certainly have heard a shot. She felt herself relaxing a bit. 'Why did you bring your gun?'

'What a silly question. I always have my gun with me, didn't you know? Your next question no doubt will be, why I am holding my gun in my hand?' She nodded. 'Well, I took my gun out of my pocket as soon as I saw the body. I imagined that I might be next, you see.'

'Next?'

'Yes, next. I thought there was someone with a gun lurking in the shrubbery. I thought I heard them. For a fraction of a second I too thought she had been shot . . . This is a dangerous place . . . People with guilty secrets, you know . . . I was wrong of course. I saw it the moment I turned her over . . . She hasn't been shot.'

Antonia had crossed to the body and was standing beside it. 'All that blood . . . How did she die?'

Dufrette's eyebrows went up. 'Can't you *see*? And you call yourself a detective! A child of five would be able to tell you how she died. No, a child of three,' he added improbably. Antonia didn't mind his unsubtle sarcasm. He had put the gun back into his pocket and that was what mattered. He went on, 'Let the lesson start. Observe that sundial closely. Notice anything unusual?'

It was only then she saw that the sundial was stained red and glistening in the sun. Blood. She nodded. 'That,' he went on, 'is where the wretched creature fell and hit her head. She landed on her temple. I don't know whether that was what killed her though . . . That's a nasty bruise. Wonder what caused it.' He pointed his long pale forefinger towards the woman's forehead. 'She seems to have been accident-prone. There's a cut above the left eye. That's not so fresh. It's been treated. It's been stitched up. Must have been really bad . . .'

'She is bruised all over,' Antonia whispered. 'Her arms and legs. Look. Bruises – *lesions* . . . Her thighs too. Her wrists. My God. She seems to have been kept bound. Some of the bruises are quite old!'

'Indeed. How curious. So you are not entirely devoid of observational skills.'

'Has she – has she been tortured?'

'Tortured? She does appear to have been kept bound, as you say, but actually some of the bruises on her arms are injection marks. She is covered in injection marks.'

Antonia gasped. '*Yes* . . . She must have been given innumerable injections.'

'Innumerable's the word,' he agreed. He then looked up and pointed. 'She must have come through there. See how the shrubbery's been disturbed? That thicket over there. There are scratches on her face and arms – and legs. I imagine she barged through, not looking where she was going, as though she was being pursued by furies,' he said thoughtfully. 'That's where the house is. She came from the house, that much is clear.'

'Was she – was she trying to run away?'

'That's a possibility . . . Why is she so pale? It's the kind of pallor that results when someone's been incarcerated. Evidently she's been kept indoors –' He broke off as the sound of twigs snapping was heard.

'What was that? Someone's been there all this time!'

Antonia cried, pulling at Dufrette's sleeve. 'Somebody's been watching us – eavesdropping.'

But Lawrence Dufrette failed to react. He was standing very still, staring before him. He had a stunned look on his face – as though he had suddenly had a startling revelation. Several moments passed. He then bowed his head – it was a gesture of resignation, of accepting defeat, Antonia reflected. Disconcertingly, his lips quivered and tears started rolling down his pale cheeks.

'What – what's the matter?' Antonia said.

There was another pause. He dabbed at his eyes with his handkerchief. Shaking his head, he said, 'I don't think I'd have been up to it. I can see they did their best. I wouldn't have been able to cope with any of it. I am terribly squeamish. If truth be told, I am an egoist. The effort, should I have made it, would have exacerbated my temper. I would have started hating her and that, inevitably, would have led to me hating *myself*.' He was talking to himself rather than to her. 'I had no idea things were so bad. If I had had any notion, I wouldn't have come.' Pulling out the letter from his pocket, he handed it to Antonia.

'You might as well read it. The English translation follows the Russian text. Rose writes a beautiful hand,' said this unpredictable man. 'It might be worth your while to go to the house and tell them that she is here, though I expect they know it already. There'd be no point in me going . . . I am sure they'd have a perfectly satisfactory explanation for the police.'

'The police?' Antonia echoed.

But Lawrence Dufrette turned round and, without another glance at Antonia or the woman's body on the ground, began to walk rapidly across the lawn away from the house in the direction of the gates. Suddenly he gave what to her sounded like a sob. *'Twice!'* she heard him call out. She expected he had parked his car somewhere outside.

She looked down at the body, at the injection marks on the woman's arms. What did he mean by 'twice'? Then, suddenly, it all came to her in a flash, and she knew with absolute certainty what had happened.

What *really* happened.

Slowly, clutching the folded letter in her hand, Antonia made her way towards the house.

25

A Mansion and Its Murder

She hadn't noticed the gargoyles before, or had forgotten all about them. They were looking down from the crenellations, leering at her unpleasantly, as though in triumphant mockery. Antonia pursed her lips. She felt a bit miffed that Dufrette had beaten her to it, that he had managed to get to the truth first. Three of the gargoyles had parts of their faces missing, either nose or ear or chin, but two looked as good as new, giving the impression they had been sculpted and mounted only recently. Twiston, it became clear to her, was undergoing renovation of some sort. To one side the stucco was so new that, she imagined, a few hundred tubs of yoghurt might have to be rubbed into it to develop some patina. But from the other two-thirds plants were protruding, gargoyles and griffins were disintegrating and streaks of damp ran down the walls.

The kind of place exiles think of when they dream of home.

It was she of course who had said that, on the day before Sonya disappeared, as it happened. She had spoken these words to Mrs Vorodin in this very garden.

Still, she didn't start reading the letter. She wanted to work out every detail by herself, unaided.

She realized she was approaching the house from the back. She smelled the sweet aroma of honeysuckle. She went up the stone steps that led to the deserted sunlit terrace. She saw a round marble-topped table and a deckchair under a striped umbrella. A tray with a silver coffee pot, a bone-china coffee cup, a plate containing a half-eaten wedge of Sachertorte, the chocolate glistening as it melted away in the sun. A starched napkin of gleaming whiteness. A small silver ashtray containing the stub of a purple-filtered Balkan Sobranie cigarette. A book lying face down on the chair. Antonia looked at the title. French. *Un Autre Moi-Même*. Mrs Ralston-Scott clearly had Continental tastes of the refined kind, acquired, Antonia supposed, in the course of her cruise down the Mediterranean. What had she said? Sailing all the way from Monte Carlo to the Greek islands.

Un Autre Moi-Même . . . How did that translate? *Another Self*? James Lees-Milne? Antonia frowned. How curious that Mrs Ralston-Scott should be reading James Lees-Milne in French, but then, Antonia decided, she was a very curious lady.

Antonia stood with her hand on the back of the chair. One couldn't have conceived of a more innocent spectacle, nor of a more reassuring one, and yet she found the sheer civilized normality of it all a bit sinister. There was a hush. She was aware of an air of expectancy.

The french windows were wide open. Although there was no one in sight, she did believe secret eyes were following her every move from inside the house, wondering what was to be done about her. Would they attempt to – No. She considered that unlikely. If they did, they'd be left with *two* bodies to account for. Still, whatever plans had been made, she and Dufrette must have upset them. She looked round. Which way had the person gone? The person who had spied on them? She didn't think they had come this way. Some side door, she imagined.

Antonia went in through the french windows and found herself inside the drawing room, as she had known she would. Most of it struck her as unchanged. There was something about its raw authenticity – floorboards so worn that they had the texture of driftwood, panes of wobbly seventeenth-century glass and 300-year-old paint which looked as though it might have been applied last week – that left her feeling disoriented. There were bowls of flowers everywhere, just as there had been on that fatal morning twenty years ago.

The cuffed leather armchair the colour of overdone veal – Sir Michael's favourite seat – and the fender stool were as she remembered them. So, for that matter, was the black Chinese screen patterned with the figures of female samurai warriors fighting dragons, which had been bought by Lady Mortlock. (Was there an encoded message? Were the dragons symbols of sexual prejudice? Not too fanciful?) On the other hand, the French nineteenth-century sofa with the woven cotton Zoffany upholstery and striped taffeta curtains were brand new. Both sofa and curtains were the colour of seashells. Some of the ancient floorboards, she noticed, had been replaced with French oak in a soft colour, in what must have been an attempt to lighten the room. The process of renovation would be resumed at some future date – if Mrs Ralston-Scott was to survive the cataclysm.

(Antonia had a good idea now how Mrs Ralston-Scott fitted into the picture.)

On the floor beside the sofa she saw a stuffed toy. She went and picked it up. A giraffe, one of whose ears bore teeth marks. It had a rather supercilious expression on its long face. Sonya's favourite toy. Curzon? Yes. Though it also brought to mind Lawrence Dufrette.

The sense of urgency had abandoned Antonia. She looked at her reflection in the oval mirror above the fireplace. She wasn't surprised to see she had a dazed air about her. There was a cigarette case on the mantelpiece. An Asprey's slide-action, engine-turned silver cigarette case. A gentleman's case. She opened it. Empty. Then she noticed the monogram on the lid: *T.N.* For some reason she felt disturbed. She looked down at the blazer button in her hand. Replacing the case on the mantelpiece, she turned round and sat down in the veal-coloured winged chair. She put her feet on the stool. She thought she heard muffled barking coming from another part of the house. Mrs Ralston-Scott's spaniels.

The kind of place exiles think of . . . Her own words, she realized, had been quoted back to her from the radio. *On top of all my problems,* Mrs Ralston-Scott had said next. She had meant Sonya of course. And she had meant Sonya again, not her dog, when she had asked her secretary to play the record that 'calmed' her. The sweet old-fashioned tune of course was 'Lavender's Blue'. That whimpering sound – Antonia shuddered. That too had been Sonya, *not* a dog. Mrs Ralston-Scott had been cautious. Extremely cautious. She had recognized Antonia's name. She had feared that Antonia might *remember.*

Antonia opened the letter. As Dufrette had said, the English translation followed the Russian text. She read it through.

I don't think it would be at all a good idea for you to come to Twiston.

That was what Veronica Vorodin had written to Lena. Antonia nodded to herself. Well, that explained Dufrette's presence at Twiston. That was how he had known where to find them.

Somewhere a grandfather clock chimed the half-hour. The next moment she heard a composed voice ask, 'Excuse me, what are you doing here? Who are you?'

She hadn't been recognized, clearly. Well, it was twenty years. Furthermore, as the mirror had shown her, she looked a sight. Grimy-faced, badly sunburnt, sweaty and dishevelled. She couldn't have presented a greater contrast to the woman who was standing beside the door, looking across the room at her.

It was a young woman with short glossy chestnut hair and glasses, wearing a caramel-coloured blouse, a heather skirt, pale silk stockings and shoes the colour of molasses that were as polished and shiny as conkers. She was the epitome of cool competence and might as well have been wearing a badge saying *Superior Secretary* pinned to her virginal bosom. Antonia saw her cast a quick glance round the room, as though expecting to see someone else. She clearly suspected Lawrence Dufrette might have managed to sneak in too.

Was that the secretary she had spoken to on the phone? What was her name? Laura?

Not leaving her seat, Antonia said, 'I came to report a body. There is a dead body outside. The body of a woman.'

The secretary gave a little controlled gasp. 'A dead body?'

Curious to see how this would develop, Antonia said, 'Yes. A middle-aged woman. Rather big. Long grey hair.'

The secretary was staring back at her, her lips slightly parted. 'How terrible . . . Where is she? I mean the body?'

'There is a clearing – a small lawn with a sundial . . . Do you mean you don't know who the woman is?' Antonia asked.

'No, of course I don't. How could I? No such woman lives here.' She was playing the part of mystification very plausibly.

So that was going to be their line. Blank stares and blunt denials. *The Lady Vanishes*.

'She couldn't have come from anywhere else,' Antonia said. 'She is wearing a nightdress. Her arms and legs are covered in injection marks.'

'I must call the police,' the secretary went on, though she made no movement. 'Oh!' She seemed to have suddenly been visited by an idea. 'Needle marks, did you say? I wonder if she's one of the patients at the psychiatric hospital. There is a psychiatric hospital a couple of miles from here. She – this woman – may have run away – must have!' The secretary spoke with a sense of shocked discovery. 'I can easily get their number and ask.'

Had they come to an arrangement with somebody from the psychiatric hospital? One of the doctors? Somebody high-up? Well, everybody had a price, or so they said. How much did a death certificate cost? Was it more expensive than, say, a fake passport? Or was all this being said only to put *her* off the scent?

Seized by a sense of outrage, Antonia said, 'Could I speak to Mrs Ralston-Scott?'

'I am afraid Mrs Ralston-Scott isn't here. She has gone abroad until the work on the house is completed. I don't know when exactly she is coming back. Next month, I imagine – or the month after.' The secretary continued standing by the doorway. Her hands were clasped before her, her head tilted slightly to one side. Was there anyone there, pulling the strings, providing instructions, prompting?

Antonia decided to change tack. She held up the letter. 'I believe this belongs to her.' She had raised her voice for the benefit of whoever might be hiding behind the door, listening.

The secretary blinked. 'Oh?'

'It's a letter Mrs Vorodin wrote to Mrs Dufrette.'

There was a pause, then the secretary said in a voice that was only slightly changed, 'I am sure you are mistaken, but I will see that Mrs Ralston-Scott gets the letter, if you really think it is hers. Just leave it with me.'

'Would you also tell Mrs Vorodin – I mean Mrs Ralston-Scott – that Sonya's father has no intention of pursuing the matter further? Lawrence Dufrette came to Twiston, looking for Sonya, but now that she is dead, he sees no point in bothering Mrs Vorodin.' Antonia paused. 'He sends a message. He said that he appreciates what Mrs Vorodin has done for Sonya. He realizes that he wouldn't have been able to cope with Sonya's deteriorating condition as effectively as Mrs Vorodin has been able to do. Would you tell her that?'

The secretary gave a little strained smile. 'I will certainly convey your message to Mrs Ralston-Scott, though I am sorry to say I have absolutely no idea what you are talking about. Who *is* Mrs Vorodin?'

'All right, Laura, that will do.' A musical voice was heard and a woman came out from behind the door, as

Antonia had felt sure she would. 'Thank you very much. You may go now. Would you see that everything is done – properly?'

'Yes, certainly, Mrs Ralston-Scott.' The secretary disappeared.

Antonia rose from her seat. 'Mrs Vorodin. You didn't really think I'd just go away, did you?'

'Mrs Rushton? That was your name, wasn't it?' Veronica Vorodin advanced upon Antonia with an extended hand, seemingly unruffled. 'We did speak on the phone the other day, didn't we? I am sorry but I didn't recognize you from the window. It has been a long time. It is too late for tea. May I offer you a drink?'

26

Another Self

The archetypal squire's lady – to the manor born – the country gentlewoman par excellence. And she had chosen the perfect name to match the part: Mrs Ralston-Scott. What was her first name now? Had she changed it to something like Charlotte or Celia? Well, it wasn't such a difficult character part to play. She had been an actress and a superb mimic, as Dufrette had said, so she could do it easily. Who was it who had said, 'If you are assuming another identity, you will never keep it unless you convince yourself that you are *it*?' Well, Veronica Vorodin had become 'it'.

She wore a bluish-grey blouse, a single string of pearls around her neck, a long black skirt and black court shoes. Her iron-grey hair was short and windswept in an uncompromising manner and she seemed to have made no concession to any current fashions. How old was she? At the time of their last meeting she had been thirty-eight, Antonia remembered, which made her fifty-eight. Twenty years ago she had struck Antonia as much younger, barely out of her teens, but now she had decided to look her age. Her face was weather-beaten and she wore next to no make-up. She had perfect cheekbones and was still what could be described as a 'handsome woman', though one had to look very hard to recognize in her the glamorous bronzed creature with the Gucci glasses, to whom Antonia had chatted in the garden about children in general and Sonya in particular.

She sat on the sofa facing Antonia. She had poured herself a whisky in a cut-crystal glass. Antonia had plumped for home-made lemonade with lots of ice.

At first sight Veronica seemed perfectly composed but it was clear that she had been crying. The lavender eyes were red and every now and then she pressed a handkerchief against her lips.

After she had listened to Antonia, she nodded and said, 'I see you know everything. You've been extremely clever. You are absolutely right in every detail. I did buy Twiston because I'd always wanted to live here. It was love at first sight. But there's more to it. I hope you will understand. I rather liked the idea of there being a symmetry about it.'

'Symmetry?'

'Yes. You see, Twiston had been made an unhappy place after we took Sonya, so I wanted to bring her back to it, to make it happy again. I meant to repair the balance. Foolish of me. I could be incredibly sentimental sometimes – fatalistic too. It's my Russian blood, I suppose. I do get these irrational fancies. You strike me as a terribly logical and sensible person, so I don't suppose you have much patience with the sort of thing I mean?'

'You'd be surprised,' Antonia murmured.

'Really? Well, that does make me feel better. But you want to hear about Sonya and the missing twenty years, don't you? What happened after we . . . bought her from Lena? Well, to start with, everything was wonderful. I mean, as wonderful as could be, given the state of Sonya's mental health. Sonya didn't seem to notice that she had a new set of parents. She became genuinely attached to us and allowed us to love her. *That* was the really important thing. She was happy, in her own way. I'd like to think that she was happier than before. Well, she didn't seem to need much, poor thing. We showered her with gifts, of course. We went to live on Simi. Have you heard of Simi?'

'Is it a paradise island?' Antonia gave a little smile.

'You might call it that. It is one of the least known and prettiest of Greek islands off the Turkish coast. The kindest people live there. We did an awful lot of yachting. Sonya loved the sea. Eventually we moved to America. Until she was twelve, she was perfectly manageable, but things started getting difficult when she entered puberty. At first, it was generally assumed that she was autistic, but it soon became clear that she was a lot more than that. She started displaying other symptoms, some, I must say, rather disturbing. She became psychotic. We kept taking her to doctors – once she was seen by seven different doctors in one month, but no one could help.'

Antonia asked what exactly had been wrong with Sonya.

'Head . . . brain . . . nervous system . . . glands . . . She had several "syndromes". Long Latin names. Something called "paranoid psychosis". A thyroid disorder known as Hashimoto's – it presents itself in a dizzying variety of ways. Oh, practically *everything* was wrong with her!' Veronica cried. 'One moment she was sweet and angelic, the next she would start writhing and screaming and kicking and biting. When she became depressed, she would hardly be able to breathe and then, suddenly, she would be possessed by this manic energy and start running about, punching things. It was dreadful. She developed headaches. Sometimes they were so bad, she passed out. We kept giving her stronger and stronger pills – painkillers, sedatives, anti-depressants, stimulants. Then she was prescribed injections. In fact, over the last couple of years she's had both pills *and* injections. Oh dear. I do sound exasperated, don't I?'

'It seems you took on more than you could handle.'

'You are right. It wasn't terribly responsible of me, what I did. It was all my idea. Anatole had doubts – it was his pragmatic French side – but he went along with me. Some may say I am like those people who buy a puppy for

Christmas and then, by the following Christmas, discover they can't cope with it, but that's not right. I did my best for Sonya. I had her for twenty years . . .' Veronica pressed her handkerchief against her lips. 'You'll agree that's a long time . . . Her health kept deteriorating. The pills and the injections she had to be given increased in number, in variety and in strength. That caused all sorts of side effects. Talking of irrational fancies! At one point Sonya became convinced that her head was full of water and that it contained a fish. The thought upset her dreadfully. She started banging her head against the wall, to let the fish out –'

'The bruise on her forehead?'

'Yes. She kept hurting herself. You can't imagine how distressing that was to watch – worse than the kicks and bites and blows I have had to suffer.' Veronica raised her forearm and Antonia saw it was covered in scratch and bite marks. 'I didn't want to send her to an institution. I could have, but I didn't have the heart. I didn't want to let her out of my sight. I felt – perhaps misguidedly – that she was my responsibility. That I had to stick to it.'

'Were you afraid someone might guess who she was?'

'Well, yes, that too . . . I *did* provide her with the best nursing care available. Two private nurses. Extremely competent – discreet. Every so often she would start smashing her head against the wall. Two months ago she broke a mirror and cut herself really badly. Her eye was damaged. It was a miracle she didn't go blind . . . Her condition wasn't something she grew out of. That, you see, was what I'd been hoping and praying for and, ultimately, believing. That she would grow out of things. I failed to assess the situation accurately. It was extremely naïve of me, I know. She didn't grow out of things. She grew worse and worse *and* worse. She kept putting on weight, so it became extremely hard to restrain her physically. She grew obese – enormous – gross. You saw her.'

'Lena used to call her *kotik* . . . Kitten . . .'

'I know . . . Well, she became as big as an ox – and as

strong. She had this insatiable appetite. She'd eat everything in sight if she came upon a table with food on it. She couldn't stop herself. Then she would throw up. And she would scream and hurl things whenever we tried to prevent her from gorging herself. She developed a passion for sweets – mints in particular. She'd put in her mouth anything that *looked* like mints. Small buttons. Pearls. Once she tore apart one of my necklaces. Pills – we had to be really careful about pills.'

Rising abruptly and holding the handkerchief to her lips, Veronica went up to the sideboard and replenished her glass with more whisky, adding only a modicum of soda water from an old-fashioned siphon and dipping the silver tongs into the ice bucket. 'Are you sure you don't want a proper drink?' She glanced at Antonia.

'No, thank you . . . Sonya looked much older than twenty-seven.'

'She aged prematurely. When she was seventeen she already looked about thirty. She changed out of all recognition. The docile affectionate *kotik* – the sweet doll-like little girl with the gentle smile – was no more. She couldn't have disappeared more completely if she had been carried away by the river that day.' Veronica resumed her seat on the sofa. 'She turned into a monster. Grossly fat, pugnacious, violent. Sometimes we had to tie her up. Put her in a straitjacket of sorts. We had no choice. Lena didn't believe me when I told her how bad it was.'

Veronica glanced at the letter which Antonia had left on the small table beside her chair. 'Lena didn't let you have the letter, just like that, did she? I expect she sold it to you?'

'No. We stole it,' Antonia said.

'*We*? Oh. So somebody knows that you are here?'

'Yes.' Antonia didn't elaborate. She knew it was absurd of her, but she felt safer now that she had suggested a 'partner' might be waiting to hear about her findings. There was something about Veronica – the mixture of the familiar and unfamiliar – the two persons in one – that made Antonia uncomfortable. She had to admit that she also felt a bit afraid.

She went on quickly, 'You wrote to Lena that Sonya's condition had deteriorated, that she was very ill, that she was not fit to be seen by anyone. You wrote that you found it unbearable, watching Sonya's misery.' She saw Veronica shut and open her eyes. 'I don't suppose Lena wanted to come to Twiston out of any maternal urges?'

'No. What she was after was lucre – filthy lucre – more and more of it. For her I was the goose that lays the golden eggs. I had to take a firm line in the end. I made it absolutely clear that "no more" meant precisely that. We exchanged several letters. She kept phoning too, but Laura managed to deal with her very efficiently. She never thought of coming in person. Too lazy, I suppose. Or never sober enough. She did try to blackmail me in a half-hearted kind of way. She said she'd tell the police, but I knew it was just talk. Well, she wasn't the only one –' Veronica broke off. 'Lena wouldn't have dared go to the police. That would have meant giving herself away. Her involvement in the affair was after all fairly central. She'd have had to admit that she sold her daughter. How ugly that sounds.'

Antonia frowned. 'What do you mean, she wasn't the only one?'

'Sorry?' Veronica looked vague.

'Did someone else try to blackmail you?'

There was a pause, then Veronica said, 'All right. You know so much already, it won't make the slightest difference. Yes. Someone else did try to blackmail us. You see, we were seen that morning –'

'By Major Nagle?' The *real* Nagle, Antonia thought.

'Clever of you. Yes. That dreadful man saw us from his window, apparently. He said he saw me pick up Sonya and carry her towards the gates. We weren't aware of it. He kept quiet about it for a long time. Nineteen years. That was his revenge on Lawrence, from what he let drop. He'd been gloating over Lawrence's loss for the whole of nineteen years. He could have told the police at once but he didn't. Dreadful man. He turned up on my doorstep in person last year. It was soon after we had moved into Twiston.'

'How did he know you were at Twiston?'

'The internet. Some stupid website. There were several of them, actually. I wasn't aware of their existence *then*. That's been dealt with now, though I wish – I do wish – I'd done it sooner! It would have saved . . . a certain amount of trouble.' Veronica's eyes narrowed and she looked towards the fireplace. 'Nagle knew all about me. He knew about Anatole's death, that it was I who had bought Twiston. Some local enthusiast who was mad about Twiston's history had set up a website devoted to it. Meddlesome fool. We caught him on the grounds once, trespassing. Set the dogs on him, but he did manage to take a couple of snapshots of me in the garden, which he added to the Twiston website. "Mrs Ralston-Scott, the new chatelaine." That kind of nonsense.'

'Nagle saw the photo?'

'Yes. He recognized me.' Aware of Antonia's eyes on her, Veronica gave a wry smile. 'I looked different then. More like what you remember, I suppose. I was still clinging to my youth. Well, I've been taught a lesson. Nagle, it turned out, had been looking up every possible source of information, trying to find my whereabouts. He had already put two and two together. He said he remembered how I used to gush about Twiston. He already had an idea he might find me here.' She paused. 'He needed money – badly. A lot of money. Now, as blackmailers went, he was the real thing. He was a menace – he presented a genuine threat.'

'Did you pay him off?' Antonia asked.

'I did. Yes.' Veronica spoke in a toneless voice.

'Won't he bother you again?'

'I don't think so. Sonya's dead now. There would be no point.' Veronica paused. 'You should have seen him that day, respectability personified, with his navy-blue blazer and bowler hat and polished boots . . . I was extremely polite. I even gave him a drink. No, he won't come again. Nagle *qua* menace is – what was that silly phrase Sir Michael used to quote? A spent egg?' She laughed. It was a musical kind of laugh. 'Is that Wodehouse? No, Major Nagle won't come a second time . . . Are you sure Lawrence won't decide to pay me another visit?'

'He won't. He admitted he wouldn't have been able to cope with Sonya as well as you. He is a very strange man . . . He lost Sonya *twice*, it suddenly occurred to him. Once twenty years ago, the second earlier today. He didn't recognize her at once, you see, and it gave him a shock when he did.'

'Yes. Terribly sad. Lawrence did love her. I know.' Veronica took a sip of whisky. 'Of course you realize that she wasn't his daughter?'

Antonia stared at her. 'Sonya wasn't his daughter?'

'No. She had brown eyes. Both Lawrence and Lena have blue eyes. Blue-eyed people can't produce a brown-eyed child, though a brown-eyed father and a blue-eyed mother can. I remember reading about it after we took Sonya. Anatole and I too have blue eyes. I was worried that someone might notice. Of course no one did. People don't usually – unless they are scientists or something.'

'Sir Michael,' Antonia whispered. 'Was Sir Michael Sonya's father?'

'As a matter of fact he was. Lena and he had an affair. It went on for some years, apparently. Lena told me about it. Michael was mad about her, she said. Lawrence had no idea – neither did Hermione for that matter. Lena believes Lawrence is sterile, though he was always too proud to go and have a test.'

There was a pause. 'How did Sonya die?' asked Antonia.

'She . . .' Veronica's eyes narrowed again. 'She emptied a bottle of pills into her mouth. She thought they were mints. We had no idea – until it was too late. I found the empty bottle. It happened between the nurses' shifts. She had been in bed, pretending to be asleep. That was why we had relaxed our vigil. Sonya *was* cunning . . . She then managed to run out of the house. We had no idea where she'd gone. We kept looking for her. She *knew* she had done something very wrong, you see. We couldn't find her. When we did, it was too late. She had swallowed some pretty powerful sleeping stuff. Zolpicone. Apparently she collapsed where you found her . . . Lawrence had already appeared on the scene . . . Then there was you.'

Another pause.

'What are you going to do now?' Antonia asked.

'I believe the ambulance has already been called. They'll be here any moment. Do we need to inform the police as well?' Veronica opened her eyes wide. Deep circles of red burned on her cheeks and suddenly she looked young and beautiful again. 'I mean, it was, after all, only a tragic accident?'

'I think you'll have to call the police, yes.'

'Oh dear . . . Poor Sonya. It was an awful thing to happen, but it's better for her to go that way, don't you think? It wasn't much of a life. It would have broken my heart to see her being led away in a straitjacket . . . That must be the ambulance.' Veronica Vorodin looked up as a car was heard drawing up outside. 'I do hope you stay on a bit longer, Mrs Rushton. May I call you Antonia? You *must* call me Veronica . . . Actually, I'd like to ask you to do something for me . . . Do you mind? We have very little time . . .'

27

The Asprey's Cigarette Case

Three days later, Antonia was entertaining Major Payne to dinner at her house and she told him the whole story.

'I'll never forgive myself for missing the denouement,' he said as he watched her pour out coffee from her new and rather superior coffee-maker. 'What a remarkable woman . . . What did you tell the police exactly?'

'Nothing much, apart from how and where I had found the body. Veronica introduced me as one of her oldest and dearest chums, you see. I explained that I'd been on my way to the house, on a visit . . . Veronica does seem to have the extraordinary knack of bending people to her own will, to get them to do what she wants. I said I'd known Sonya as a little girl and confirmed that she had been extremely ill. Veronica had all the necessary papers. Funnily enough they had gone on calling her Sonya. No one made a connection between the psychotic young woman whose death was clearly a tragic misadventure and the disappearance of the little girl from that same house twenty years ago. The policemen were all rather young . . . I hope I did right.'

As distant thunder signalled the end of the heat wave, Major Payne said, 'You think she killed her, don't you?'

'I do. I believe it was a case of mercy killing. Veronica couldn't bear to watch Sonya's misery. She said so in that letter. I believe she made up the story about Sonya's fondness for mints and how she'd put pills and suchlike in her mouth. *It's all too neat*. You probably think it's my imagination again?' She paused. 'There was also the way her eyes narrowed when she told me what Sonya had done . . . She had a certain *look*. Not ruthless exactly – I can't quite explain it.' Antonia frowned. It had occurred to her that she had surprised that same look on Veronica's face not once but twice . . .

Major Payne produced his pipe. 'Well, Veronica Vorodin is a Yusupov on her mother's side. She and Lena are cousins. Prince Yusupov first tried to kill Rasputin with poison, remember? He put cyanide in the cakes, and it was only when it didn't work that he shot him. What I mean is, poison was his first choice. It's probably all rot, but I suppose it can be argued that it's in her blood? Veronica is descended from a poisoner . . . It would have been easy for her to crush a lethal dose of sleeping pills, slip them in a drink and give it to Sonya –'

'Wait a minute,' Antonia interrupted. '*Drink* . . . Oh my God. Hugh, she is a poisoner all right. She did it twice.'

'What do you mean?'

'She killed Major Nagle too.'

'What?'

'That's when her eyes narrowed and she got that same look. She said, "I gave him a drink. No, he won't come again." It ties up with several other things. Nagle's disappeared – no one knows where he is. *And* he was wearing a blazer when he paid Veronica his second visit!'

Payne stroked his jaw with a forefinger. 'The blazer button you found in the garden? Beside the Edwardian game larder, did you say?'

'Yes. The button had been there for some time. It was a bit rusty. The game larder's covered in some creeper plant. I did have a funny feeling when I saw it. Thought it looked like a shrine.'

'You think that's where she put Nagle's body?'

'Yes. And if you are still not convinced,' Antonia went on, her eyes very bright, '*there's the Asprey's cigarette case on*

Veronica's mantelpiece. It has Major Nagle's initials on it. T.N. Tommy Nagle.'

'Crikey,' Payne said. 'It must have fallen out of his pocket when . . .'

Antonia nodded. 'She kept it.'

After a pause, Major Payne cleared his throat. 'Do you think we could go to Twiston again? Just the two of us? You said that Veronica would be going abroad soon. We could sneak into the garden and see what's in that game larder. Then we'd know – um – beyond any reasonable doubt? We don't have to involve the police . . .'

Antonia nodded again.